SUN, MOON, AND STARS

VOLUME ONE

E.J. RUSSELL

Sun, Moon, and Stars, Volume One
Copyright © 2024 by E.J. Russell
Partnership (as Sun, Moon, and Stars) copyright © 2016 by E.J. Russell
Principles copyright © 2024 by E.J. Russell

Cover art: L.C. Chase, http://lcchase.com
Partnership edited by Amanda Jean, Meg DesCamp
Principles edited by Meg DesCamp

ISBN: 978-1-947033-96-2

First edition
July 2024

Contact information:
ejr@ejrussell.com

SUN, MOON, AND STARS

VOLUME ONE

E.J. RUSSELL

For the misfits

PARTNERSHIP

SUN, MOON AND STARS

About
PARTNERSHIP

When Sun-born mage Zal is called to a remote village after an explosion on a nearby mountaintop, he's stunned at what he finds in the gaol under the town hall—the last Moon-born on the planet, apparently a rogue mage, and someone Zal is duty-bound to haul to the capital to face judgment.

But although nonbinary Torian is Moon-born, they're no mage. Rescued as an infant from the plague that wiped out the rest of their race, Torian is as much cybertronic as human, and desperate to escape their former Star-born overseers.

Zal has never felt the desires of the flesh, and as an avowed celibate Sun mage, he couldn't indulge them if he did. Torian has only known value as a sexual surrogate, and isn't sure how to prove their worth to a man who has no need of their abilities.

As danger looms from both Zal's world and Torian's, mage and cyborg must find common ground, because only together can they hope to survive.

Chapter One

Zal

Just bloody marvelous.

From the moment I'd gotten assigned to the northern circuit, the bridge to Corvel-on-Byrne had been a pain in my arse. Every time I passed through on my rounds, I had to slap a new reinforcement spell on the rickety span. Sun magic never lasted long over water, but that wasn't the problem today.

No, today's problem would be the boulder the size of my cottage standing where the bridge *used* to be, sending the Byrne off-course to eat away at its banks. One more blasted thing for me to deal with before I left off traveling and returned home for my annual respite. I'd be lucky if I made it halfway to the Inland Sea before the winter storms roared in from beyond the mountains.

"Why anybody would choose to live this far north is more than I can fathom," I muttered as I shrugged off my pack.

But this canton was part of my circuit and therefore my responsibility, so I shed my cloak and coat and prepared to rebuild the bridge. Even if the present emergency hadn't called me to Corvel-on-Byrne, the river-locked village at the base of Star Mountain, I could hardly leave its citizens without a way to escape their homes all winter.

Planting my staff with its captive Sun Stone into the ground, I grasped the handle with both hands, calling on the Sun—its size, its strength, its irresistible pull—to convince the boulder to rise from its landing spot. The glow of the Stone bathed the river bank, a sunrise contained in an amber gem the size of my two fists.

I clenched my teeth, muscles straining. Although Sun and Stone delivered the power, a mage still had to control it. And that boulder was *heavy*, unwilling to abandon its new home in the river bed. As it rose in the air, I saw why: Its base was easily three times the size of the bit that had peeked above the water. I was lifting something the size of the House of Mages.

I gave one last mental shove, levitating the boulder until it was safely away from the river, and let it thud to earth. I ought to have moved it beyond the fields, rough with stubble from the harvest and already rimed with frost, but without stronger sunlight to power my Stone, I couldn't manage it. I'd need to come back in early spring when the Sun was on the ascendant to move it before first planting.

That would mean cutting my respite short, but that was a worry for later. For now, I needed to conserve enough power to remake the bridge.

Luckily, the villagers kept a goodly supply of replacement slats and coils of rope on the far bank so I didn't have to forage for materials. I used up the lot, my Stone twining wood and hemp together in a dance above the water until the bridge was back. The villagers could spend their fierce, interminable winter replenishing the stock for the next time the bloody thing needed repairs. And it would. It always did.

I walked across the bridge, skirting the inner fields planted with winter-hardy vegetables where a few of the citizens were occupied with their end-of-season tasks.

The village streets were busy enough. Here and there among the brown-skinned Earth-born, I caught a glimpse of darker skin like my own. *Hmmm.* Unusual for a Sun-born to venture this far north unless, like me, they had duties that required it. None of my people appreciated the cold.

I strode down the muddy main street, past citizens bustling about their business as if the mountain hadn't exploded over their heads not a fortnight ago. As I approached the town hall, the village reeves hurried out to meet me. The man, Barkon, outpaced Netta, the women's representative, as he always did. I was constantly surprised that the men of the town didn't elect a different reeve, one who wasn't so nervous.

"Magister, thank the Earth you've come." Barkon panted to a stop in front of me, wringing his hands. "We have a... a situation."

"I'm aware of that, Elder. That's why I'm here." I gestured to the top of Star Mountain—or rather, to where the top of Star Mountain had been until something had blown it off.

"Yes, yes. But this is a *real* emergency."

"What Barkon means," Netta drawled, dusting her hands on her breeks, "is that this affects him personally. So it must be more important."

Barkon scowled at her. "That's not the point. If the mountain decides to fall on us, how can we stop it? It will fall or not, no matter what we do. But this other problem is right here, in our village, in our *hall*."

I glanced between them. Barkon avoided looking at my face, as the sight of my eye-patch apparently made him even more nervous. He always focused his attention on my collar-bone. Netta at least met my single-bored gaze but didn't offer any clarification.

I was tempted to sigh, but I'd been a circuit mage long enough to hide my impatience. "Suppose you tell me of this situation then."

Barkon swallowed audibly, his throat working behind his collar of office. "After the... the event on Star Mountain, the next day, we found a... a person. On the river bank."

My attention sharpened. "Someone was caught by the river when that boulder came down? Were they injured? Sun and stars, man, where are they? You stand here, whining in the street, when—"

"Peace, Magister." Netta showed her palms. "No one in the village was hurt. This person is a stranger. We suspect he came from the mountain."

I blinked, which made Barkon wince. "A Star-born? Here?"

Netta's brows drew together. "Not a Star-born, no, although who can tell? Nobody's ever seen one that I can remember."

"Then what? Earth-born? Sun-born?"

She shook her head, grim satisfaction in the set of her mouth. "*Moon*-born."

My fingers clenched on my staff. "Impossible. The Moon-born are gone. Dead these thirty years and more."

"Nevertheless…" She shrugged. "We found a person, not Sun-born and not Earth-born, naked on the river bank."

"Naked? In this weather?"

"Well, mostly naked. I wouldn't call what he was wearing fit for a dash to the privy, let alone a swim in the river."

"Where is he then? I should examine him. Treat him for exposure."

Barkon licked his lips and jerked his head toward the hall. "She's in the cellar. In the gaol."

I frowned. "She? Netta said *he*."

"Yes, well, there's the issue. We have a bit of a disagreement on that point."

"How long"—I tightened my grip on my staff to keep from throttling Barkon—"has the *person* been in gaol?"

"Since, ah, we found her." Barkon tugged at his collar. "The day after the explosion."

My Sun-driven rage began to build, a burn in my belly. "You've kept him—"

"It's not a him," Barkon insisted.

"Then you've kept her—"

"It's not a her," Netta countered.

I clenched my teeth. "You've kept this person locked up underneath the town for a bloody fortnight? I ought to report you for hospitality infringement."

"You don't understand, Magister. She—"

"I told you, Barkon, he's a man."

"Elders. Please. Obviously the person in your custody is two-natured at minimum." The reeves looked blank. "You've heard of the two-natured, surely?"

"Hearing is one thing, Magister," Netta said. "But seeing? We've never—"

"Apparently you have now. But let us leave the issues of sex and gender out of this discussion. It's irrelevant to your treatment of a stranger."

"Not just a stranger, Magister." Barkon fiddled with his collar again. "A mage. An unregistered one. Has to be. No other way to account for the..." He glanced over first one shoulder, then the other, earning a snort from Netta. "... the *spell*."

I pulled my staff across my chest in a double-handed grip, my head whipping around to check my blind left side for a rogue mage who might be creeping up on me. *Ridiculous.*

I straightened, planting my staff at my feet. "A spell, you say? What spell?"

Barkon edged closer. "Anyone who goes in there, anyone at all, gets overcome with a... well... a *need* if you get my meaning. An *urge*."

"Earth and sky, Barkon, when did you turn into a stripling?" Netta crossed her arms and glared at me. "Whoever goes into that cell turns into a bitch in heat."

Barkon bridled. "I never—"

"You did. Your pants were around your ankles, man, and your pecker in your hand. If it weren't for the bars between you, you'd have—"

"Enough!" I thrust my staff between them before Barkon's head exploded like Star Mountain. "Regardless of the details, it sounds as though the hospitality laws aren't the only violations here. Barkon, did you seriously expose yourself to a captive stranger? Did you bother to ask their leave? Give them a proper choice?"

Barkon's throat worked. "I— It was the spell, Magister. You know I would never— No one in *our* village would ever do such a thing!"

"Much as I hate to agree with Barkon," Netta said, "he's right. The same thing happens to everyone. Once they're within ten feet of him—"

"Her," Barkon grumbled.

"—they're suddenly desperate to swive. Do you know how difficult it's been to keep all the apprentices out of there? We need you to take him away to prison in the capital."

I shuddered. *Prison if they're lucky.* An unregistered mage, using sexual coercion spells? That was enough to get anyone beheaded, drawn, and quartered, in whatever order the Congress was in the mood for on Judgment Day.

"Right, then. Let's waste no more time." I waited, but neither Barkon nor Netta moved, both of them gazing at the muddy ground at their feet. "Well? Which one of you is the gaoler?"

"The thing is, Magister..." Barkon swallowed noisily again. "We don't like to go in there because of, well..."

"He's afraid he'll have another uncontrollable *urge.* Although to be fair—" Netta patted her coronet of braids. "—so am I."

"Very well. The key?" I held out my hand, and Barkon handed it over.

"Could you take him his meal?" Netta snapped her fingers and an apprentice who'd been lurking nearby hustled over with a burlap bag and a water skin.

"You haven't even fed them?" My rage rose higher, power bleeding from my Sun Stone until my own braids lifted and swirled around my torso.

Barkon spluttered. "Of course we have. Er, we *do.*"

"He doesn't eat much." Netta took the provisions from the apprentice, who scuttled away—no doubt to put distance between him and the angry one-eyed mage. "I think he may be sickening for something."

I bared my teeth. "Did you bother to pass them a healing stone?"

This time, Netta wouldn't meet my gaze. "We're, ah, running low. With several confinements coming this winter—"

I snatched the bag and water skin. "I expected better of you," I growled. "Of the whole village."

"Don't judge us until you meet her, Magister." Barkon puffed his chest out like an indignant hen. "And if I were you, I'd don your fiercest protection charms. There's not a man, woman, or child in this village—"

"Child?" I roared. "The adults are afraid of uncontrollable urges, and you send *children*—"

"Stay, Magister." Netta held up her hand, patting the air in a placating gesture. "The children don't have the same reaction. Yes, they're drawn to him, but as if he were a kindly uncle with a bag of sweeties."

"That's what I'm worried about," I muttered.

I left Barkon and Netta staring one another down and stormed up the steps into the hall.

Just my luck to run into another rogue mage. I was the one who'd had to track down Loriah at the Congress's decree. I'd resisted for as long as I could. Loriah and I had grown up together, trained together, taken our mage oaths together. But I couldn't hold out forever, not against my superiors' direct orders, and I'd been instructed to deliver her to the Congress of Mages and Seigneurs personally.

I delivered her, all right, but not before she'd half-blinded me.

Her execution was the first thing I'd seen one-eyed, and I'd have closed my remaining eye if I could. They'd ripped her Stone from her—almost worse than death for a Sun mage, although her death hadn't been an easy one.

The Congressional tribunal hadn't been in a merciful mood that Judgment Day.

I descended the stairs from the hall proper to the cellar that housed the gaol. The rough stone walls breathed damp and chill, a discomfort just shy of pain to my Sun-born blood. Would a Moon-born be similarly afflicted?

The chair at the bottom of the stairs, where a guard should have been stationed, was empty.

"Cowards," I muttered and stomped down the short hallway to where two tiny cells were cut out of the bedrock. The one on the right was empty. I had to turn my head to compensate for my missing left eye to view the other cell.

"Sun, moon, and stars," I breathed.

The person in the cell stood under the narrow horizontal window slit. They wore a ragged brown robe, an obvious cast-off from the Earth temple's charity box. The fabric had fallen away from their arms as they stretched them up toward the window, fingers straining for the sliver of light that was all that made it past the screen of dirt and weeds.

Even in the near-dark of the cell, I could tell those arms were as pale as new milk.

Shite. The reeves were right.

Moon-born.

My gut tightened. I wasn't qualified for this, the first encounter with a Moon-born mage since the Lunaria plague had swept through the population over three decades ago, killing every last Moon-born on the continent, yet leaving Sun-born and Earth-born untouched. This was a job for the Congress, not a half-blind circuit mage patrolling the arse-end of beyond.

I had no idea what Moon magic was like. When the plague hit, I hadn't even been born. Later, when I was old enough to understand such things, the Moon-born were spoken of rarely, and then only in furtive whispers, as though folk feared the mere mention of the lost race would call down the same fate on their heads.

Sun mages specialized in healing, in counseling, in dispensing justice outside the capital. The Earth-born held no magic potential whatsoever, content with farming and government. What had the Moon-born done? What magic had they wielded? At this point, they were as mysterious and unknowable as the Star-born in their mountain fastnesses.

I cursed the boulder for draining most of my reserves. If I had to face down a rogue Moon mage, I needed every trick at my disposal, every scrap of power. I'd learned, however, that what I couldn't counter with magic, I could often handle with physical intimidation. I'm tall—one of the tallest of the Sun-born and we're all taller than the Earth-born—broad across the chest from chopping my own firewood, lean from constantly walking the length and breadth of my circuit for ten months of every fourteen.

Plus the eye-patch made everyone uncomfortable.

"You." I put an extra growl in my voice.

The Moon mage flinched but didn't turn. I noticed their hair hung lank and matted, only reaching the base of their neck. Its lack of cleanliness was one thing—the reeves could have at least allowed their alarming prisoner a bath—but its length was another story. Only criminals had their hair shorn. My own dozens of narrow braids hung past my hips. Barkon kept his gathered in a loose-woven snood, not as tidy as Netta's plaited crown.

Had the villagers cut the mage's hair because of the alleged spell? If so, they had more to answer for than simple hospitality violations or even choice infringement. Only the Congress or a mage on the circuit, as the Congress's official proxy, could order a shearing, and then only after clear proof of guilt.

I steeled myself against an unwelcome surge of pity. "You have serious charges laid against you. What do you have to say?"

The Moon mage lowered their arms. Their shoulders rose and fell once, and then their fingers clutched their ragged robe as though they were gathering power for a strike.

I braced for attack. I'd never felt sexual desire before, but what if Moon magic was stronger than my nature, than my will? If I were overcome by the spell—if I broke the vows I made when I took up my Sun Stone—I'd lose more than my reputation.

I'd lose my life.

Chapter Two

Torian

The man looming outside the cell was enormous. He was taller than any of the Infomancers or Lab assistants and easily twice my breadth, even accounting for the bulk of his sheepskin vest and heavy, fur-lined cloak. The shivers that had chased across my skin since the moment I'd stepped out of the Lab—woefully underdressed for the climate, despite the meteorological data at my disposal—increased exponentially at the promise of the warmth inherent in those garments.

I recognized the man as what the Infomancers called the J-4 strain, what the planetary subjects referred to as Sun-born: dark skin, dark eyes, black hair braided close to his scalp with dozens of finger-narrow plaits falling to below his waist. Square jaw—smooth, of course. The Originators had engineered all subjects, regardless of their strain, to be beardless.

He held a wooden staff. *Oak equivalent, heartwood, twenty-seven point three cycles old*, according to the cybertronic sensors threaded along my veins. The huge chunk of amber chrysocite contained in the cradle atop the staff identified him as a solar energy manipulator.

A mage. Higher in status than anyone else in this primitive habitation. None of them had been any use at all. Perhaps this man would be able to help. To get me away from the Laboratory and its chaos before the Infomancers noticed I was gone and mounted a recovery operation.

This helplessness was intolerable. If I had been allowed even an hour to charge my power grid in the sun, this prison would have been laughably inadequate. But I had lost consciousness after fighting free of the icy river. I had awoken after full dark, a captive in this dreadful hole. With no artificial lights to provide even a glimmer of power, I was close to emergency shut-down.

If I didn't act quickly, I would have insufficient power to drive my body enhancement modules and convince the mage that I could fulfill his needs. Contingent, of course, on release from this cage.

I studied the mage, who glared balefully out of his single eye, but could get no sexual preference signals at all. He registered as null on my sensor array. *Why can't I read this one? Is it because he's a mage?* From my studies of the Lab databanks, I'd reached the conclusion that the Infomancers, in their hubris, had grossly underestimated the subjects' abilities, particularly those of the mages.

Or perhaps it was nothing more sinister than my lamentable lack of reserves.

Very well, then. As the Infomancers told the Lab assistants, nothing can be verified without experimentation. *Frame your question. Test your hypothesis. Reframe the question. Test again.*

I could apply their methods here, although as always, I shrank away from the subterfuge of the enhancement modules. Male, female, balanced—all three were intrinsic to my nature without the need of additional programming. But the Infomancers had installed the modules anyway, claiming it was for my benefit, so I wouldn't slip and adopt an unsuitable aspect for whoever happened to be my current assignment.

In the absence of more complete data, therefore, I would begin with the default. *If male, then female.*

"Well?" The mage's voice was deep, as befit his barrel chest.

I activated the female module. The changes were subtle. Attitude, posture, presentation. I looked up from under my lashes as I'd learned to do when servicing the Infomancers who preferred the female in manner. I could manufacture few of the supporting pheromones any longer, not without a recharge, but

I'd found that most males seeking a female didn't require much in the way of enticement.

Not so with the mage. He continued to glare at me, seeming angry as opposed to aroused.

"What are you playing at?"

Not the default then. I reversed the polarity to male, standing straighter, shoulders back, meeting the mage's eye without any overt subservience. The Infomancers who sought male sexual partners typically preferred stronger, less pliant behavior. It gave them something to subdue and added to their illusion of superiority.

Since the mage looked strong enough to break me in two should he choose, the need to pretend physical inferiority was clearly moot. A tiny frisson of fear sparked my sensors before I damped down my feedback circuits. No Infomancer had ever damaged me beyond the odd bruise or two. I was too valuable a resource. This man, though, had no such restriction.

Nevertheless, if the mage was a means of escape from the Infomancers, I was prepared to take the risk.

I raised my chin and smiled, forcing the last of the pheromone enhancement from my depleted backup stores.

It did no good. The mage still glared.

"I see why the reeves couldn't agree on your nature. What are you?"

I lowered my gaze. "I can be whatever you like."

"What I like is for you to be yourself. Or do you know who that is, since you seem determined to play turnabout?"

"I… I suppose I am both." I deactivated the module and reverted to my preferred balanced state. "Or neither. It depends on circumstance."

"Such as who you're trying to seduce into getting your way?"

The warmth of a blush, the one involuntary response the Infomancers hadn't been able to program away, started at the base of my throat and rose all the way to my forehead. While mortified at being caught out, I was nevertheless grateful for the heat.

The mage blinked. With a single eye, it almost looked like a wink, although the way the rest of his face went slack, I didn't mistake it for a response to my sexual overtures.

"I apologize," I said, low-voiced. "But you have me at a disadvantage, you realize. If you... If I... Oh." My knees buckled, and I reached out, but missed the wall entirely.

Reserves depleted. Shut-down commencing in three... two... one.

Chapter Three

Zal

The Moon mage crumpled like a broken doll, landing gracelessly in the cell's scuffed straw.

"Shite." I'd been so startled by their impossible presence, mesmerized by the way color rose across their skin like sunrise after a night of rain, that I'd forgotten my duty, just as I'd forgotten the water skin and food still clutched in my hand.

Clearly the Moon mage—fool that I was, I hadn't bothered to ask for a *name* yet—was on the edge of starvation. Their face was thin to the point of gaunt, cheekbones sharply prominent, dark circles under eyes the color of storm clouds.

Ah, bugger it. Whatever Moon magic had affected the villagers had had no effect on me. The mage seemed dazed and nearly unconscious in the noisome straw. Not much of a threat.

I unlocked the cell and walked in, propping my staff in the corner and calling forth a low glow from the Sun Stone, just enough to see better in this miserable hole. I lifted the mage, settling the dark head in the crook of my arm. I pulled the cork from the water skin with my teeth and set it to their parched lips.

"Here. Take a sip. Not too fast."

I needn't have uttered the warning. They ignored the water, focusing instead on my staff.

"Oh." They reached out a trembling hand, and for an instant, the light from the Stone seemed to flow through their long, thin fingers like honey. "Chrysocite. It emits solar power. I'd forgotten."

Chryso-which? What in the name of the Sun were they on about? "Listen you—what's your name, anyway?"

"I'm called Torian."

"Torian, then. Zal here. Take a drink before I have to force it down you. You're dehydrated. I can tell."

Something else was going on with Torian too. Their life energies felt peculiar, jerking along in uneven bursts rather than flowing smoothly. After they took a few sips of water and turned away to stare avidly at the Sun Stone, I set the water skin on the floor, then placed two fingers on the pulse-point in Torian's wrist.

Shite! I snatched my hand away, fingers tingling. I tried the other pulse point, at the angle of the jaw, and got the same tiny jolt. Oddly, it was the same sensation as when I touched my Sun Stone directly—not that I was fool enough to do that, not unless I was dead certain it was fully depleted.

Did Moon mages carry magic in their very skin? Could Torian hold other secrets, pose other threats? They might seem no more dangerous than a half-drowned catamountain kit right now, but wasn't the appearance of helplessness the best way to lull an enemy? That ploy had certainly worked for Loriah.

I sighed. So much for getting home before the storms. I'd take Torian to the capital, as the reeves wanted, to let the Congress of Mages and Seigneurs sort it out. That was their job, after all. My job was simply to deliver Torian to the tribunal for judgment.

Sun willing, I'd survive this go-round with a rogue mage without losing any more body parts.

"Can you stand?"

Torian hesitated, turning away from the staff with obvious reluctance. "I think so."

"Good. We've got a long journey ahead of us. You've got to face the Congressional tribunal. Explain your magic. Justify using it against citizens with no consideration for their will."

"I have no magic."

"Bollocks to that. You cast your seduction spell on everyone who came near."

Torian studied Zal somberly. "But not on you."

"No. But wasn't for lack of trying, was it?"

Remorse flickered across Torian's face, but was it regret for the spell itself or for its failure? Until I knew for certain, I wasn't about to let my guard down.

"Will you be the one to take me to this tribunal?"

"Nobody else seems up to the job."

"Then I will go."

"You don't have a choice. I'm sorry about that."

They blinked those luminous gray eyes, eyes that seemed all the larger because their face was so gaunt. "I see."

I stood and helped Torian to their feet. At least they didn't seem to be playing gender guessing games with me anymore.

As I helped them negotiate the stair, I noticed they were barefoot. "Haven't you any shoes at all? Clogs? Boots? Slippers, even?"

"No. I left in rather a hurry."

"Even so, who forgets shoes?"

Torian glanced up at me and lifted one dark eyebrow. "Someone who's never worn them?"

My jaw sagged. "Never? Who never wears shoes? Especially in winter?"

"It wasn't an issue. The Lab is climate-controlled." Fear shadowed their eyes. "Or was."

"That so?" I had no idea what this Lab was, but that was the tribunal's problem, not mine. "Well, it's an issue now. Welcome to the edge of winter in the north."

We stepped out the door into the street. The instant they cleared the roof of the hall, Torian gasped and scrabbled at the neck of their robe as if they were about to strip it off.

I gripped their wrists, bracing myself against the zing of almost-familiar power. "Oi. None of that. You're already in a world of trouble for that kind of thing." I squinted at Torian's soft white hands. Was that a glint of gold under their skin?

"But..." They peered up at the pale winter sun, such longing in their face that I nearly relented. "Very well." They shrugged their ragged robe back over their shoulders, but surreptitiously kept their hands out, palms up, as if to cup the watery light.

I released their wrists and ran a hand over my head. "Ah, bugger it. You can't make this trip barefoot and in rags."

Torian didn't respond, simply stood shivering in the muddy street, eyes closed, their face turned up to the wan sun with an expression as if their last, best dream had come true.

I spotted Barkon hovering in the lee of the blacksmith shop, Netta at his side. A gang of village youths, boys and girls old enough for apprenticing, lurked behind the livery stable, watching Torian's every move. I glared at them until they dropped their gazes. *Up to no good, that lot.* I beckoned to the reeves, but they wouldn't come closer than a dozen yards away.

"You're taking her, then, Magister?"

I glanced down at Torian, who hadn't reacted to Barkon's pronoun use. Maybe it didn't matter to them. Or maybe, as they'd said, they became whoever the other person wanted. Barkon wanted female, so Torian was *she*.

Not my problem.

"I'm taking them, but not like this. They need a proper kit. Leggings, shirt, tunic, vest, cloak, boots, pack. A hat."

"But... But... We... The village stores... We can't afford—"

I glared at him. "Don't push me, Barkon. I've half a mind to report you for hospitality violations on food, water, *and* shelter. Not to mention you deprived a citizen of choice. You know what that means."

Barkon clutched his snood. "No. Not a shearing. I didn't—" He turned to Netta. "It was her, too."

Netta cast a disgusted glance at Barkon. "Give over, Magister. What were we to do? Seemed like a rogue mage to us." She peered at me from shrewd dark eyes. "Clearly you don't know what to do with 'em either."

"I know enough to feed them and keep them from dying of exposure. For that, they need clothing, and that's your duty under law."

"Much as I hate to agree with Barkon, you've caught us at a disadvantage. A number of our citizens are decamping, heading south for winter, in case Star Mountain decides to spew on us again. We've not got much to spare."

I sighed. I had no time or heart for bargaining right now. I swung my pack off my back. "How much?"

Netta's eyes gleamed. "We could do with some extra healing stones. As I said, we're running low and it never hurts to have spares."

"And prosperity stones," Barkon blurted. "For protection. From the mountain."

I dug in my pack, pulling out two of the leather scraps I kept for dispensing supplies. I wrapped up four healing stones and handed them to Netta. I glanced at Barkon, who fairly danced in place at the notion of four prosperity stones. *Not likely.* I wrapped a single prosperity stone and handed it over—to Netta.

"Will that do?"

"In a pinch." She pointed to the gang by the stable. "You, there. Farren. Morvan. I've a task for you." Two of the older apprentices slouched over, cutting a wide berth around me.

While she gave them low-voiced orders, I turned to Torian. "We'll get you sorted with some essentials. I worry about your feet, though. No boots Netta can scare up will fit you properly. You'll likely be rubbed raw by the time we make camp every night. I can treat you then, fix them up for the next day, but during the day's trek?" I shrugged. "I'm afraid it'll be brutal."

Torian lowered their chin, turning their face from sun contemplation, but I didn't miss the half-fearful glance at the mountain. "Will we be going away from here?"

"Aye."

"Then I'll make do."

Chapter Four

Zal

I didn't force the pace the first afternoon—or at least I didn't think I did. But Torian was a good foot shorter than me, still recovering from near-starvation, and unused to hard tramping, if indeed they'd ever done any at all in this Lab of theirs.

The way they lifted their feet, as if the boots Netta had found were leaden weights, made their claim of having never worn shoes believable.

By the time I found a reasonably protected campsite in a fall of rocks that shielded us from the vicious wind, Torian was limping visibly. But they'd never complained. Not once.

I shed my pack and my cloak and pointed to a fallen tree. "Sit there. I'll gather wood for a fire, then see to your feet."

Torian sank down on the log. "Thank you. Can I be of assistance?"

"I don't know. Can you? Ever made a fire?"

"Of course." They struggled to their feet. "Where's the accelerant?"

"Don't know what that is, but I'm pretty sure we don't have any. Just sit. I'll handle it." I unstrapped my ax from the pack and turned toward the woods.

"Wait. Are you... That is, you trust me here alone?"

I grunted. "Not a matter of trust. I don't think you could move another step, not if the whole of Corvel-on-Byrne was after you with fire and pitchforks."

I strode into the trees. By the time I got back with a double armful of wood, Torian had removed their boots and the three pairs of socks Netta had come up with to try and make the things fit better.

Their pale, narrow feet were rubbed raw at heels, ankles, and toes. Guilt curdled my belly. After I'd given the reeves shite about cruel and unusual, I'd done the same by forcing this march.

I dropped down in front of Torian, my hand hovering over one of their feet. "May I?" At their nod, I cradled it in my hand. This time, the ping against my skin was stronger, running up my arm in a not-unpleasant way. I ignored it—*no harm so far*—and turned the poor foot this way and that, my healer's skills assessing damage, considering treatment.

Torian sucked in a breath. I glanced up to see them clenching their eyes shut, teeth sunk into their full lower lip.

"I'm sorry. Did I hurt you?"

"No. It's just... One of my regulars had a... a thing for my feet."

"Your regulars. What regulars?"

Torian opened their eyes, shadowed and wary now, and I cursed the accusatory tone of my voice.

"I... One of my jobs at the lab was sex aid."

"Sex aid? You were a sex worker? Like in a Comfort House?"

"I suppose you could say that. If the Infomancers or Lab assistants required release, it was my duty to provide it."

I narrowed my eye. "Your duty? Not your choice?"

"It was my *job*. I was compensated, like any other Lab assistant."

"Could you have gotten a different job if you'd wanted?"

"I wasn't qualified for anything else."

"So you *didn't* have a choice." My fingers tightened on Torian's foot, and they flinched. "Shite. I'm sorry." I gentled my hold. "Look, we need to talk more about this. But for now, I need to treat your wounds."

Torian nodded, hunching deeper into their oversized jerkin and dusty second-hand cloak.

I considered the medicines I had in my pack. Rudimentary for the most part. Magic was a marvelous thing, but sometimes it was as well to treat a cut with a little protective salve, keep it clean, and give it time. But this wasn't one of those occasions, not if I expected Torian to be able to walk tomorrow.

I'd have to use my staff, despite the fact it was still depleted from moving that thrice-blasted boulder and rebuilding the bridge, followed by a half-day's march under heavy cloud-cover.

I pulled a crumbling meatroll from my pack and held it out to Torian. "Here. Eat this while I get things ready."

They attempted to refuse it. "I don't really—"

"Eat it. You're nothing but bones, and you need your strength."

Torian's eyes widened at the fierceness in my tone. "I'm sorry."

"Don't be. I'm not angry at *you*." But I was completely out of charity with the citizens of Corvel-on-Byrne and the Infomancers, whoever they were, in this Lab, whatever *that* was.

We'd been following the river all day, so I stumped down to the bank and filled both of our water skins and the cook pot, considering my options. While it was the duty of the circuit mages to serve the citizens of their jurisdictions, it was the duty of *all* mages to advance learning and to share that knowledge for the betterment of all.

Who else had had the opportunity in the last two decades to speak with a Moon-born? To understand their magic? I had no illusions: Once I turned Torian over to the tribunal, there was little chance I'd see them again, let alone have this opportunity for uninterrupted conversation. The sin of all mages was insatiable curiosity.

Curiosity and, in my case, a very inconvenient compassion.

When the Congress had sent me to arrest Loriah, I'd almost let her go, believing her tale of misunderstanding and persecution. Then she'd gone for my eyes, the look on her face as feral as any mad cur.

This time, I'd keep my guard well up.

I stalked up the trail to the campsite and set the pot on a flat rock next to the fire to warm the water. Planting the staff so it would stand at my back, I took my place in front of Torian, my medicine kit next to me, a length of rough toweling across my lap.

Before I picked up Torian's foot again, though, I remembered to ask again. "You permit?"

Torian nodded, still hunched and clearly miserable.

I lifted one foot and wiped the raw flesh gently with lambs-wool soaked in a mild cleanser. "You know, don't you, that what you did in the village was wrong?"

"You mean trying to convince them to let me go?"

I stilled, the sponge resting on Torian's instep. "Is that what you were doing?"

"Of course. I needed to get away." They looked back the way we'd come. Although the village was out of sight, the topless mountain loomed over the trees. "I still do."

"Doesn't matter, you know. Using magic that interferes with free will is illegal. Our whole society is based on the right of every citizen to choose. When you bespelled them—"

"I'm not a mage. I can't bespell anybody."

"You cast the same spell at me. Twice. It didn't work, but that doesn't make it any less unlawful."

I set Torian's foot on the toweling and tested the water in the pot. Warm enough. I tossed in a handful of soothing herbs to reduce the discomfort of the healing process. Rogue mage or not, Torian had had precious little pleasantness lately. "This may sting for a moment." I eased their feet into the warm water, holding their ankles firmly when their feet twitched. "If you're to be able to walk tomorrow, I'll have to speed the healing with a spell."

"Isn't that illegal?" A faint note of irony laced Torian's voice. "Aren't you bespelling me?"

"Technically, I'm bespelling the water. You have the choice to remove your feet if you wish." I lifted my hands, nodding at the pot. "Up to you. You're the one who has to walk on them tomorrow, and we'll be on the trail for a full day rather than just a half."

"Very well."

Sulky, now, are we? I hid a grin. Perhaps Moon mages weren't so different from anyone else. "Right, then." I focused my attention on my task, reaching for the link to the Sun.

"I'm not certain I understand the nuances, but—" Torian sucked in a breath when my Sun Stone began to glow. "Oh. Yes." The word was spoken like a prayer.

I circled a fingertip over the water, and it began to swirl, turning from clear to opaque to white to gold. I murmured the healing words under my breath.

"That's so... I've never... Please don't stop."

Sun, moon, and stars—Torian sounded as if they were deep in the throes of lovemaking, not in the midst of medical treatment in the wilderness. If this was another attempt to ignite my non-existent sex drive...

I glanced up, and the words of reproach died on my lips. My finger stilled, and the water stopped swirling and lost its glow, but the light didn't fade. Because the light was *inside* Torian, illuminating them, a pattern of gold weaving under their pale skin like a web of fire.

They blinked, disappointment clouding their gaze. "You've stopped."

"What *are* you? A parasite? Is this what a Moon mage does? Suck up the light of the Sun?"

"I'm not a mage. I told you. I'm not a parasite either."

I scuttled backward, knocking my staff to the ground and dousing my Sun Stone. "That's for the tribunal to decide. But I warn you, I'll have to give testimony about what I've seen you do."

"I understand." The gold lattice under their skin faded. Torian looked unhappy—who wouldn't, when faced with legal action?—but less malnourished.

I pretended I believed it was from the meatroll, but I wasn't fooling myself. Torian had absorbed magic from my Sun Stone, taken it in like they were *feeding* on it.

Think about it, man. Isn't that what the moon is? It had no light of its own, only reflected light stolen—or at the very least, borrowed—from the sun. Is that what Moon mages were? Leeches who could drain the power from a Sun Stone, from a Sun mage, whether the Sun mage chose to allow it or not?

Perhaps it was a good thing there weren't any more of them —and perhaps this was why.

I tossed the second bedroll at Torian's now-healed feet. "Here. Get some sleep. We march out at first light."

I'd get Torian to the capital. Once I turned them over, they'd be somebody else's problem and I could go home and forget all about them.

Chapter Five

Torian

The torture of the next few days almost made me wish I was back in the Lab.

The morning of the second day, Zal gave me a quartz-laced pebble and told me to keep it in a pocket so my feet wouldn't get quite so raw during the journey. Consequently, my feet fared better, although my legs and back were not so fortunate. Apparently the pebble's healing properties were quite localized. I stored that piece of data for later consideration, automatically framing a report to the Infomancers, recommending further study.

But then I remembered: That life was over now, and well over at that.

I repeated that litany as I marched, but every night, my gaze was drawn to the broken top of the mountain, which never seemed to grow further distant. The ruins of the Lab, since I knew where to look, still faintly glowed in the dark like a misplaced star, neither fading nor flaring, giving no clue whether anyone remained inside.

After four long days on the trail, I had at last begun to believe pursuit unlikely, that the Infomancers had all either perished in the attack or fled off-planet as they'd been scrambling to do when I escaped. After all, what was one cyborg compared to all their lives, particularly a cyborg manufactured from one of their own failed experiments?

To keep my mind off my discomfort, and to bury the fear that they might yet be tracking me, I began to log information about the journey, simply because I wanted to and because no one was there to forbid it.

The trees, as an example, in their endless variety and aspect. Somehow, the information in the data banks didn't do justice to the way the deciduous specimens bent in the wind, their bare branches creaking, dry leaves crunching underfoot. Or the soughing of the evergreens, their pungent smell, the prick of their needles as we pushed through a close-grown stand.

Just as well I was accustomed to the company of my own observations and thoughts because Zal hadn't spoken to me again since the first night. Or only orders, such as "Sit here," and "Eat this," or warnings such as "Mind the ledge."

My energy reserves were another problem. If I could lie bared to the sun's rays, allowing the solar network on my back and shoulders to absorb the light and recharge completely, I'd be able to manage the discomfort myself with my body enhancement modules. They weren't only good for complementing secondary sex characteristics: They amplified my recovery subroutines. They could ease aches and pains, even subtly augment my muscle mass so I wouldn't be so pathetically weak compared to the strapping mage, who apparently never tired, never hurt, and never slowed down.

Just when I thought Zal would continue to march until dark again, he announced camp in his bass growl while the sun was still above the horizon but below the persistent cloud cover. After he stomped off to gather wood, I quickly stripped off cloak, jerkin, and shirt, baring my back and shoulders with their embedded solar grid.

I sighed with relief as power thrummed along my circuits, even though my skin pebbled in the cold. While soaking up the last of the sun's rays, I scanned the edge of the clearing, my awakening systems allowing access to data on edible flora. Perhaps, if I were to prove my good will and ability to assist in the journey, to become something other than a burden and a duty, Zal would relent and *talk* to me again.

At sunset, while Zal still crashed about in the woods, I resettled my clothing and scouted the immediate undergrowth and along the river bank, collecting wild onions, a handful of desiccated berries, and the leaves of a kale-equivalent. By the time Zal returned with a bundle of wood under one arm and a string of fish dangling from his other hand, I had a fairly respectable selection spread out on a rock.

Zal stopped, letting the wood drop to the ground. "What's that?"

"A salad. I thought our diet might benefit from some fresher items."

"Salad, you say?" He scratched the back of his head through his heavy braids. "Looks like a mess of weeds to me."

I tilted my head to look up at him. "Technically, they *are* weeds. That doesn't mean they're not edible. Don't you eat greens?"

"Of course. But not on the trail. And not in winter."

"Do you object to them?"

Zal scowled as he squatted to build the fire. "No."

"I'm afraid we'll have to eat them plain. I have nothing to dress them with."

He snapped his fingers and a flame leaped onto the kindling. "I might have something that'll do." His gaze flicked up to me, the fire dancing in the depths of his eye. "Thank you."

In the end, we had the greens and a fish stew flavored with the onions and wild thyme. I didn't normally concern myself with organic food since my cybertronic energy could sustain me, provided I remained sufficiently charged and hydrated. But there was something satisfying about sharing a meal with Zal, a meal we had prepared together.

Zal apparently felt the same way because he began to talk again, to my intense relief. The Infomancers had spoken *at* me rather than *with* me, but I'd missed communication, however utilitarian.

Zal fed another log into the fire. "Are you really Moon-born?"

"Yes. Or so they tell me."

"'They'? You mean these Infomancers you talk about?"

"That's right."

"What under the Sun is an Infomancer anyway?"

I gazed into the flames, their warmth comforting even if the firelight couldn't add to my energy reserves. "It's... a joke, I suppose. You call them Star-born, and in a way, that's more literal than calling you Sun-born or me Moon-born. Those terms originated as references to your genetic make-up, expressed in skin and hair color, body characteristics and aptitudes. But they —the Infomancers, that is—are literally from the stars."

I leaned back and peered into the dark sky until my eyesight recalibrated. I pointed to the lower-most star in the constellation the subjects called the Galleon. "That star right there, as a matter of fact."

Zal scoffed. "Get away with you. You mean they're not even from here?"

I returned my gaze to Zal. "Neither are you, you know."

Zal frowned and tossed a twig into the flames. "I was born outside the capital, in the same cottage where my mother was born, and her father, and his father. Of course I'm from here."

"Not originally. All life on this planet was seeded by people from the third planet orbiting that star. The Lab on the mountain was constructed so the Originators could monitor their experiment."

"I mislike that notion," Zal growled.

"Nevertheless, it's true. They set the basics of your society in place and let it spin. But the latest researchers to staff the Lab have taken more onto themselves than was intended by the Originators. They're starting to interfere."

"Interfere how?"

"The virus that eliminated the C-27 strain." At Zal's blank look, I scanned my lab report files quickly and located the local nomenclature. "Lunaria."

"You mean the plague that wiped out the Moon-born?"

I inclined my head. "Yes. That was a mistake. An experiment gone wrong. They'd intended to seed a new ability into the population, instantiate a C-28 strain. But they miscalculated somewhere, and it turned lethal."

Zal stabbed the air with his forefinger. "You see? This is why it's illegal to practice magic on someone who doesn't choose the path."

"It wasn't magic. It was science."

Zal's lips set in a stubborn line. "I don't care what you call it. It was wrong."

"I can't disagree."

For a few minutes, Zal glared into the flames. Then he sighed and looked up at me. "So how did you escape? And how did they get their hands on you?"

I shrugged, readjusting my cloak when it slid off my shoulder. "They rescued me as a baby, but I would have died too. They"—I gestured, the sweep of my hand indicating my body—"*improved* me. Replaced the dying parts with synthetic ones. Over the years, they've made other modifications."

Zal lifted an eyebrow, the one above his eyepatch. "Told you all this as a bedtime story, did they? Rocked you to sleep with the tale to keep you grateful?"

I snorted at the notion of the Infomancers deigning to provide any justification for their actions. "Hardly. They never told me anything about it at all. However, one of the modifications they made was to refit me for information storage. With the data cells in my spinal column, I hold the Lab's entire data bank, including the files on my origin and subsequent schematics." I swallowed against an unexpected lump. It had been years since I'd come to terms with the dry, factual—and yes, brutal—account of the death of my entire race. "Theoretically, I can access the data, provided I'm given the correct search parameters. I was… motivated to find them in this case."

But now, I held more data, data that would never be merged with the Lab's computers—my escape, my captivity, our journey. Direct experience was a heady thing. Empowering. *All because I chose to leave.* Perhaps the planet's populace had a point when they valued choice above all else.

Across the fire, Zal's expression had turned speculative. "So you know everything they know?"

"I contain it. My data access protocols aren't very efficient. My brain is one of the only fully organic parts of my original body that remains."

"Did you choose this?"

"I was an infant. I had no concept of choice."

"What about later? All these modifications of theirs?"

I shrugged, sending my cloak slithering off my shoulder again. "By then, it was habit."

Zal frowned. "I don't like it."

"I owed them. If they hadn't taken me out of the village after they unleashed the virus, I would have died too."

"If they hadn't caused the bloody plague," Zal growled, "you'd have been in no danger in the first place. They murdered a whole race, Torian. There's no excuse for that. No way they can ever atone."

I picked at the edge of the travel-stained cloak, unable to meet Zal's furious gaze. "So you think they should have let me die?"

"Shite, no!" Zal's big hand was suddenly there, covering my own chilly fingers, stilling my fidgeting. "You deserve to live, but you shouldn't have to thank them for it. And they shouldn't have expected you to keep paying for it forever."

The warmth of Zal's hand sent an entirely anomalous data set coursing through my secondary processors. His touch didn't come with the expectation of sexual release—and I wasn't entirely sure that was a good thing. Zal was a very impressive specimen, and kind. I wouldn't have minded if he wanted the one thing I was certain I was proficient at.

Could that be respect I detected in Zal's earnest gaze? Simple affection, perhaps? I'd never received either from anyone at the Lab. Little wonder my sensor array was going haywire.

Zal took his hand away, and I was immediately colder than ever.

"I don't think much of your Infomancers. *Infomancers*. What a stupid-arsed name. You said it was a joke?"

I nodded. "There's a quotation from an ancient author from their home world. He wrote speculative fiction. He said, 'Any technology, when sufficiently advanced, is indistinguishable from magic.' So the researchers like to joke that the subjects—"

"You mean us. The citizens of this world."

"Yes. They call you subjects." *Probably the better to dehumanize you in the Infomancers' minds.* "They joke that if any of you, being primitive and believers in a system of magic, were to witness their technology, you'd consider them magicians. But they wield the magic of advanced information. So, Infomancers."

"Arrogant arseholes," Zal muttered.

I found his attitude unexpectedly comforting. "Indeed. That was their downfall."

Zal gazed into the dark, toward where the moon hung low over the mountain. "They've fallen then? The Star-born? Is that what the explosion was about?"

"Yes. Word reached their supervisors of the nature of their experiments. The supervisors... disapproved. And reacted strongly. With ionic weapons."

"Serves them right."

I ducked my head and peered at Zal from under my lashes. "Do you think I deserve punishment too? For what I did in the village?"

He sighed. "I'm not so sure now. You say you're not a mage, and I begin to believe you." He leaned forward, resting his elbows on his knees. "What's likely to happen to your Infomancers, assuming they survived the... the ionic weapons, was it?"

"I think—I hope—that they've gone, either dead, fled, or taken into custody. Their trip back to face justice will be far longer than ours. Although"—I lifted one foot in its heavy, ill-fitting boot—"much easier on the feet."

Zal's mouth dropped open for an instant, and then he laughed—a great, rolling, basso profundo laugh that echoed through the trees. *I could listen to that laugh to the end of days and not get enough.* The Infomancers had never laughed for joy. I'd forgotten that such a thing existed.

"Do you sing, Zal?"

Both his eyebrows popped up. "Now and again, if nobody's around to complain of the noise. Why?"

"Your voice is pleasant. So is your face and your..." I swallowed and averted my gaze. "... your body."

In my peripheral vision, I glimpsed Zal shift on his tree-stump chair. "Thanks, but best not get into that or you'll get us both into trouble."

I peeked up at him. "You weren't affected by the body enhancement program, nor the pheromones. Granted you haven't seen me at my best"—*understatement*—"but why weren't you affected? They've never failed on anybody else."

Zal shrugged. "You say you know all about this world. Can't you guess?"

"I only know what was in the Infomancers' data sets, and I'm beginning to think they missed more than they realized."

"Did they know that Sun mages are celibate?"

Chapter Six

Torian

Celibate? I blinked. "I— No, I don't believe so. Is that a recent development?"

"Only for the last three centuries or so." Zal's tone was dry.

"So you're resistant to the enhancements because of your magic?"

"I'm resistant, as you call it, because I don't feel desire. Not that way."

How could the cultural anthropologists have missed this? "So when you take up your vocation, your desires are... are extirpated somehow?"

"No. I've never felt any. Used to wonder what all the other lads were on about, strutting around after their manhood trials, telling lies about their conquests. I never saw the point."

"Never?"

"Not once." He smiled wryly. "Never felt I was missing much, if you want the truth. Of course, if you pass the magical aptitude tests and qualify to take up a Sun Stone, you have to take the celibacy vow or have your potential stripped from you. Pretty effective way to weed out the folks who aren't serious."

"But you are."

"Aye. That celibacy vow was the easiest promise I ever made. Not like I was giving up anything I truly wanted." His gaze turned unfocused. "Although I do miss my sister and her family. Once you take to the road as a circuit mage, your time belongs to the land, not yourself. I don't have the chance to see them but once every three or four years."

"That must be lonely."

Zal squinted up at the stars. "There are compensations, although many think they're a poor replacement. Every year, fewer candidates present themselves for training. Fewer of those who qualify are willing to make the sacrifice."

"Why did you?"

"The work's important, and somebody's got to do it. I'm qualified. I'm competent. Why not me? Everyone is expected to give back to our society somehow. This is my way."

Give back. If I wanted to fit into this world, I needed to find a way to contribute. But how? The only job I'd ever held was providing sexual release to people too consumed with their own importance to find another compatible partner. While I was well aware that this world placed no shame on honest sex work, the notion of returning to that occupation held little appeal.

I wanted something else. Something different. Something I had no name for.

"Zal."

He had been staring into the fire again, but he met my gaze over the flames. "Hmmm?"

"If I pass whatever tests your tribunal sets me, what happens then? I don't have any outstanding skills. The tools I know how to use aren't available here. How can I give back?" *How can I find a place to belong?*

Zal grinned. "That's an easy one. You know everything." He chuckled. "Well, except how to make a fire without your *accelerant*. But things no Sun-born or Earth-born has ever dreamed of. Things only the Star-born know. So tell us."

Could it be that easy? A simple sharing of information? "Is that all? Just... talk?"

"Or write it down." He lifted that single eyebrow again, the one that didn't have an eye below it. "You *can* write, can't you?"

"Of course. But—"

"Try it on, then. Tell me something from the old world, the one where you say we came from."

Suddenly, my mind was a complete blank. "What?"

"I don't know." He waved one hand. "Anything. A joke."

"A joke." There had been few reasons to laugh at the Lab, but the archives held everything. I sent a query through the appropriate channels, although the resulting data was dubious. "Knock knock."

Zal stared at him. "That's it?"

"No. It's a challenge-response sequence. You say, 'Who's there'?"

"Who's there?"

"No, wait until I start again. Knock knock."

"Who's there?"

"May."

Zal scowled. "That's not very funny."

I buried a sigh. "You have to say 'May who'?"

"Why didn't you say so? Do I have any other lines?"

"No. That's all. You just respond to the challenge. Knock knock."

"Who's there."

"Justin."

"May who?"

"No, you see, I changed the challenge, so you need to change your response."

"But you said to say 'May who.' Now it's different?" Zal threw a pebble into the fire. "Your Infomancers have a piss-poor sense of humor. We'd best leave off the jokes."

"All right." Zal might not appreciate the joke, but I hadn't been this amused in... in... well, ever. "I've told you something of the old world. It's your turn to tell me something of this one."

"I don't think that joke counts. It wasn't funny, or even finished."

"That was your choice." I allowed a hint of slyness to creep into my tone and was rewarded with Zal's flashing smile.

"Point taken. What do you want to know?"

I laced my hands around my knees. "I've never seen this world through anything other than a monitor, or lived anywhere other than the Lab. What is your home like?"

"My home? It's not much. Just a cottage. Couple of rooms below. Loft above for sleeping."

"Does it have indoor plumbing?"

"What's that?"

"Never mind. Please go on."

"The cottage isn't all that grand, but it sits on a cliff overlooking the Inland Sea. When the sun rises in midwinter, the light skates a red path across the water, right to my door. That's a beautiful sight, let me tell you."

"It sounds lovely." I couldn't keep the note of wistfulness out of my voice.

"Of course, the canton where I live is south and west, so winters aren't so vicious there. Truthfully, I enjoy winter. I don't have to travel. I can sit at home by the fire of an evening, or walk on the shore when the wind is from the west and brings the scent of other places, places I've never seen and likely never will."

"Yes. Scents. I hadn't imagined their diversity. Although not all are pleasant. The cell in the gaol?" I wrinkled my nose at the memory. "I hope never to smell *that* again."

"What, doesn't that Lab of yours have privies? Don't your Infomancers shite and piss?"

"They do. But that's what indoor plumbing is for. I'll show you when we—" I wouldn't be showing Zal anything, would I? The point of this journey was to turn me over to some other group, who would judge me and categorize me and compartmentalize me just as the Infomancers had. None of those unknown people would have a liquid dark eye, a voice to rattle bones, or a touch to soothe the most jangled nerves.

I am a prisoner still. I cannot forget. I cannot mistake Zal's moral center for liking or even for grudging tolerance.

Zal seemed to remember too. He picked up the long stick he'd used to roast a bit of fish and poked the fire, sending a shower of sparks leaping up to die in the dark.

"Your turn again. This time give us something that makes a bit of sense."

Something that made sense? Nothing made sense anymore. Certainly not the Infomancers' absolute certainty that they owned the subjects—the *people*—on this planet to do with as they pleased.

I had never considered the *rightness* of the workings at the Lab. It was simply how things were done. Form a question. Conduct experiments. Draw conclusions. Repeat.

Inside that sterile world, I had been the anomaly, both subject and co-worker. Had I truly been a colleague, though? I'd been part of experiments and research, but primarily as the subject, not the scientist. I'd never refused an enhancement proposal or turned down a sexual release assignment.

Would I have been allowed to refuse?

Choice. The only true choice I'd ever made was to run.

The Infomancers considered themselves superior, benevolent. Their research here was designed to improve the lives of others —but the others on their home world, not these people here on this planet, whom they treated like a live-action simulation. *Expendable.*

But these people weren't simulacra. Zal was real. His concern for his world, for his duty, for *right*, was far more benevolent and yes, *superior*, than the Infomancers had ever dreamed of being.

Assuming they dreamed at all.

From the music data banks, I lifted a song that had always fascinated me, both from the concept of natural consequences and because the tune was so haunting.

"This ae nighte, this ae nighte,
Every nighte and all,

Fire and fleet and candle-lighte,
And Christ receive thy soul.
When thou from hence away art past,
Every nighte and all,
To Whinny-muir thou com'st at last;
And Christ receive thy soul.
If ever thou gavest hosen and shoon,
Every nighte and all,
Sit thee down and put them on;
And Christ receive thy soul.
If hosen and shoon thou ne'er gav'st nane
Every nighte and all,
The whinnes shall prick thee to the bare bane;
And Christ receive thy soul."

While I sang the ancient tune about the rewards of charity and the penalties for its lack, Zal's gaze never wavered from my face. When the last note died away, he heaved a deep sigh.

"Sun, moon, and stars, Torian. I've never heard the like of that before, how your voice rises and falls. What do you call it?"

I frowned. "The name of the song? It's called 'Lyke Wake Dirge.' Dirges as a class were rather bleak songs, as a rule, but the tunes make them worth the singing nevertheless."

"The Earth temple priests claim what they do is singing, but it's nothing like that. Those sounds... The way they fit with the words..." Zal held out his hands helplessly. "Put it all together and it runs right down the spine and shivers there, doesn't it?"

I nodded. "That's exactly how I've always felt."

Zal rubbed the side of his nose. "One thing, though. Who's this Christ?"

Unwilling to go into the details, I shrugged, although I remembered to hold onto my cloak first. "I think they may be a bit like me. Three-natured. They seem to be in a lot of songs, although many of the lyrics are rather depressing. I fear they didn't come to a very pleasant end."

"Do you know more songs?"

"Of course. My data stores include the Infomancers' entire music catalogue." I smiled wryly. "They encoded much of it in my DNA, so sometimes retrieval can be complicated, but I can sing at least the melody of all of them." I could automatically transpose them into my own optimal range, although the limitations of my vocal chords meant that I couldn't manage any multi-voice pieces.

"I'd like to hear more sometime, if you've a mind to share. But for now, you get some rest." He stood, picked up his pack, and swung it onto his shoulder.

"You're leaving?" Anxiety bubbled up in my chest, and none of my disaster recovery programming could tamp it down. True, Zal disappeared each evening to tromp around in the woods, but he'd never been so far away that I couldn't hear him. Nor had he ever taken his pack with him before.

"Not for long. Got a bit of scouting to do. Might trap something for our meal tomorrow. You've plenty of wood here, so keep the fire stoked." Zal tapped his staff on the ground. A subtle wave of energy flowed outward, ruffling my hair and stirring the branches of the trees surrounding our campsite. "That'll keep the wildlife at bay. I'll be back in an hour or two."

"An hour or two." I huddled next to the fire as Zal disappeared into the woods. Surely I could manage for that long. I'd spent hours alone at the Lab. *But the Lab had walls.* The Infomancers and Lab assistants hadn't been friendly, but they'd been predictable. Here, with the vast, unknown dark pressing at my back, I was suddenly cognizant of how dependent I'd become on Zal in such a short time.

Unacceptable. Zal wasn't a constant. He would turn me over to the tribunal and move on without a second thought. *Best to learn some self-sufficiency now, while I still have the opportunity.*

Best to consider options as well, because if it looked as though the tribunal would treat me no better—or perhaps even worse—than the Infomancers, I intended to be ready to run.

Chapter Seven

Zal

I batted the branches out of my way as I stomped off through the woods. I couldn't deny I was running away like a coward, but I also couldn't deny I was beginning to doubt my own convictions. My training and my knowledge of the laws screamed that Torian was a rogue mage—a practitioner of unknown power who used illegal spells of coercion, depriving citizens of proper choice.

But with everything Torian had told me about their life in that Sun-forsaken Lab, about the Star-born Infomancers, about the origins of this world—*my* world—my doubts grew.

Why did our world not have a story of its beginnings? Wasn't it human nature to wonder, to find answers, even if the answers were pure guesswork and total shite? Had the Star-born, these Originators, somehow *prevented* us from even asking the questions? With what they'd done to poor Torian—I'd seen the mess of metal glinting on their back and shoulders when they'd thought I was off gathering wood—who knew what the arrogant arseholes were capable of?

I'd begun to doubt everything I'd ever learned, chiefly whether I should turn Torian over to the tribunal at all. Would they bother to listen, to understand what Torian had to say? Would they take the trouble to be kind?

Shite, that song, all about reaping what you sow. It had squeezed my heart enough to make it weep. If someone were to sit in judgment on me, on the Congress of Mages and Seigneurs, on all the Sun-born and Earth-born inhabitants of the world, would we be found lacking?

I needed clarity, and for that I needed to cast the divination stones so I could see the paths before me and make my own bloody choices.

I broke out of the tree cover onto a plateau that overlooked the river. The gibbous moon rode high over the mountains, and the tattered remains of the earlier clouds didn't obscure the stars. Perfect.

I tossed my pack down, then drove my staff into the earth amid the frost-killed grass and sat, cross-legged, the staff at my back. I pulled out the worn square of leather with its four lines —peace, prosperity, principles, partnership—and spread it on the ground in front of me.

Had this come from the Infomancers too? Had they imposed rules on the world so deeply and subtly that no citizen had ever suspected they all danced to someone else's tune?

Can't think like that. Didn't matter anyway. My spells worked. My connection to the Sun was real, palpable, *useful.* So to blazes with the Infomancers. I refused to let them choose my path for me.

I pulled the pouch on its leather thong from under my shirt and shook the divination stones into my palm. Still warm from my skin, they shone in the combined light from my Sun Stone and the moon.

"You've always spoken true for me. I have faith you'll do so now. What must I do with the Moon-born?"

I closed my eye and selected the opal by touch, its surface smooth and cooler than the others. "Moon for peace." I tossed it toward the divination mat, heard the soft *spat* as it landed.

Next, the agate, its roughness familiar, unmistakable. "Earth for prosperity." I cast it after the opal.

The flake of Sun Stone thrummed against my fingers. "Sun for principles." *Yes, principles. That's the crux of the matter, isn't it?* Which principles took precedence: the ones I'd vowed to uphold as a mage, or the ones I lived by as a man? For the first time, they seemed to oppose each other. Nevertheless, I flicked the tiny bit after the others.

"Stars—" Shite, I didn't want to cast the quartz chips. It seemed too much like giving in to the Star-born and all their plots. But the stars didn't belong to the Infomancers. The stars were there for all, shining in the sky every night. So. "Stars for partnership."

I flung the handful of quartz in the direction of the mat and took a moment to breathe, praying to the Sun that the answer would be obvious because I'd never felt so uncertain in my life. Learning to live with a single eye had been less disorienting than having the foundation of my beliefs upended by one slight, impossible person.

I opened my eye.

The Sun Stone flake and opal were aligned, touching in a tentative kiss, directly on the partnership line. The quartz chips were off the grid entirely, and the agate lay between principles and prosperity.

"Bloody wonderful. How am I to make sense out of *that*?" My own divination stones had a worse sense of humor than the fragging Infomancers.

Chapter Eight

Torian

After Zal left, I moved closer to the fire, settling on the same tree stump he had used. The flames should have warmed me, but they didn't.

I had no notion how to make my way in this world. I'd nearly died twice over—once by underestimating the power of the river and once in the dark of the village gaol.

I stared into the heart of the fire, where the flames danced orange and blue, and tried to formulate the query that would return the information I'd need to survive in the wilderness on my own, should the outcome of the tribunal be less than optimal.

For that matter, perhaps I should research ways to escape prison. Or methods of self-defense. If I could—

"You're wearing my cloak."

My head jerked up at the unfamiliar voice, and I blinked, trying to recalibrate my vision to see beyond the circle of firelight, into the dark at the edge of the clearing.

A male, just shy of full maturity, stepped out of the trees. A quick scan of my short-term memory circuits identified him as one of the crowd in the street the day Zal had rescued me from captivity.

"I... I beg your pardon?"

"My cloak." He jerked his chin at my feet and his thumb at the male standing at his right shoulder. "And Morvan's boots."

"My jerkin, Farren," said a third, whose face I'd seen more than once peering through the cell's miserable excuse for a window. "Don't forget that."

Two more joined the first three while I was still attempting to formulate an appropriate response.

My gaze pinged from one to the other before returning to Farren, the obvious leader. "But Zal paid."

Farren sneered. "Oh, aye. He paid the *reeves*. Din't pay *us*, did he? Din't give *us* no prosperity stones, nor anything to trade with in place of our kit." He took a step closer, the fire casting distorted shadows on his face. "You could pay, though."

Five of them, and no sign of Zal. *Now would be a good time to locate those self-defense files.* Since my query processor seemed inexplicably offline, I shrugged out of the cloak and removed the jerkin with trembling fingers. I held both out, the wind raising gooseflesh along the edge of my power grid. "Here. You can have them back. I'll manage without."

The third male started forward, but Farren held him back. "Leave off, Avram. Go keep watch for Magister."

"But, Farren—"

"Go!" Farren turned back to me as Avram slunk off into the dark. "Why'd we want 'em after they've been *used*?"

I glanced down at the worn edges of the cloak, and the darker cloth at the seams of the jerkin where it had clearly been taken out at least once. "I believe they'd already been used."

Farren waved my words away, his eyes glittering with reflected flames. "Second wearing means they're not worth as much as before, eh? But Comfort House folk pay in trade, same as anyone else. They just got different goods to offer." He licked his lips. "I was there with Barkon, first time he talked to you in gaol. You're just like those as work in the Comfort House."

I let the clothing fall to the dirt at my feet, dangerously close to the fire. "That was different. I didn't have a choice."

"Maybe. But out here, looks like nobody's depriving you of choice except Magister."

"He's taking me to the capital. It's his duty."

"Aye. *Doooty*. Know what happened to the last rogue mage he took to the capital on account of duty?"

I shook my head. "No." My whisper was nearly inaudible over the crackle of the logs and the wind soughing in the treetops.

Farren grinned, the firelight turning his teeth red, and drew a finger across his throat. "Cut off her head, they did."

Morvan nudged Farren with an elbow. "Don't forget the..." He pointed to his middle. "You know."

Farren nodded, pursing his lips. "Right. Slit open her belly and filled it with hot coals. But that was after they tied her up to four horses and whipped 'em up. Ripped her arms and legs right out of their sockets. Left her there in the square, screaming, for a good two days, I hear, with them other mages keeping her from death. *Then* they cut off her head. Not from mercy, but 'cos they was sick of the noise."

I hugged myself, hands clamped under my arms, willing the tremors to stop chasing across my skin, the danger alarms to stop pinging in my survival circuits. "He wouldn't allow it. Not Zal. He's not like that."

"They're all like that, those mages. Say they're holding up the laws, but who made the laws, eh?" Farren sidled closer. "You don't have to go with him, you know."

I shook my head. "I must. Zal wouldn't compromise his duty, and I..." *I have no place else to go.*

"We'd hide you 'til he leaves," Farren said, as if he'd heard my desperate thoughts. "Take you back to our village. Then you could work in *our* Comfort House." His gaze was hot enough to sear my skin. "'Cos we don't got nothing like you there now. Pale as snow, you are. You like that everywhere?"

"I—"

"Farren," Morvan murmured. "What about choice? Shouldn't we... you know... ask?"

"Oh, aye. Let's see about that, eh?" Farren took another step forward. "All you got to do is say no and we'll be on our way. Leave you to the Magister's mercy. Well?"

I tried. Oh, how I tried. But when I opened my mouth to refuse, my throat closed up, and nothing emerged. *What? Why?* I traced the decision pathways and tried again but... *there*. A block in my programming, diverting it back to the *Yes* decision node, no matter how I tried to activate *No*.

But worse, Farren's obvious desire instantiated the secondary sex characteristics and behavior body enhancement modules, the ones I'd always believed were under my control.

No no no.

I could think it but not say it. Although I fought against it, I pulled in, rounding my shoulders, dropping my gaze to peer up through my tangled hair in the submissive female aspect. *I don't want this. I don't choose this.* Had the Infomancers coerced me after all, and I had never even realized it?

"There, see?" Farren held out his palms as if delivering my fate on a platter. Then he grinned. "Maybe we should make sure though." He began to unbutton the front of his breeks.

Morvan tugged on Farren's cloak. "We should go. Before Magister comes back."

"He's casting the divination stones. When's he ever figured their meaning in less than an hour? We've got time. Time to be sure." Farren stared avidly at me. "Go on. Say no."

My thoughts flew in a dozen different directions, searching for a way around that blasted block, a way to control my own programming, my own destiny. Suddenly, I flashed on Zal as he raised a sardonic brow: *"Technically, I'm bespelling the water."*

Could I use my own traitorous circuits to bypass the *Yes* command? To bypass it, or at least side-step it sufficiently to send Farren and his gang away?

I didn't know if I'd succeed, but I was determined to try. So I allowed Farren to approach, desperately formulating the question that would turn the situation to my own advantage.

Chapter Nine

Zal

After staring at my casting for a good half-hour, I gathered the stones again. Tradition dictated that nobody got a second chance with divination, not with the same question. Once the stones had fallen, you had to interpret the results and choose a path.

Bugger that. I warmed the stones in my palm, but before I could begin the ritual, a faint shout echoed through the trees from the direction of the camp. Not just one shout—a chorus of raucous hoots and catcalls.

Torian.

Shite, I was a fool—I'd protected the camp against wild animals, but I hadn't thought to ward it against *people*. Yet people were Torian's greatest threat.

I tossed the stones onto the mat without a glance and leaped to my feet. I grabbed my staff but left my pack where it lay and took off, crashing through the trees and letting my downhill momentum propel me into the camp clearing.

A handful of Earth-born young men were gathered near the fire. All of them looked to be in that unfortunate stage between their manhood trials at fourteen and citizenship initiation at nineteen. I recognized the biggest one—Farren, was that his name?—as the apprentice from Corvel-on-Byrne who'd run Netta's errands and fetched Torian's kit.

Farren faced Torian across the fire, his hands, rot him, fumbling at his trouser buttons.

And Torian—Torian had shed their cloak and jerkin, nothing but the thin linen shirt covering their moon-pale skin. Their head was bowed, tilted slightly to look up at Farren from beneath the sweep of their lashes. Everything about Torian oozed *promise*, and their attitude was having a predictable effect on the young men. All of them sported cock-stands under their breeks, and a few, like Farren, had already taken their flesh in hand.

The effect on me was not the same. Heat—not desire but fury—rose from my belly to my chest to the top of my head, my braids whipping around me as though I stood in the center of a cyclone.

"Stand down!" I bellowed, my roar startling an owl from its perch in a nearby tree and sending it winging into the night sky.

Most of the men flinched, the ones with their peckers out hurrying to shove them out of sight. Farren, though, hadn't budged, seemingly mesmerized. Torian didn't so much as glance at me. They kept their attention on Farren.

Spellbound. That's what Farren was, and if that wasn't magic, I was blind in both eyes, not one.

I swept my staff in a circle overhead, the Sun Stone glowing brighter than the fire's embers. The men cried out, stumbling back outside the circle of my rage.

"You." I thrust the end of my staff toward Farren. "I said stand down. You—"

"Zal! On your left!"

At Torian's cry, I whirled to my blind side to face a reedy youth hefting a rock the size of his head. "Oh no, boyo. When you threaten a Sun mage, you need a much bigger weapon." One wave of my staff sent the rock spinning away with the boy stumbling after.

Although Torian had dropped their seductive pose when they warned me of the attack, Farren hadn't moved. I took two strides across the clearing and lifted the young idiot by the scruff of his neck, giving him a shake before shoving him to join the rest of the lads.

"Do you know what you've done, the lot of you? You know what it means to violate a citizen's right to choose."

Farren rubbed the back of his neck. "But she *did* choose. We asked. She din't say no."

"You mean *he* didn't," another boy muttered.

"Enough!" I roared. "Did they say yes?"

Four of the boys shared uneasy glances, but Farren jutted his chin. "Din't say no. That's what counts."

"All five of you fools have cleared your manhood trials. Farren, you look to be on the brink of initiation. You should all be well aware that *not refusing* is not the same as *choosing*."

"Seems like you're not offering a choice either, Magister, hauling her off to the capital. Did *you* ever ask?" Farren crossed his arms. "Go on. Ask."

Guilt twisted in my gut. It wouldn't matter what Torian said. The two of us had to make the trip, whether either of us wanted to or not. I faced Torian, whose gaze was riveted on the ground by their feet. I could see the shudders racking their thin shoulders. *Shite, they must be frozen.* I picked up the crumpled cloak and draped it over their shoulders. "Torian. Tell me the truth. Do you want to go with me?"

Torian took a deep breath and raised their chin, although they kept their eyes downcast. "Yes."

Farren's mouth dropped open. "But... but I asked. I gave her the chance to say no."

Torian finally lifted their gaze, glaring at Farren with more anger than I had ever seen in them before. "You asked the wrong fucking question!"

I blinked at the venom in Torian's tone. We clearly had some things to discuss, including the meaning of the unfamiliar word: *fucking*. But later. Now though...

I turned to Farren and the other boys. "The way I see it, you lot have to answer for violating the reeves' decree to send Torian away from Corvel-on-Byrne." I counted their transgressions down on my fingers. "For interfering with a mage's duty. For *attacking* a mage." I glared at the boy who'd nearly brained me with a rock. "For failing to see the difference between *no* and *no answer*. All basic lessons you've had ample time to learn. But since none of them seemed to stick, here's something to remind you."

I gestured with my staff and in an instant, with the overwhelming stench of singed hair, each boy's braids were burned up to his ears. They all shouted, slapping at the smoldering ends.

"You tell your village elders what you've done to earn a shearing. When next I make my rounds, I'll have a talk with them to make sure you've come clean and that you've learned to be decent citizens." I pointed my staff at them. "Go."

They went, although not without a baleful glance or two over their shoulders.

I turned back to Torian, who had shed the cloak again in order to pull their jerkin over their head. They wouldn't meet my gaze, and no wonder.

"Torian, it's not your job anymore to service anyone who asks."

They stopped fumbling with the jerkin's laces. "Is that what you think I was doing?"

I dropped my own gaze, scraping the dirt next to my boot toe with the end of my staff. "Didn't look like they were giving you much choice. And that's on me. I shouldn't have left you alone."

"You think I would submit to them? On *purpose*?"

I shifted my grip, but my staff didn't seem to fit in my hand comfortably anymore. "That's how it worked with those Infomancers, didn't it? Back in Corvel-on-Byrne, too, or nearly."

Torian's eyes flashed in the firelight. "Be fair. In the Lab, it was my *job*. And what options did I have when I was shut up in that awful cell, behind bars, in the *dark*?"

"Aye, well..." I parted my braids to rub the back of my neck. "That's how all rogue mages justify themselves when they're cornered. That they didn't have a choice."

Torian's mouth turned down. "Maybe if they'd been allowed more time, they'd have found one."

"Now *you* be fair. If I'd given the last rogue I faced more time, she'd have taken *both* my eyes."

"Do you know why?"

I leaned on my staff, seeking strength from my Sun Stone because Torian's attitude was completely unlike them. Was this the first sign of rogue instability? The notion sent my heart tumbling to my knees. "Wasn't a lot of time for asking questions."

"Maybe you should have *made* time. Because from where I stand, Zal, *you're* the one who failed to *ask*."

Chapter Ten

Torian

I yanked my cloak off the ground and flung it across my shoulders. I wanted to rip, to tear, to throw things. Was this what it was like to be angry? I'd never felt like this before, as though some primal beast were hatching in my chest, trying to claw its way out.

It was *glorious.*

Glorious yet also frightening and disorienting, and those feelings were far too familiar from my flight from the Lab.

But the look on Zal's face, the revulsion, the disappointment. I had been foolish to imagine for one nanosecond that Zal believed I had no sinister magical agenda, and that I had no desire to repeat any part of my life in the Lab. If Zal—who had spent time with me, talked to me, *knew* me in a way no one ever had—could think the worst, what of the other mages? If Zal no longer believed in me, could the hideous fate Farren described be waiting for me in the capital?

Why was that thought so much less distressing than the loss of Zal's good opinion? Why did I crave the humor that lurked in his eye? Or the integrity that seemed to shine from him like the light of the chrysocite on his staff?

But how can I expect anyone, no matter how decent at their core, to accept me for all that I am?

Different. Three-natured. Moon-born. *Cyborg.*

My eyes burned in an unfamiliar way. I rubbed them, sniffing, and huddled next to the fire.

"Torian."

"Yes?"

"What should I have asked?"

An odd tightness gripped my chest, making it difficult to speak. "It doesn't matter."

"Yes, it does. Tell me."

I met Zal's gaze across the dying flames. I read nothing but concern in his face now, and for some reason, that constricted my chest even further. *A malfunction? Must run a diagnostic later.* I shook my head.

Zal tossed his staff aside and hunkered down so he was at eye-level with me. "Please? I promise I'll listen. No judgments."

"You…" I pressed the heels of my hands against my eyes for a moment and took a breath before meeting Zal's perplexed gaze again. "You should have asked what was wrong."

Zal blinked, his eyebrows lifting. "I could see what was wrong. A pack of idiots forcing themselves on you."

"Not what was wrong with *them*. What was wrong with *me*." I clutched the edge of my cloak. "You were right."

"I was?" Zal frowned. "You mean you *were* coercing them?"

I shook my head wildly. "No. Of course not. But I *couldn't* say no. No matter how hard I tried. The Infomancers put a limiter in my programming. Every time I tried to say *no*, it rerouted me to *yes*."

Zal pinched the bridge of his nose. "Ah, shite."

"And the way Farren phrased the question. He said, 'Say no.' And I couldn't. Not only that, but the behavior modification module activated too."

"Did you know about this?"

"No! I never even suspected." Suddenly, it was difficult to swallow. "All along, I had no choice. I still don't."

"Of course you do. You're not a slave to those Infomancers anymore."

I met his solemn gaze. "But aren't I just as captive to you and your laws? I don't know anything about your people, Zal. My only experience has been with you and those villagers. How do

I know whether the rest of the populace will be like you or like them or perhaps worse than the Infomancers? Farren told me what happened to the last mage you delivered."

"That was different. She'd gone rogue."

"But that's what everyone thinks *I've* done. What if..." My lungs had turned to lead. "What if they don't believe me? What if they don't *listen*? Will they do the same thing to me?"

"I can't—" Zal ran one big hand across his face. "Look. I like to think everyone wants to do the right thing. That deep down, we all believe in the precepts of our society, the basic rights laid out in our charter and the laws in place to ensure those rights. That we'd never punish someone unless their guilt was beyond question. But what can I say? People are idiots."

I was surprised into a laugh. "The Infomancers would agree to that in regard to all of you. Not themselves so much."

"Aye, well, from what you've told me, they've got no room to judge." He let his hands drop between his knees. "Those young fools from the village just now? By this age, they ought to know better. Respect a citizen's rights. Perhaps they'll think twice before they go haring off on another half-arsed quest, but I'm sorry their lesson came at your expense. I should have protected you."

I shrugged. "You didn't know they'd follow."

"I saw them eyeing you in the village. I should have known they'd never be able to resist. You are unique in more ways than I can count."

Zal's words washed through me, leaving my chest hollow, as if my human heart had been replaced by the pulse of a cybertronic relay. *I'm alone. The only one of my kind.* Even if the Moon-born still existed, after all the modifications, there could be no other like me.

Perhaps the tribunal would find it more convenient—and safer for their status quo—to eliminate such an anomaly.

I hunched forward, burying my head in my arms as shudders racked my body. A small part of my processing cycles registered the new experience.

So this is crying.

All things considered, I preferred gaol.

Chapter Eleven

Zal

"Torian?" Ah, shite, I'd put my big, clumsy foot in it now. I forced my hands to stay where they were, dangling between my knees, hesitant to touch Torian's huddled form without permission. There'd been far too much of that in their life already.

"I may not hold much sway in what happens at the tribunal —I'm just a circuit mage when all's said—but I'll do my best. I can explain what your life has been like, bear witness in your stead if you'd rather not say."

"Will you wave your staff at them?" Torian's voice was muffled by their arms. "Singe off their hair like you did with those boys?"

"Hardly. They'd have my Stone if I came over insubordinate to the Congress. But even though I don't have the status I once had, they'll still listen to me." I hoped.

Torian peeked up from the folds of their cloak. "Why did you lose your status?"

I pointed to my eye patch. "Some don't believe a one-eyed mage can see the paths clearly enough to do his duty. Others think any mage who'd be careless enough to lose his own eye won't be able to care for the people in his charge. To be a mage, you must command the respect of the citizens. If they think you can't master your own bloody element, they won't trust you to master their problems."

"If people think you can't manage," Torian said with a lift of one dark brow, "they've never seen you in action."

I chuckled. "You've not had any basis for comparison. I patrol the hinterlands. The mages who serve around the capital and down in the delta, where it's more temperate and populated? They're far more impressive than I am."

"I don't see how they could be."

Warmth infused my chest at the muttered praise. I wasn't sure Torian even realized it had been a compliment. "Wait until you meet them. You'll see."

Torian hunched over again. "Is it terrible that I don't want to meet them? If I had a choice—"

"Everybody has a choice."

"Then my choice would be to stay out here with you. At least I understand what you want. I mean, not that you want *me*, not the way I'm used to."

I studied their bowed head. "Does that bother you?"

"It's... different. Everyone at the Lab, they all wanted something from me. They logged their preferences as to what aspect I should display to best please them when it was their time for release. If I don't even have that to offer, why would you want to keep me around?"

"You really don't see yourself, do you?" I shifted off my haunches and sat next to Torian. "Let me tell you, we've got a story. The way to kill a mage is to put a man-eating beast in a cage, cover it with a curtain, and put up a sign that says 'Don't go inside!' We'd all go. Every one of us, every time." Torian was peeking over their arms again, so I smiled at them. "Being a mage isn't just working with the power of the Sun. It's learning. Chasing down knowledge. Bending it to new uses. Now you— you're like a whole *maze* full of doors, all marked 'Don't look!' No mage alive could resist talking with you, learning all you have to tell."

"There's a lot of it." Torian's voice was rueful. "You'd get tired."

I nudged Torian with my shoulder. "If I did, you could sing to me again, and I'd forget all about being tired."

Torian raised their head at last, a smile trembling on their lips. "You like my singing?"

"Can't imagine anyone *not* liking it. It's brilliant."

"But would other mages feel that way? They wouldn't see me as some kind of artifact to keep locked away, would they?"

I frowned, considering what I knew of the mages elected to positions of authority in Congress. Surely some among their number were old enough to remember the nature of the Moon-born. But what if they treated Torian's science as magic, the way the Infomancers had mockingly declared? What if they decided it was forbidden?

If Torian's presence, their stories, made me question my convictions, would it do the same to the other mages? Would they see Torian as a resource, a way to learn about the Star-born, about our own beginnings? Or as a danger that threatened the foundations of our society?

I wanted to believe the mages would do the right thing. But I'd said it myself—people were idiots, and mages, no matter how much power or responsibility they held, were still people. "I—"

"Are they all like you? Desireless?"

I blinked. "I have desires. Just not fleshly ones. Other mages? They've got 'em." I shrugged. "They might be tempted, but they can't act or they risk the loss of their Sun Stones and possibly their heads."

"I hadn't realized." Torian bit their lower lip. "It's a good thing you find me repulsive, then. I wouldn't want you to risk your head."

I held my hand suspended over Torian's knee. "May I?" When Torian nodded, I rested my hand there, the lightest of touches. "I may not have sexual desires, but I can appreciate beauty. Believe me when I tell you that you're the first thing in a long while that's made me regret not having two eyes."

"Oh." Torian ducked their head, and that slow flush rose along their neck and to the tips of their ears. *Adorable.* "I— Thank you."

"Do you really like it out here in the wilderness? Far cry from your mountaintop citadel, isn't it?"

"Yes. But it's so much more... real. Immediate. Alive. I'm not sorry for escaping. But..."

"But?"

Torian raised their chin, their smile tremulous. "I had no idea it would be so *cold*."

I laughed. "Aye. The north'll freeze the bollocks off you if you don't wear your woolies. Here."

I stood and shook out my bedroll, then added Torian's on top of it, doubling up the blankets.

Torian watched me with wide eyes. "What are you doing?"

"One way to keep warm is to share blankets. Twice the wool. Twice the body heat."

"But... but you don't want me."

I propped one arm on my bent knee, gazing at Torian where they sat on an overturned log, the waning firelight catching the glint of gold under the pale skin of their cheek. "This isn't about sex. It's about comfort. We could both use that, I'm thinking. Because I've got no idea how to interpret the divination I just— Shite! My pack! Here, you crawl in. I've got to go rescue my things from up the hill. Unless— are you afraid the lads'll be back?"

Torian clambered under the blankets. "After what you did to them? Not likely. Go on."

I raced up the hillside, unwilling to leave Torian alone for any longer than necessary. *Comfort.* That's all this was, but if Torian should drop that word in their testimony, could it be misconstrued a Comfort House offering? I pushed the thought aside—time enough to worry about that later. I was sure I could set the matter straight, but we had to get there first and request an official audience.

When I got to the spot where I left my pack, I stared down at the mat, where I'd tossed the stones when I'd heard the shouts from the campsite.

The stones were in exactly the same formation as my first throw.

And what that meant, the Sun only knew.

Chapter Twelve

Torian

For the first time since leaving the Lab, I awoke warm. Zal's big body, spooned behind me, radiated heat like his Sun Stone. This was a new feeling for me altogether. I'd never slept with a partner before. The transactions at the Lab had been restricted to the prescribed hour during regular work shifts. My nights had always been my own.

But this, the comfort of another body—moreover, the body of someone who would never ask for more than I was willing to give—made me want to snuggle in and never arise.

Another thing that close proximity under a double layer of blankets brought to pungent attention, though, was that the two of us had been on the trail for nearly a week, with only minimal opportunities for washing. Not that Zal's earthy male scent was unpleasant, precisely. It was definitely different from the Lab inhabitants, who all smelled of antiseptic cleansers and formaldehyde.

I wasn't certain if my own scent would be pleasing to Zal, however, and I desperately wanted to please Zal. Not *that* way, not now that I knew the cost, but enough to be a desirable trail companion.

I eased out from beneath the blankets, loath to leave Zal's heat. For once, the big mage had slept beyond the first pinking of the sky. Perhaps he was glad to have someone to generate extra warmth as well. I knew I was good for that, and for the first time, I was pleased about it.

I took the cooking pot and the toweling and made my shivering way to the river. I filled the pot with water and set it on the bank, then stripped, gritting my teeth as gooseflesh rose over every square centimeter of my body. It would be worse once I dumped the frigid water over my head, but I had no choice.

Or do I?

Zal had expelled the solar power stored in his chrysocite to ward off the local fauna and to singe off the village boys' braids. What was I but a living solar storage unit? Perhaps I could discharge energy as well as absorb and consume it.

I hunkered down next to the pot and thrust in my hands. *Cold!* Concentrating despite shivering so hard it was a wonder my cybertronic connections didn't shake loose, I traced the neural pathways to the power cells at my core. If I reversed the input *here* and redirected the output *there… Ah.*

The water warmed around my hands, heating until it was almost uncomfortable. I grinned, dipped a corner of the toweling into the water, and scrubbed away the grime of my days on the trail and my time trapped in the cell.

True, it wasn't the same as the perfectly regulated temperatures of the Lab showers. In a way, though, it was better because I'd managed it myself—altered my programming for a new purpose to suit this new existence.

What else might I be able to do if I questioned a few of my assumptions? *Frame your question. Test your hypothesis. Reframe the question. Test again.*

By the time I was clean and clear of soap, I had compiled a mental list of my most pressing concerns, chief among them how to say *no*.

I rubbed myself with the rough toweling, my skin turning an unbecoming shade of pink from the cold and the friction. I wrinkled my nose at my stained and travel-worn clothing. What would it be like to put on freshly laundered clothes again?

I pulled on the shirt, and as my head emerged from the neckband, I caught the white stroke of a com-trail, like a tether linking the ruins of the Lab to the sky.

I froze with one arm through a sleeve. Were the Infomancers still inhabiting the Lab? Had there been other launches that I hadn't witnessed? Was that an evacuation pod en route to a ship in orbit? Or a contingent of armed personnel coming the other direction, on a mission to eliminate inconvenient loose ends?

Like me.

I scanned the sky, activating my infrared sensors. *There.* The signature of a cloaked shuttle, coming this way on a landing trajectory—a shuttle that could track my Lab-manufactured implants with pinpoint precision.

I hurried into the rest of my clothes and stumbled up the trail to camp, my bootlaces still untied. Zal was just strapping the bedding to his pack. He looked up with a grin, but his smile faded when he took in my state.

"What is it? What's wrong?"

"I think... I think the Infomancers may still be here. There's been a glow in the Lab ruins every night, but I thought it was just the residual energy from the breach in the walls. I thought it would fade eventually, but it hasn't. And now there's a ship on its way."

"A ship? You mean a boat on the river?"

I shook my head impatiently. "No. An airship."

Zal's eye widened. "A ship that flies through the air? Now that I'd like to see."

"No. No you wouldn't. Because the ship comes with at least one Infomancer. And I think they want me back."

Chapter Thirteen

Zal

I grabbed my staff and stood up. "Why? Just for the sex? They can bloody well get that from someone else. You've paid them back and more."

"Not just that. The data stores. The archives. They're here." Torian thumped their chest with a flat palm. "All of it, stored inside my cybertronics. I hadn't thought. I hadn't considered. But if the attack destroyed the Lab computers, I'm the only backup they've got left."

"No fear. I won't let them take you. Unless..." I studied Torian, who looked flustered, frightened, and half-frozen. "Unless you *want* to go with them. I know this world isn't what you're used to."

Torian clutched my arm. "I don't want to go. I want to stay here. With you."

"Now, we talked about that, my friend. That choice won't be mine to make."

"But shouldn't it be mine? You're always saying your society is founded on free will, on the right of every citizen to make their own choices. I choose here. I choose you. Unless... oh, *fuck*." They carded trembling fingers through still-damp hair. "You don't want sex. I keep forgetting. There's nothing I can offer you in exchange for keeping me with you."

"Oi. You've got way more to offer, believe me. But just so we're clear, if *you* want sex, I can't give it to you. So if that's what you need—"

"No. It was only ever a job for me. I've had enough to last for quite a while, possibly forever, trust me."

I gazed down into their troubled face. "Aye. I do."

"You... trust me?" Torian's eyes widened. "I don't think anyone ever has before."

I brushed Torian's cheek with the backs of my fingers. "What did I tell you? People are idiots."

"Torian." A gravelly voice spoke from the forest behind us and Torian flinched.

I whirled, my staff held across my body, shielding Torian from the threat. "Who goes there? What do you want?"

The man who stepped out of the trees was shorter than me but taller than Torian and soft around the middle like Barkon. He wasn't Moon-born pale or Earth-born mid-brown or Sun-born dark. He was somewhere in between earth and moon, with near-black eyes, a broad nose, and an expression of total irritation.

So this is a Star-born. I wasn't impressed.

The man didn't pay any attention to me. "Torian. We're evacuating, and this stunt of yours has put us seriously behind schedule."

Torian stepped out from behind me. "Then by all means, Edric, feel free to go. I, however, am staying here."

Edric's thin eyebrows shot up, astonishment joining the irritation on his face, as if his breakfast egg had grabbed his fork and stabbed him in the belly. "Don't be ridiculous. The facility is compromised. The recidivist faction... well, they don't intend to allow us to rebuild. It's time to regroup."

"I told you. I choose to remain."

"Have your circuits been damaged? I said we have no time. We have to activate the destruct sequence before we go, and the mother ship won't wait for us."

"Destruct sequence?" My gaze bounced between Edric and Torian. "What's that? Is something in danger?"

Torian's fists clenched at their sides, their attention fixed on Edric. "You intend to go through with it, then? Destroying the whole planet, the civilization that *you* started, murdering all these people, just to cover your tracks?"

"Clearly you need a complete system diagnostic. I'll start it as soon as we've docked in orbit." Edric looked Torian up and down, his glance cold, dispassionate. "I hope the backups haven't been corrupted."

I'd had enough of Edric's attitude. "Let me see if I understand you. You don't want Torian from affection or loyalty. You want them for what they know? As if they're nothing more than a book to open and discard at your whim?"

"It doesn't *know* anything. It's a repository and a sexual surrogate. Nothing more."

I took a step forward, fingers tightening on my staff. "They're not an *it*. And they're far more than a fragging book. You don't deserve them."

"If not for for the Lab, for my work, for *me*, it wouldn't exist, so I own it, legally and wholly, and I intend to take it with me." Edric beckoned to Torian. "We've a task to accomplish. If you continue to behave irrationally, I'll have to wipe your memory. As if I didn't have enough to do."

I turned to Torian and grasped their wrist, the little zing that always accompanied contact with their skin sizzling along my veins. "Don't go with him. You can't want this. They *exploited* you."

Torian's gaze cut to Edric. "He's right, Zal. This is all I am. All I've ever been, but for this time with you. It's better this way."

"It's not. It's not better for you. And it's not better for me."

"Enough." Edric held a strange object in his hand, pointing it at me as though it were a mage's staff.

"What in the name of the Sun is that?"

"It's a blaster." Torian's murmur was strained. "Don't move."

"Come now, Torian." Edric gestured with the blaster. "Or do I silence this fool for good?"

"Please, you needn't do that. I'm coming." Torian gripped my arm. "Don't follow."

My heart gave a painful lurch. "Torian—"

"You said you trusted me," they murmured. "Trust me now."

Chapter Fourteen

Torian

This has to work. But in case it didn't, I allowed myself an indulgence. I stretched up and kissed Zal's cheek. "Thank you."

Zal blinked rapidly, a sheen in his dark eye. "Ah, shite. Don't go." His voice, laced with pleading, resonated painfully with the implants in my chest. "You said you were done with them. That you wanted to stay here. With me."

Edric laughed, a thin, arrogant sound. "What foolishness. Torian is a logical construct. We've made it that way. Why would it want to stay here and be destroyed when it could return to comfort, convenience, and usefulness?"

"Usefulness? Making them think all they are is a machine for you to tinker with or a hole to stick your pecker in? I'll wager you've never even heard them sing."

"Sing? Ridiculous." Edric shuffled his feet, clearly on edge. "No more delays, Torian. You can commence data retrieval for the detonation protocol codes on the way to the site. Thanks to your antics, our launch window is too narrow as it is, so if you don't move your mechanical ass—" Edric gestured at Zal with the blaster.

"I'm coming." I walked toward Edric, keeping my body in direct line with the blaster. I was in no danger. As long as I held the backup files, Edric wouldn't fire for fear of scrambling the data. But Zal—no, I would not allow harm to come to him.

I'd nearly reached Edric when Zal strode forward, dodging in front of me to face down Edric.

"Don't do this. We—my people—we're not some trifling annoyance, like a swarm of insects for you to swat. We have homes, families, a *civilization*."

"Really? How long do you think your so-called civilization can go on without our support?" Edric waved the blaster, his finger far too close to the trigger, and I flinched. "That chrysocite, for instance. *We* gave it to you. *We* turned those worthless rocks into massive solar cells to study how a society policed with magic would work. You've got fewer than half the original number now, and lose more every year. What will you do when your magic doesn't work anymore?"

"I reckon we'd learn to cope."

Edric snorted. "You couldn't. You're too dependent on it. We're doing you a kindness by making the end short. Perhaps not painless, but at least quick. A brief flare and you're done, rather than a long, drawn-out descent into chaos and starvation."

Zal's eye blazed. "You've no right—"

"I've had enough of you." Edric adjusted the setting on his blaster. "The rest of the planet can wait for the destruct sequence. But you? I'm ending you here."

Edric pointed the blaster square at Zal's chest.

I didn't pause, didn't think, didn't hesitate. I *acted*, grabbing Edric's bare wrist with both hands and wrenching it downward. *I did it with the water, for my own convenience. This time, it's for the planet. This time, it's for Zal.*

Edric struggled, but my infrastructure was reinforced with materials of the Infomancers' own making, and no matter how degenerate their morals, they knew their cybertronics. "What— let go. Torian, what are you doing?"

I bared my teeth. "Choosing."

I pushed the entire charge in my reserve banks through the conduits in my cybertronic network, out the sensors in my fingertips, directly into Edric. This time, I encountered no hidden feedback loops. No safety bypasses. The Infomancers hadn't coded for this scenario—obviously, they'd never imagined one of their own constructs would rebel.

Their mistake.

Edric juddered and twitched, and his eyes rolled back in his head. I sensed his heart stuttering, but still I discharged.

More, more, *more*.

Reserves depleted. Shut-down commencing in three... two...

With a jerk of my chin, I disabled the safety protocols and *pushed*. All of it. Every last joule. Whatever it took to keep Zal safe.

As Edric collapsed to convulse on the ground, I followed him down until the very last spark of energy flowed out of me and into Edric's corpse.

Danger! Cascading system failu—

Chapter Fifteen

Zal

"Torian! Sun, please, no. Torian!" I dropped to the ground next to where they lay beside the lifeless Star-born.

I ripped Torian's shirt apart and pressed a hand to their chest. No little zing of awareness, not even a ghost of a heartbeat flutter. The gold lattice under Torian's skin was gray and dull, exactly like my Sun Stone when its charge was depleted.

Wait a moment.

Depleted charge? Hadn't I noticed the similarities between Torian and my Stone? Hadn't I seen that network of metal on their back, exposed to the sun the way I recharged my staff? They needed fuel for their—what did they call them?— cybertronics, and those were solar powered, just like my staff.

My bloody half-charged staff. But with the sun still hidden behind the mountain, it was all I had.

"Please let it be enough."

I stripped Torian to the waist, their slender body already cooling on my lap. I turned them gently, exposing that astonishing metal latticework on their back.

Grasping my staff, I *willed* the Stone to life, the sudden flare so bright I had to squint. The light bathed Torian's back. I felt the heat on my own wrist where it supported Torian— scorching, as if the sun had drawn too close to the earth. Would it burn that pale skin? Did the lattice have a limit on what it could absorb at one time?

I eased back on the Stone's output and knelt there, in the imprisoned light of the sun, and prayed for all I was worth that it would be enough.

Too soon, the light began to fade, although the gold beneath Torian's skin had barely begun to glimmer.

"No! *More*, blast you."

I can't fail now. Not with this. Not with them. Torian had sacrificed themself for me. How humbling that the person I'd been half-convinced meant nothing but chaos for the world might have been its salvation.

I exerted my will, further than I'd ever tried before, forcing every last bit of energy out of the Stone until, with a crack as loud as the death of Star Mountain, the Stone shattered, scattering shards over me, over Torian, over the ground, and cleaving my staff in two.

Yet Torian didn't move.

Dimly, I wondered why the destruction of my Stone didn't gut me, why it was insignificant, trivial against the monumental pain of Torian's death.

I cradled Torian in my arms, held tight against me. My hair, a curtain around my face, lay in limp black ropes across their skin as dry sobs shook my shoulders.

"Zal?" I caught my breath at the thready whisper and eased Torian away from my chest, nearly breaking down anew when they blinked at me, confusion clouding the depths of those luminous gray eyes. "What— How did I—" They pushed feebly at me. "Why am I functional? Did Edric—"

"Shhh." I laid my palm against their cheek, for my own comfort as well as theirs. "Edric is no longer a threat."

Their eyebrows bunched. "No longer a threat?"

"No." I angled myself so that Torian, still in my arms, could see the Star-born stretched out on the ground, but at their swift inhale, twisted again to hide the body. I doubted they'd ever seen death up close before, and I was certain—as certain as the Sun—that they'd never killed anyone. That kind of thing left a mark, be the punishment ever so justified. Every circuit mage knew that. We all bore the scars of our calling on our souls.

"He's dead?" they whispered brokenly.

"Aye."

"Good." They gazed up at me. "I know that's wrong, that I should never be glad of anyone's death, but I *chose* to...to *eliminate* Edric. For you. For your people. And I can't be sorry."

I smiled down at them. "They're your people too. You're as much of this world as I am, no matter how the Infomancers tried to remake you into a tool for their own devices." I hugged them tight again, murmuring into their hair. "Sun, moon, and stars, Torian, I thought I'd lost you. Don't you ever do something like that again."

Torian coughed. "No promises, but I'll try to keep the near-death experiences to a minimum."

For a moment—a long moment—I held them, their hands warm now against my chest, their hair tickling my cheek in the chilly morning breeze, until they began to shiver in my arms.

"Zal?"

"Yes, my own moon?"

"Why am I half naked?" They pulled back to peer up at me. "For that matter, how am I alive? I forced myself into a cascading system failure. I should be as dead as Edric."

"Ah. Well. As it happens, I made a choice of my own." I plucked a Sun Stone shard out of Torian's hair and tossed it aside.

Their eyes widened as they scanned the remains of my staff. "You...you rebooted me? But that must have taken—"

"Everything I had. And I'd do it again in a bloody heartbeat." I kissed the top of their head. "Now let's get you warmed up." I helped Torian to their feet and eyed their clothes that I'd tossed willy-nilly in my haste to save them. They were covered with Sun Stone shards, and I knew from experience that even the tiniest could slice like the sharpest dagger, or work their way beneath skin like a needle. So I took off my cloak and draped it around Torian's shoulders and led them to the fire. "Wait here while I make sure your clothes won't shred you like mincemeat. I have precious few healing stones left, and since without my Stone there'll be no more, we'd best practice a little prevention, eh?"

Torian nodded numbly, pulling the cloak tight as they sank down on the log next to the embers. I took a moment to stoke the fire back to a crackling blaze, and for good measure, settled the blankets from our bedrolls around Torian.

I left them staring into the flames and strode over to shake out their shirt, jerkin, and coat. After I'd made doubly sure that no Sun Stone flakes remained in the worn folds, I took them back to Torian. "How about you put these on while I"—I glanced over my shoulder—"deal with yon Infomancer. I'm sorry I'll have to bury him, but a proper pyre would be—"

"The Infomancers!" Torian shot to their feet, the blankets and my cloak pooling at their feet. "Fuck! I forgot."

One day, I'd have to ask them what *fuck* meant, because clearly it was a word that held weight. "Whatever you forgot, it can wait until you're rested and properly dressed."

"No." Their mouth set in a determined line. "It can't."

And they took off across the clearing, leaped over Edric's corpse, and disappeared into the trees.

Chapter Sixteen

Torian

How could I have been so stupid? Eliminating Edric wasn't enough because he wasn't alone. The Infomancers' professional reputations, their freedom, their very lives depended on keeping their interference here, their *failures*, hidden from their supervisors on the home world. If Edric didn't succeed, they'd send somebody else until the mission was accomplished.

So they needed to believe the mission *was* accomplished.

It wasn't hard to retrace Edric's path through the woods—he hadn't been concerned with concealing his movements. Why would he? He believed the entire planet would be nothing but interstellar dust and debris before long.

I ran, ignoring the sting when brambles striped my still-bare chest and back. Edric would have needed a relatively clear spot to land the shuttle, and it would be nearby. He was a firm believer in minimum effort for maximum results. He'd never volunteer for a long hike just to retrieve an *asset* gone astray, not if he had the choice.

Choice. It was a heady thing, but also a burden, because every choice carried consequences. When I'd made my choice to kill Edric, I hadn't expected to survive to face those consequences. And that, I was beginning to believe, had been both cowardly and short-sighted.

Because I hadn't *thought*, hadn't considered that Edric wasn't the only threat, or that Zal might be left to face the fallout from my actions. He would have had two corpses to explain, specimens of two races not seen on this planet for years, maybe not in living memory. Would the tribunal have believed his explanation? What would they have done to him if they hadn't?

I lurched into a clearing barely large enough to hold the one-passenger cargo shuttle. *Of course he brought the cargo shuttle.* To Edric, I was cargo, a construct, so why worry about my comfort in flight?

His landing had splintered several trees at the perimeter, not that he would have cared. He'd also left the pilot's hatch open. The consequences of that could be— I shuddered, imagining what any of the planet's inhabitants would do if they stumbled across this literally alien technology. The cognitive dissonance alone would be massive, setting aside the danger should any of them deduce how to operate the onboard weaponry.

I raced up the short ramp, through the open airlock, and onto the small bridge. I allowed myself a grim smile when I was able to pull the launch protocols from my data storage in an instant. Naturally the Infomancers would allow me easy access ship's operations. It meant they could leave me on watch while they slept or occupied themselves elsewhere.

Edric hadn't powered all the systems down, and the comm array flared to life with an incoming message. "Doctor al-Mohindes? Our departure window is closing. Your status?"

My knees buckled, and I flopped gracelessly into the pilot's seat. *Just in time.* I cleared my throat and activated the mic. "Asset secured. Stand by."

"Torian?" At Zal's whisper from the airlock door, I quickly muted the mic and spun the chair to face him. He was gazing at me, his eye wide, clutching my clothing to his chest. "That... that was... You spoke in Edric's voice."

I nodded warily. "Yes. I'm able to mimic voices and sounds if I'm especially familiar with them." I didn't believe Zal would view this as another instance of rogue magery, but he was clearly uncomfortable. I rose and crossed the two steps to reach him, gently taking my clothes from his arms. "Could you do me a favor?"

He swallowed audibly, then nodded. "Aye. Anything you need."

"Could you please bring Edric's"—it was my turn to swallow —"Edric's body here? There's something else we must do to keep the planet safe." *To keep* you *safe.*

"Very well." With one last worried glance, the glow and blink of the instrument panel reflected in his beautiful dark eye, he turned and left.

I drew in a shaky breath and blew it out in a huff. I had no time to dither, no time to surrender to shock and guilt. I sent a quick command down my primary neural pathway to my emotion circuits. I couldn't switch them off completely, but I could at least suppress them enough to allow me to focus. I'd done the same when I'd escaped the Lab, burying my fear of an unfamiliar environment. I needed it far more now, when the fate of the entire planet rested on my actions in the next—I checked the digital readout over the viewscreen—twenty-seven minutes.

I yanked my shirt over my head, not bothering with its laces, nor with the jerkin or jacket. Those could wait. Besides, despite the cold air drifting in from the open hatch, the shuttle's environmental controls were set to the warmer temperatures the Infomancers maintained in their facilities. What did it say about me that after less than two weeks, I preferred the wilderness, with its bitter winds, frigid waters, and lack of shelter?

It also has Zal. And being with him had made me feel warm *inside* for the first time in my memory.

Think, Torian, think. What could I strip from the shuttle to make our journey easier? The bridge was intentionally spare, to minimize the possibility of injury to the pilot from unsecured detritus once the shuttle escaped the planet's atmosphere. Unlike the mother ship, the shuttle was too small for an artificial gravity generator.

But surely there had to be something useful here, something easily portable. I accessed the ship's schematics in a picosecond, astonished at the retrieval speed. Clearly, Zal's reboot had charged my energy stores to the limit. It was… exhilarating, but also a bit disorienting. I wasn't used to operating with this much power.

However, with a mission this critical, I'd take it thankfully and run with it.

Ah. There. I knelt next to the bulkhead by the airlock and pressed on an almost seamless panel. It detached, revealing the emergency medkit. I freed it from its clamps and set it aside. An adjacent panel revealed a toolkit and a neat package of electronic components, and I laughed softly. *Conveniently located for all your cyborg's maintenance needs.*

What else could I scavenge that was small enough for us to carry? Fully charged, I was nearly as strong as Zal, perhaps stronger. But I couldn't depend on maintaining that charge in weak sunlight, and we needed to be able to move swiftly.

I scrambled to my feet and keyed open the cargo bay door. "Shit."

The bay was so jammed with plasformed storage crates that they almost didn't need the straps dogging them to the deck. I checked the ID on the nearest one. I didn't have to unlock it, although the key code was instantly accessible, because the cargo manifest also popped up, floating a foot in front of me in a way that used to be second nature, but now felt oddly foreign.

I scrolled through the list with a swipe of my finger. While Edric was transporting a few customized pieces of lab equipment, most of the cargo consisted of the staff's personal effects. I scanned it quickly. One name was notably missing: mine. Not that I had many possessions, but despite the emotional dampener, I felt a pinch in my chest. I hadn't been important enough to them as a *person* for them to consider that my *effects* might have value to me. That I'd like to keep them with me.

I pushed the pain aside. It didn't matter anymore, especially since everything here would be destroyed in—I checked again —nineteen minutes.

According to the manifest, the crate at the top of the nearest stack held the belongings of *Drina, P.*, a Lab assistant whose job had been studying the inhabitants' maker skills. She'd also been fascinated enough to replicate them in the Lab, so... *Yes!*

I undogged the straps and pulled the crate off onto the deck to key in the unlocking code. I didn't bother to unpack neatly, just dug through the crate, tossing the contents aside until I found what I sought: a leather pack, worked in the planetary style. *Perfect.*

As I shoved the medkit and tools into the pack, I reviewed the rest of the cargo. The equipment could be rebuilt off-planet, and while the staff might have a sentimental attachment to their belongings, there was nothing that wasn't replaceable elsewhere, nothing that was worth a costly retrieval mission.

I froze, one hand on the pack's buckle.

Nothing except me.

I was not only their most complex project and their data backup, I was witness to their crimes. They'd keep coming for me. Unless...

Unless they didn't believe I was here.

Zal ducked through the airlock door, Edric over his shoulder. "Where should I put him?"

"The pilot's chair, please." My knuckles whitened as I clutched the leather straps. Could I do this? I had no choice, not really. The alternative was the destruction of an entire world. "The needs of the many," I murmured, quoting an ancient film.

There ought to be a lancet in the medkit, but I didn't bother to retrieve it. I had no time for finesse. "Zal, could I borrow your belt knife, please?"

His eyebrows quirked, conveying his confusion at my request, but he was Zal, so of course he said, "Aye," and slipped it from its sheath. He passed it to me, hilt first.

I hefted it in my hand. The blade was sharp, thicker than a lancet, but not clumsy. It would do. It would have to do. I closed my eyes for a moment, then opened them, my own schematics visible in the virtual panel.

And shoved the knife into the base of my neck.

Chapter Seventeen

Zal

"Shite!" I lunged forward, fist closing on air as a grasped for a staff that was no longer there, reaching for Sun magic that was no longer mine, because Torian was... Torian was...

"Fuck, that hurts," they said matter-of-factly, although their face was twisted in obvious pain, blood soaking the back of their shirt.

"Then for the Sun's sake," I said desperately, gripping their wrist gently, ready to pull the knife away, "*stop.*"

They glanced at me out of determined gray eyes. "Don't, Zal, please. I must do this."

"What? Sever your own spine?" I cast around the strange metal ship for something to stem the blood flow and spotted a scatter of unfamiliar items on the slick floor beyond Torian. "I don't blame you for being upset." I scrambled over, staying low to keep from knocking myself out on the low ceiling. "I'll wager you've never killed anyone before. But that's no reason to—"

"I'm not trying to kill myself, Zal, if that's what you're thinking." They angled the knife, teeth gritted.

"You could have fooled me," I muttered. I grabbed a tumble of white fabric. It was finer and softer than any linen I'd ever seen, but I didn't care if it was silk or cloth of gold. I needed to stanch Torian's bleeding. I held it out, loath to jostle Torian in case I caused the knife to slip. "Let me—"

"In a moment." They grimaced, digging into their own flesh as though it was of no more moment than gutting a fish. "Ah.

There it is." They withdrew the knife, glancing at the bloodied blade ruefully. "Sorry about the mess."

"Bugger that." I grabbed the knife and tossed it aside with a clatter. "You need to— Shite!"

Because rather than taking the fabric and pressing it to the wound, Torian reached up and dug finger and thumb into the gash, widening it, and from the expression on their face, causing even more pain.

"I have to... make sure... *fuck!*... that the others... don't come —*got it!*—looking for me." They pulled a bloodied *something* out of their neck and threw it toward where Edric's body slumped in the odd chair. It ricocheted off the wall with a *ting* and spun across the floor, leaving a trail of blood—Torian's blood—in its wake. "All right, *now* I'll take that T-shirt."

I was still gaping at the thing Torian had pulled out of their body. It had sounded like metal, not bone, and certainly not flesh. "The what?"

"The T-shirt." They waved a shaking hand at the fabric I held. "That."

"Oh. Aye." I gestured to Torian's neck. "May I? That wound is in an unchancy place for treating yourself."

They chuckled weakly. "I suppose you're right." They bent their head, pushing their ragged hair aside, and I pressed the... the *T-shirt* to their neck. "I'm sorry if I frightened you, but we don't have much time."

"Time for what?" I murmured, checking the wound under the soft fabric. It had already stopped bleeding, something I wasn't sure I could have managed with my Stone intact and a pouch full of healing stones.

Torian laid their bloodied fingers over my hand on their neck. "Zal. Edric isn't alone, remember? The other Infomancers are still up in the mother ship, waiting for him to return. With me."

I sank down on my arse next to Torian. "I see."

"The only way to keep your world safe is if they believe returning is both impossible and irrelevant." They pointed to the bloody object. "That's my primary tracking device."

"So they won't be able to find you without it?"

Torian smiled, although their lips were pinched with pain, and I cursed my broken Stone that I couldn't help them. "They could still track me by my cybertronic signature, but only if they look." Their jaw firmed with steely determination. "So I plan to give them no reason to look." They glanced at a series of glowing red numbers on the wall. "Shit. Only eleven minutes. That's not much—" They scrambled to their feet, still clutching the T-shirt to their nape, and pointed to a leather satchel. "Take that, please, collect your knife, and wait for me outside."

"No chance of that. I'll gather the kit, yes, but I'm waiting here with you." I shouldered the pack and grabbed my knife. With a grimace, I wiped the blade on Edric's trousers before sheathing it. "We'll leave together."

They gave me an exasperated glare. "Still think I'm trying to off myself?"

I shook my head. "Nay. But I've learned my lesson. I'll not leave you to fend for yourself. Never again."

"Oh," they breathed, blinking rapidly. For an instant, I thought they might kiss my cheek once more—which I wouldn't have objected to in the least—but instead they tied the T-shirt around their throat, strode to the oddly illuminated metal table in front of Edric's corpse, and touched a glowing glass panel.

"Detonation countdown commenced. Ready for dust-off," they said in Edric's voice. "Be advised. Destruction radius is estimated to be wider than first calculations. Be ready to proceed at full speed to heliopause with immediate transition to slipdrive."

"Understood," said a tinny voice, apparently from midair. "Standing by for shuttle docking on your arrival."

Torian's fingers flew over the table, touching a panel here, a button there, with occasional glances at the numbers on the wall. At last, they blew out a shaky breath. "There. Course laid in and comms cut." They shot me a crooked smile. "Now for the tricky part."

As they turned, I spied a line of blood trickling from under the T-shirt, so I moved next to them and laid my hand over their nape, pressing gently. "I've got you," I murmured.

They met my eye for an instant, their gaze soft. "Thank you." Then they turned, held down three buttons at once, and cleared their throat. "Al-Mohindes, Edric," they said in Edric's voice again. "Authorization delta gamma five seven one bravo charlie nineteen auto-destruct sequence alpha. Engage on my mark." They glanced at me, swallowed, and said, "Mark."

"Now what?" I asked.

Torian touched the central glass panel in two spots. "Now we haul ass."

They grabbed my elbow, but I needed no urging to lunge for the door at their side. We had to leap to the ground because the short ramp had already disappeared. Torian kept running through the trees, back toward our camp, and I kept pace as a rumble and whine grew behind us.

We burst into the clearing by our fire, both of us breathing heavily. Torian shaded their eyes, peering into the sky. I looked up too, but couldn't see anything.

"Did it work?" I asked. "Should that... that ship be in the air?"

Torian nodded. "It worked, and it is." They pointed to a faint distortion above the trees, dwindling even as we watched. "The shuttle's hull is coated in an alloy that bends light." They smiled crookedly. "Hard to conduct clandestine experiments on primitive populations if you flaunt your tech every time you do a flyover." They gazed down at their bloodied hands and grimaced. "I think a wash is in order."

Since my own hands weren't much better, and since I still needed to dress Torian's wound, I couldn't disagree. I was a little off-balance as I followed Torian when they snatched up a pot. True, I hadn't ordinarily used my staff as a walking stick, but it—and my Stone—had been a part of me for so many years, I felt almost as though I were missing a leg.

At the river, Torian filled the pot. With an almost mischievous grin, they swirled one finger in the water. "No more cold washes for us. I've learned a thing or two from you, Magister."

I chuckled weakly, dipping my hands in the pot beside Torian's, the water almost too warm against my chilled flesh. "I'm not entitled to that honorific, not any more. Learning a new trade at my time of life won't be easy, but I can't very well be a Sun mage without a Stone."

Torian's fine eyebrows bunched, and they paused, hands shedding crystalline drops in the morning light. "But you've got the ability. The training. The… the magic."

"Aye. But I can't harness it without the Stone."

"Can't your College of Mages give you another one?"

I shrugged. "Your Edric had the right of it about that, even if he was full of shite otherwise. We've no Stones to spare." I pointed to my eyepatch. "Especially for mages who are already damaged."

Torian's scowl deepened. "That's nonsense. You—"

A boom like distant thunder sounded overhead, and we both looked up. A glow—yellow, orange, and red—bloomed in the sky, rivaling the sun in radiance.

"It worked," Torian murmured. "I hope the Infomancers buy it."

"Buy what?"

"That"—they pointed to the sky—"was the shuttle self-destructing. If the Infomancers scan the wreckage, they'll find evidence of Edric's DNA as well as mine, along with my tracker. I'm hoping they'll believe that both Edric and I were aboard and not come looking for us." Their expression turned almost savage. "I also hope they're fleeing as fast as their engines can cycle to ensure that their ship doesn't meet the same fate when the planet explodes." They must have seen my alarm, because they patted my arm with their damp but blood-free hands. "Don't worry. No more explosions. I promised to keep the near-death experiences to a minimum, remember?"

I frowned at them, pointing to the makeshift bandage around their throat. "Aye, but you've already gone back on that promise."

They waved one hand. "I was in no danger."

"Be that as it may, I'm taking no chances with you." I dumped the murky water and scooped out a fresh potful. "Come."

Torian didn't object, trailing me back to our camp and discarded bedrolls. They sat on the log next to the dying fire while I collected the healing supplies from my own pack.

When I turned back, Torian was shaking droplets off their fingers, probably from warming the fresh water.

I laid a gentle hand on their shoulder. "May I remove the... the T-shirt?" They nodded and bent their head, allowing me to untie the knot and expose their neck. The T-shirt was a bloody mess, but the wound itself was less dire than I'd expected. "I've got a few healing stones yet. With those I should—"

"Don't bother." Torian didn't look up from beneath the curtain of their hair. "You've juiced my power grid so much that I'll be able to seal it myself before long. Just neaten it up and we'll call it good."

"Allow me a little professional pride. I can't take you before the tribunal with an untreated wound."

"Must we go?" they asked, their voice soft, hesitant. "To the capital? You don't owe the College of Mages allegiance anymore, do you?"

With a tuft of lambs-wool from my pack, I sponged the wound with warm water, blinking when the gash seemed to stitch together as I watched. "Aye, that's true enough. However,

I owe them the story. Otherwise, if I don't report in, they'll be thinking I've gone rogue."

"Will they... will they think *I'm* a rogue mage? After all, I murdered someone. I used technology, not magic, but..." They glanced up at me and then away. "Like I said before, that may not be a distinction they're able to make."

I tied a strip of linen around Torian's throat to protect the wound while it healed, although I surmised that no covering would be necessary by evening. I settled their cloak over their shoulders. "That's another reason for us to go. I'll offer my testimony. Tell them of your remorse—"

"But that's just it." They shifted on the log so they could face me. "I don't have any. Remorse, that is. I know I should. Taking someone else's life is wrong."

"When you think about it, he and his lot took your life long ago. This is turn-about, eh?"

"Revenge? That's not why I did it." Torian shivered, and the breeze tossed up a strand of dark hair that snagged in their eyebrow. They pushed it aside irritably. "I did it for you."

My heart warmed as though my Stone weren't in a million useless pieces. "For me?"

"For you and everyone on the planet. When I weighed his life against your whole world, the choice was easy. But choices have consequences." They bit their lip, shoulders rounding as they shrunk in on themself. "Do you think the tribunal will... will execute me? As they punished Loriah?"

The warmth in my chest turned to a burn, both anger and resolve. "Loriah planned to slaughter an entire Earth-born village. She was condemned because she was a threat. You aren't."

"Am I not?" Their smile was crooked. "New knowledge can seem as perilous as an ionic cannon to people with an established power base dependent on the status quo."

"I have no notion what an ionic cannon is, but I won't allow the tribunal to hurt you."

"But if you're not a mage anymore, will they listen?"

"They must." I refused to consider anything else. "I'll need to brief whoever takes over my circuit, and if they accept my words there, they'll accept them elsewhere too. And with all you have to tell them about the Star-born, about our history, about our *future*, they'll fall over themselves to listen to you too."

"Promise?"

I captured Torian's hands and held them against my chest. "I promise. If they don't make a place for us in the capital, we'll find another. You and me."

Torian offered me a trembling smile. "Does that mean you like having me around?"

I remembered my incomprehensible divination spread—sun and moon together on the partnership path; stars no longer in play; earth suspended between peace and prosperity. *It was a true casting, after all.*

I understood the meaning now—and thanked the Sun for the disaster that took me to Corvel-on-Byrne. This was my destiny —working with Torian for the good of the world, the Infomancers be damned.

"I'm bloody sure I can't do without you now."

"Nor I you. You need someone to guard your left side. And I need…" Torian shrugged and pulled their oversized cloak closer around their shoulders.

"What do you need, love?"

Torian ducked their head, as if they'd suddenly come over shy. "I need someone who thinks I'm important. Necessary. Beautiful without the body modification protocols, regardless of the aspect I'm wearing."

"Aye, well, you're always beautiful to me. Have been since I first saw you, filthy and half-starved in that odious gaol. But don't imagine you can't choose to leave my sorry arse behind if you want. The Sun knows I'm no prize. Got only one eye. An uncertain temper. No useful trade. Won't swive. A bad bargain all around."

Torian leaned over and kissed my cheek again. "There are other reasons to be with someone. Companionship. Support. Caring. After you report, we could travel together. I'd like to see your home."

I pictured Torian on the beach below my cottage, their soft dark hair blowing in the breeze as the sun rose across the sea. Aye, I'd give a lot for that sight. "The life of a circuit mage was a rough one, my dear, and the life of a former circuit mage won't be much easier. Are you ready for that?"

They met my gaze squarely. "I am. I could ask for nothing better."

"Well then." I stood and offered Torian my hand to help them to their feet. "We'd best get started then. Without my Stone, though, our journey will be a sight less comfortable, and I won't let you march all the way to the capital in ill-fitting boots and threadbare clothing. I've some healing and prosperity stones put by that we can use to barter, but we'd best go out of our way a bit for provisions."

"Why?"

I chuckled. "I want to avoid anyone on my old circuit. Not all my judgments have been popular, and with no magic at our backs, some of those folk might try a spot of payback."

"Ah. I understand."

They joined me in striking our camp, insisting that we gather the pieces of my broken Stone. Their vision was far sharper than mine, clearly, because they could spot the tiniest chips amid the grass and brush. By the time Torian was through, and I'd bundled the lot in a square of heavy leather, I'd wager we left nothing more than a few specks of dust behind. Then, despite my protests, they used the satchel they'd scavenged from Edric's ship to redistribute our kits more evenly.

As we shouldered our packs and headed for the trail beside the river, Torian chuckled.

"All right, I'll bite," I said. "What's so amusing?"

"This reminds me of something from the archives. A film."

"Film? What's that?"

Torian looked blank. "It's a... if you think of a—"

"Never mind. I'll take it as given. A film, then."

"At the end of a very famous one, after one character has killed a very bad person, his companion, against all expectation, protects him. In return, he says, 'I think this is the beginning of a beautiful friendship.'"

I tweaked a lock of Torian's hair. "You know, my own moon, I couldn't have said it better myself."

PRINCIPLES

SUN, MOON AND STARS

About
PRINCIPLES

Zal and Torian make their way to the capital at last, but things don't go precisely as planned…

Chapter One

Zal

"Are you all right?"

At Torian's soft question, I tore my gaze away from the vale below us where the village of Market Spinney was just waking in the wan morning light. A chill breeze stirred the bare branches of the copse where we stood, tugging at Torian's dark hair—soft, loose, and still short enough to make it appear that they'd committed a crime that warranted a shearing.

"I think I should be asking you that question," I said.

A dark lock blew across Torian's face and they pushed it aside with a pale, impatient, gold-latticed hand. "I'm operating at only slightly suboptimal levels. You needn't worry about me."

"No? I think I do."

When Torian chose to escape the world they'd always known, in the Infomancers' Lab on Star Mountain, they couldn't have expected the journey that followed, trekking miles through the wilderness with me on the cusp of winter, clad in poor clothing and ill-fitting boots.

They couldn't have expected being faced with taking a life. But they had. And they did.

It had been barely a fortnight since Torian had sacrificed themselves to save me from injury or death at the hands of one of those blasted Infomancers of theirs—the Star-born who'd been playing with my people, my planet, my *home*, from the very beginning, as though we were no more than a child's poppets.

While I'd been able to bring Torian back—*reboot* them, they'd called it—that hadn't erased the fact that they'd killed another person—Edric, the very Star-born who'd threatened me, who'd treated Torian as though they were nothing more than a tool like my Sun Stone.

Or the fact that my Sun Stone had shattered as a consequence, rendering me no longer a Sun mage. And *that* was something I'd never expected.

I had no regrets. I'd choose the same path again in a heartbeat. But my life had altered just as drastically as Torian's had, so perhaps they were right to inquire about my welfare. I'd told Edric that Torian was more than the Infomancers gave them credit for. Perhaps I should remember my own words.

I sighed, gazing down at the scatter of wood-shingled buildings and thatched-roofed cottages that lined the muddied snarl of the village's meandering streets, the faded awnings of its central market square like a cluster of drooping wildflowers in a frost-killed field.

"It's still... unsettling. Peculiar. Like I'm missing a leg at every third step."

Torian moved closer to me so that our arms pressed together. "A period of adjustment is to be expected. You've been traveling with a staff taller than you for, what? Ten years?"

"Closer to fifteen." My fingers flexed on the sturdy branch that, at Torian's suggestion, I'd fashioned into a walking stick. It wasn't the same as my old staff, not without my Sun Stone affixed to its crown.

Not without my magic.

But at least it made hiking rough trails easier.

Torian laid their hand on my forearm. Through my heavy sleeve, I didn't feel the little fizz I'd have felt if they'd touched my bare skin, but their presence, their concern, was welcome in any event.

"I know it's not the same. But you're not helpless, Zal. You're big. You're strong. You're kind. You know how to navigate your world. That counts for as much as or more than the clutter of facts and theoretical information in my data banks. So I'll ask again. Are you all right?"

I smiled down at them, smoothing the crease between their dark brows with a fingertip. "I will be. If you can learn to manage without... What was it again? Indoor plumbing? Surely I can learn to manage without my Stone. After all"—I gestured to the town below us—"the Earth-born do so all their lives and are perfectly happy."

"Yes, but..." They shook their head. "Never mind." They squinted down at the village. "What is our plan?"

"Once we get down off this hill, you mean?" I asked, straight-faced.

As I'd hoped, Torian cut a sidelong glance at me, their full lips twitching. "Yes, Zal. Aside from the obvious."

I chuckled as we started down the path toward Market Spinney, adjusting my longer stride so Torian could keep pace.

"First, we'll head to the shoemaker. Even if we're lucky and they've got a pair of boots that's close to fitting you, chances are they'll need time to perfect them. The boots will also be the most expensive, so best we know how much we've got to work with when we head to the market stalls for everything else."

I winced a bit. I hadn't intended to let on to Torian that I was worried about how we would pay for our purchases. In the past, I bartered for what I needed with magic: stones imbued with healing, peace, or prosperity spells. I still had a few stones in my pack, but my stock was running dangerously low, and I had no power to make more.

I was loath to part with the healing stones particularly, because despite Torian's proven ability to heal themself when they were... what had they called it? Operating at only slightly suboptimal levels? When their energy was close to fully depleted, they weren't able to mend so much as a hangnail. Gradually, as we'd traveled, Torian's well-being had become essential to me, so I was determined to save the healing stones for them. Just in case.

Torian hummed, a tune that I recognized from our time on the trail, when they'd sing to me evenings around our fire. This one was about something called *money*, and it seemed like the Infomancers' world had more words for it than were necessary. Marks? Yens? Bucks? Pounds? Just call it a trade and have done.

According to Torian, the names weren't the only things that differed. In order to barter, people in other places, on other worlds, needed to first establish an *exchange rate* so they could figure out how many *marks* were the same as how many *yens*.

Our way was much simpler. Decide what you want, and what you're willing to give away in order to get it. The other party decides whether what you're offering is worth losing what they've got. Certainly there was haggling—everybody wanted to get their best possible bargain—but far easier to negotiate when you had actual *things* to see, to touch, to *use*.

We reached the foot of the hill and joined a straggle of people heading into town, clearly coming in from their farms for market day, their bundles of trade goods looped over their shoulders or strapped to their backs or stacked in their barrows.

Those were material goods. Touchable. *Real*. And they'd go home with things equally real. When I'd argued with Torian about that, they'd retorted, "And exactly how touchable is magic?"

I'd spluttered, because while you couldn't *see* the magic itself, you could measure its results easily enough. But Torian had just shaken their head and bent over the herbs they'd collected, tying them into neat packets with deft fingers.

We'd merged with the foot traffic and had been walking for a few minutes when Torian edged closer to me.

"Zal?"

"Hmmm?"

I was peering ahead, trying to remember the way to the shoemaker. Market Spinney wasn't in my circuit—it had been part of Loriah's—but I'd passed through it more than once. The last time I'd been here, however, was when I'd been tracking Loriah after she'd gone rogue.

The last time I'd been here, I'd had both eyes.

So the difference in my depth perception was making navigation... challenging.

"People are staring."

My attention snapped from the village outskirts to the path near us. Torian was right: If the others heading into town weren't gawking at us outright, they were at least casting us furtive sidelong glances.

"Shite," I muttered.

It stood to reason no one had ever seen anyone like Torian before. They were the last Moon-born on the planet, and most of the Earth-born trudging toward town looked to be too young to have seen a Moon-born before the Lunaria virus wiped them all out over thirty years ago.

The only reason Torian had survived was because the Infomancers had kept them alive with *technology*. I was more grateful than I could say that the Star-born had done so, but still as angry as I'd ever been about the way they'd treated Torian like a *thing*, not a person.

I slowed my pace, taking Torian's elbow and drawing him off the path. "I'm sorry. I should have realized. I should have had you wait—"

"No!" Torian's protest was loud enough that a tall, stocky fellow who'd just passed paused and looked back around the enormous bundle of firewood strapped to his shoulders.

Torian shrank against me, tucking their chin so their hair obscured their face. "No," they said more softly, "that wouldn't have served. First, the shoemaker can't fit my boots unless I'm there. We'd be in the same situation as we are now in that case, and although my feet are a lot tougher than they used to be, breaking in another ill-fitting pair is not on my preferred agenda. Second..." Torian pressed their cheek against my chest. "Second, I don't want to wait alone. I don't want to *be* alone."

"It's all right, love." I kissed the top of their head. "We'll get you a cloak with a hood to hide your face and hair. Gloves, too. You need them anyway for warmth, and they'll help mask the most obvious differences."

Torian nodded, but didn't say anything, not then, and not the rest of the walk to the shoemaker. Once we stepped into the shop, its rough floorboards creaking under our feet, they finally stepped away from me and raised their chin.

The ceiling inside the door was high enough for me to stand, but it sloped down sharply to where the shoemaker hunched on a stool behind a counter, a wooden last in his lap. His silver-gray braids were gathered neatly at his nape with a leather thong, their ends trailing nearly to the floor. Their length and color, as well as the creases on his mid-brown skin, spoke of his age.

The shelves that lined the walls behind him and along either side of the room spoke of his experience: They were full. Pairs of boots, shoes, and slippers were arranged neatly along each shelf, not crowded together, but not widely spaced either.

I blinked in the early light filtering through the distorted but spotlessly clean window. For a village this size, this vast selection was startling.

On the other hand, Market Spinney was on a main trade route between the northwest cantons and the capital, which was why I'd chosen it in the first place.

The shoemaker set aside his awl and last. He squinted at us for a moment before removing his spectacles and wiping at his eyes with the back of his wrist as though he was having trouble seeing in the dim light, too.

Or perhaps because he couldn't believe what he was seeing.

He settled his spectacles back on his nose. "Good morning," he said. "I am Ranolt. How may I serve you today... Magister?"

I shook my head. "Not a mage, good citizen." His assumption was reasonable. Most Sun-born, folk with skin as dark as mine, stayed in the milder south climes unless they were circuit mages as I was. As I *had been.* "Just a customer. My friend is in need of boots. Do you think you can help us?"

Ranolt slid off his stool and circled the counter, hands tucked behind his back beneath the fall of his braids. He came to a stop in front of Torian and tilted his head as he studied Torian's boots.

"Hmmmph." He made a circling motion with one finger. "If you wouldn't mind turning about?" Torian complied. "I'm surprised you can walk at all." He gestured to a low stool in the corner. "Sit. Sit. And remove those abominations from your feet."

After a rather startled look at me, Torian did as they were told. Ranolt, pacing along the shelves, said, "Stockings too."

Torian hesitated a bit at that. They'd told me that when they'd acted as the sole sex worker in the Infomancers' Lab, one of the Star-born had been fixated on their feet. Nevertheless, they removed all three pairs of socks that had been the only thing making the second-hand boots even a passing fit.

"Aha." Ranolt selected one pair of ankle-high boots and two pairs that would reach nearly to Torian's knees. "These should do."

I cleared my throat. "I beg your pardon, Ranolt, but I fear I can only afford a single pair."

He glanced over his spectacles at me. "Perhaps. But these are not for you, are they?"

What was that supposed to mean? I frowned as he crossed to Torian, the square heels of his own brogues clacking on the floorboards. He hooked a lower stool with one foot to drag it in front of Torian and sat, setting the footwear on the floor next to him. Leaning forward, elbows on his knees, he peered down at Torian's feet, his forehead bunched in a scowl.

"It is a crime to subject feet such as these to objects such as"—he sniffed, casting a disdainful glance at Torian's boots—"*those*." He extended a hand. "Do you permit?"

I exhaled, relaxing a trifle. Torian had a problem with the way some questions were phrased, but this one seemed safe.

"Yes." Although their shoulders were clearly tense, Torian nevertheless lifted one foot and placed it in Ranolt's hand.

Ranolt lifted it closer to his face, as though bringing it into focus. With a jolt, I realized that at his age, his eyesight must be failing despite the spectacles. That had to be devastating to a craftsman whose livelihood depended on close, precise work. As I thought about it, Ranolt was possibly the oldest craftsman I'd ever seen still plying his trade. Most had already ceded their business to their apprentices by this time and retired to live out their last years in peace with family.

I swallowed, shifting my gaze to the window. *If they hadn't already died*. Life on our world wasn't easy. It took its toll, often early. Anger simmered under my breastbone. Was that the Starborn's doing, too? While they had been toying with us, using us, had they chosen to make our lives harder than they needed to be?

"We are heading into winter," Ranolt said, "so you need sturdy boots with room for heavy stockings." He held up a finger and shook it at Torian. "A single pair at a time, mind. Wearing many pairs at once doesn't help the fit, merely presents more opportunities for chafing. Since you are not from Market Spinney, I deduce that you are on a journey, so you must be able to tramp over rough ground in comfort." He looked up and grinned at Torian, revealing two missing teeth in his lower jaw. "But when you reach your destination, you won't want such heavy footwear. With spring and summer coming, stockings need not be so heavy either."

"Ranolt," I said, "we really have not the funds—"

"Hush," he said. "I am not trading with you." He looked up at Torian. "I am trading with the Traveler."

Chapter Two

Torian

The Traveler? My jaw sagged. What did that mean? Was Ranolt referring to our journey that he'd already flagged because we weren't village residents? But if that were the case, Zal would be a Traveler, too, and Ranolt had implicitly excluded him from the label with that last statement.

Zal's brows were drawn together, his lips downturned, worry evident in his dark eye, so I shunted the questions to temporary storage to review later and smiled tentatively at Ranolt.

"I don't need so many shoes. One pair that's closer to fitting will do."

"Nonsense," Ranolt said. "You don't want to be wearing winter boots in the summer, nor traveling boots in town. Wear the proper boots at the proper time, in the proper place, and all will last longer. Now these…" He held up a knee-high pair in brown leather.

My vision automatically recalibrated. *Upper thickness: 3.8mm. Sole thickness: 6.4mm. Hide type: Bovine equivalent. Surface treatment: Plant-based oil.* They looked sturdy, yet supple. I curled my fingers against the urge to stroke them, to add their *feel* to the data.

"Inside is lined and padded, so they'll do you on your journeys," Ranolt continued. He reached into a basket on the shelf by his elbow and pulled out a ball of knitted wool that he unrolled to reveal a pair of striped socks, at least as tall as the boots. "Slip into these and we'll see how they fit, hmmm?"

I did as I was told. If I were to be honest with myself, anything would be preferable to continuing to wear the old boots. Some days, just looking at them sent me back to that moment at the campfire when the apprentices from Corvel-on-Byrne had appeared out of the trees and I'd discovered the truth.

That I couldn't say no.

Not with any certainty. If Zal hadn't returned at that moment, I might have been hustled back to the village—assuming we even got that far—and into sex work at their Comfort House, providing the only services for which I had any real or extensive experience.

But now, despite the uncertainty of what we would face in the capital, I wanted nothing to do with my old life. Perhaps this new one would be hard, existing without the convenience of the Lab's advanced technology, but at least it would be one of my choosing. The longer I spent with Zal, the more I was coming to embrace the planetary inhabitants' fundamental belief in the sanctity of choice.

Yes, the sooner I could shed everything related to that night, the happier I would be. Another step forward, another step away from my existence as an oddity, an experiment, an inconvenient reminder of a drastic miscalculation.

Another step toward *choosing*.

I shivered as Ranolt slipped one boot on my left foot. Because *choosing* had turned me into a killer, too.

I didn't regret Edric's death at my hand. He would have murdered Zal had I not acted, would have destroyed the planet and everyone on it. But when I made *that* choice, I hadn't expected to survive.

If I were to be honest with myself again, I had moments of anger at Zal for bringing me back where I had no alternative but to face the consequences. To live with the memories. To shoulder the guilt.

Ranolt muttered to himself as he laced up the boots. Once he'd tied both securely, he said, "If you could stand, please, Traveler."

There was that term again. What did it mean? From the way Zal's forehead creased, he didn't know any more than I did.

Ranolt felt the way the left boot fit snug around my ankle and my calf, pressed down at the tip to judge where my toes lay. "How does it feel?"

I wiggled my toes and lifted my heel. "Perhaps a bit wide in the heel?"

He hmmmphed. "Can't have that. Blisters." He grasped my heel with a surprisingly strong grip. "I've the way of it. Let's try the rest."

We went through the same process with the right boot, and, despite my protests, with the other knee-high pair, its uppers thinner than the first, its soles not as heavy, and with the ankle-high pair as well.

"These'll be ready in a candlemark or so."

Candlemark.

I inhaled sharply, causing Zal to step forward and Ranolt to look up.

"Is aught amiss?" Ranolt asked. "I fear I can't have them done any sooner."

"No. No, that's fine."

The problem wasn't with the boots. The problem was with me. My retrieval protocols should have returned the definition of *candlemark* in a nanosecond. But it had not. I tried again, framing the query completely:

Linguistic equivalency; local jargon=candlemark; Return result.

But still nothing. My breathing sped up enough that Zal stepped forward again, concern in his dark eye.

"Torian? What's the matter?"

I shook my head. "Nothing. It's nothing."

It wasn't, of course. If my search protocols on something so simple had failed, what did that mean about the rest of my programming? Could I depend on it? Had I damaged a circuit when I'd removed my tracking device with rough frontier surgery using Zal's belt knife? I had no scar on my neck—my repair subroutines had healed the gash without a trace. But if I'd somehow disrupted an internal circuit... If the tracker had a failsafe, something that could cascade through my systems and compromise other code, there was nothing I could do. Not out here, not without the Lab's diagnostic tools.

Yes, I could run my own system diagnostic, but I'd need to go offline to do it. And even that would only tell me something was wrong, not exactly what it was, and not how to fix it.

And I already knew something was wrong, didn't I?

In an attempt to reassure Zal, I smiled at him. Judging from his deepening frown, however, I failed spectacularly.

"Now, about payment..." Ranolt said.

Zal unslung his pack. "I've some stones to trade." He unlaced the flap and pulled out a roll of leather tied with a thong. A shout outside in the street made him flinch, though, and he fumbled it, loosening the thong when it caught on one finger. The leather unrolled partially, and a scatter of bright amber shards pinged onto the floor.

"Shite," Zal muttered, and knelt to gather them into his palm.

Ranolt, meanwhile, was staring at the chrysocite chips with wide eyes. "Are those... Can it be..." He raised his chin and glared at Zal. "*What have you done?*"

Zal blinked at Ranolt's fierce tone. "Naught but my duty, I assure you."

Ranolt jabbed a finger at the chrysocite in Zal's hand. "Does the mage still live?"

Zal grimaced and rubbed the back of his neck under his braids with his free hand. "That's as may be."

Ranolt folded his arms. "I don't trade in stolen goods, nor in those gained by blood."

Understanding dawned on Zal's face. "Ah. I see. These are the remains of my own Sun Stone, one I carried for nearly fifteen years. However, it met with an accident and shattered, as you see. Therefore, the man to whom it belonged lives"—he spread his arms—"but does the mage?"

"Ah. I see." Ranolt's attitude softened, a flicker of pity in his faded brown eyes. "Well then. I can't deny that bit of Sun Stone would pay for these boots and more. Nothing is better for working with the hides, for it's sharper than the sharpest blade and never dulls. But if it does not truly belong to you, you will not be able to give it away."

I raised my eyebrows. Was that true? The Infomancers claimed they'd instantiated the solar manipulation aptitude into the genetic makeup of the J-4 strain, the race the inhabitants called Sun-born. But I didn't recall them mentioning that chrysocite could be *keyed* to a specific person, enough that it couldn't be stolen.

Tentatively, I sent another request down the query pathway.

Chrysocite; attributes; security features; Return array.

When I got an immediate response—*Investiture ceremony establishes secure link between manipulator and solar interface; single use, no transfer; ensures no manipulator may be eliminated for their interface*—I heaved a shaky sigh.

So. I wasn't completely broken, but unreliability was nearly as bad. I redirected the issue to temporary storage. I'd worry about it later.

Zal flattened his big palm and teased the shards into a single layer with one fingertip. "Tell me which three you wish."

"Three? Nay, one will do."

"Nevertheless, I choose to give you three for your good work and your care for Torian."

Ranolt gazed at Zal's face for a moment, and then studied the mineral splinters, his hands clasped behind his back as though he feared to touch them. Then he pointed, his finger hovering above each choice. "This one. And this. And this." He glanced up at Zal again. "If you are sure?"

"I am." Zal pinched the first shard between thumb and forefinger and held it out. "Here. Please take it. I swear to you that it is mine to give."

Ranolt hesitated for a moment, then allowed Zal to drop it into his palm. The little chip bloomed with light for a moment and subsided, although it still shone in the pale light filtering in through the irregular glass of the window.

"Ah," he said. "Then it is well." He let Zal transfer the other chips to his palm and tilted his head to one side. "I will include a pair of soft slippers as well."

Zal's eye widened. "I didn't—"

"Pish. Everyone deserves a pair of slippers." He smiled slyly. "Even you." He closed his fist over his prizes and flapped his other hand. "Now, shoo. Come back in a candlemark. And if you're seeking new clothing? Go to my cousin's stall. Annice, her name is. It's in the northeast rank, on the side nearest the smithy, third from the end. She'll give you good value for your Sun Stone bits." He winked. "Double perhaps, because it'll give her boasting rights over her friends."

As much as I hated to do it, I put my old boots back on. Ranolt had already turned away with more of that sotto voce mumbling, seemingly dismissing us. I stood and followed Zal out the door and onto the plank walkway that lined the muddy street.

Traffic had picked up now that the sun was fully up. People led large, heavy-hoofed dray animals that resembled a cross between old Terran Clydesdales and water buffalos down the middle of the street, churning up even more mud and trailing the inevitable droppings. Others guided laden barrows along, their rag-wrapped wooden wheels picking up more mud and, from the curses of their owners, making them harder to push.

People called to one another or shouted commands to their beasts. Mud *schlurp*ed beneath hooves and wheels and boots. Footsteps—our own and those of others who hurried past us—rang hollow on the walkway.

I wasn't used to the chaos and the noise, and every new sound made me flinch. The lab had always been quiet except for the hum of machinery, or the murmur of low conversation, or the coded chatter of the AIs, something I'd barely registered after the Infomancers had installed the module that let me decode the AI data stream without a translation interface.

Once traveling with Zal, I'd gotten used to the softer silence of the outdoors. I wished fervently that we were back on the trail.

"Are you all right?" Zal asked. "You look a bit spooked."

I shrugged, but then winced when someone whistled loudly from the street right next to us. "It's bigger than I'm used to. More people. More noise."

"Big? This is naught but a speck. If you think this is big, you're going to hate the capital. It's bigger. Noisier, too."

I wrinkled my nose as a dray animal dropped an odiferous load not a meter away. "Smellier?"

"Some parts." Zal pursed his lips. "Most parts." He chuckled. "Who am I fooling? All parts."

"Lovely," I said faintly.

On the opposite side of the street, the droning chant of many voices emanated from a building that stood apart, nearly three times the size of its nearest neighbor.

"What's happening over there?" I asked.

Zal followed the direction of my gaze. "Earth temple. Priests leading morning prayers." He chuckled again. "Although on market day, they're probably only leading each other. Their flock is either on the way to shop or already there, preparing to sell." He stopped at a cross street, holding my elbow until a barrow nearly overflowing with smooth gray rocks trundled by, pushed by a grunting youth with black braids gathered in a top knot who didn't look nearly strong enough to move the load.

After they'd passed, Zal helped me down off the walkway—which was elevated a good two feet above the ground—and into the soupy mud of the street.

We picked our way across, and for a moment, I was glad I had on the old boots. Ranolt's handiwork would be the first new shoes I'd ever possessed. The first shoes, actually, since in the Lab, I'd only ever worn disposable synthetic booties. *New boots.* The notion was unexpectedly thrilling, and I had no desire to cake them with mud... et cetera.

After we reached the other side of the street, Zal didn't mount the walkway in front of the Earth temple. Instead, he led me beside it along a narrow alley that opened onto a square populated with canvas-topped stalls.

The paths between them weren't churned-up muck like the streets, but neither were they raised walkways. Instead, wooden planks lay directly on the ground. I was glad not to sink up to my ankles again, but in truth, there was nearly as much mud on top of the planks as underneath.

"Zal, may I ask you something?"

He glanced down at me from where he'd been scanning the square. "Of course."

"What did the Moon-born *do*?"

He blinked down at me, his steps slowing to a stop, much to the irritation of the people behind us who were forced to go around. "Don't you know?"

"I was raised in the Lab, among the—" I winced, and glanced around to see if anybody was close enough to hear. Regardless, I probably shouldn't mention the Infomancers, particularly as Star-born. "Among the *others*. How would I know anything about their lives?"

Zal gestured to my middle. "But you have the... the *stores*. All of their records. Can't you check?"

I inhaled shakily. True, I could check. I'd researched some of the events around the Lunaria virus in the past, after all, but I'd never probed any farther. Had the Infomancers bred curiosity out of me, out of my kind? Zal had told me that the besetting sin of Sun-born mages was insatiable curiosity. If the Originators could code for that, surely they could code for its inverse.

But I *had* been curious. I *was* curious. Furthermore, I'd been delighted to add to my data stores from the new experiences of my journey with Zal. The true answer, I suspected, was that I had probably feared I wouldn't like what I found about my... my kind. And now?

Now I was afraid to look for fear I wouldn't be able to retrieve the data at all.

"I... Could I ask you something else?"

His brow wrinkled in confusion. "Aye."

"What's a candlemark?"

Chapter Three

Zal

Ranolt had been right. His cousin cackled gleefully the entire time she kitted Torian out with new clothing—half a dozen new shirts, smallclothes, a leather jerkin as well as a woolen one, three pairs of breeks, a heavy waterproof cloak with a hood, one pair of fleece-lined leather gloves, and one pair of knitted mittens.

After Torian had changed from their old clothes in a curtained-off corner of her stall, Annice took those in trade too, as well as the three Sun Stone shards, so I had no fear she'd come off the worse in our bargain.

By the time we'd finished, we had just enough time to pick up some food supplies—a small sack of grain, a half dozen tubers, and a small jar of honey—before heading back to Ranolt's shop. I didn't part with any Sun Stone chips for the food, though. Instead, I traded for several packets of dried herbs that were hard to find in this canton, two bundles of wild onions, and a coney pelt.

"Zal?"

"Hmmm?" Weighing the merits of two belt knives—Torian needed one of their own—I didn't turn at Torian's murmur.

"We're being watched."

That got my attention. I set both knives back on the cutler's table, much to her disgruntlement, considering how many questions I'd already asked, but I didn't face Torian immediately. I didn't want to betray to the onlookers that they'd been spotted.

Instead, I glanced sidelong at Torian, where they'd sidled up next to me, so close they were almost inside my cloak. Their hood was up, hiding their short, unplaited hair and shadowing their pale face, and they were wearing the mittens, so none of their skin was showing.

I took Torian's arm and ambled away from the cutler to the next stall over, a leatherworker with dozens of belts, harnesses, and satchels on display. "Still watching?"

"Yes."

I could feel Torian trembling. "For how long?"

"I don't know. I didn't notice them at first, or not them in particular. But when you were buying the honey, I saw someone staring. They darted into the smithy, so I lost track of them, but then they came out with a large man in a leather apron, whom I assume is the smith. Then the smith watched us while the first person dashed off and returned with a third. They were still there when you were talking with the cutler."

"The cutler is likely selling the smith's goods, or that of his apprentices. Perhaps he's merely keeping an eye on her."

"They wouldn't have been concerned with the honey, though. You didn't move on to the cutler until after that."

I gazed down into Torian's worried face. "Folks have been staring at you since you came down off Star Mountain, love. I expect that's all it is. Are you worried someone might accost you?" I thumped my walking stick on the plank under our feet. "You said it yourself. I'm not completely defenseless."

Torian peeped around his hood, shooting a quick glance back at the smithy. "Do you think that's all it is?"

I was about to reply stoutly that I was certain, but then a niggle of doubt wormed into my belly. *Perhaps it's not Torian who's drawing attention.*

This village had been on Loriah's circuit, so the folk hereabouts likely had a long-standing relationship with her from before she went rogue. Chances were, seeing how gossip seemed to spread across the cantons as though it were carried on the wind, that news had reached them of the one-eyed mage who'd turned Loriah over for judgment.

Would they view me as a savior, then, or as a traitor? I ranked the odds at dead even, which meant the sooner we got out of Market Spinney and on our way, the better.

Torian could continue to share my knife for now.

"It's been near a candlemark." I took their elbow and hurried them away from the stalls. "Let's see if Ranolt has your boots ready."

When we got back to the shop, I waved Torian over to Ranolt for a final fitting. "Go ahead. I want to rebalance our packs."

They nodded and met Ranolt at the stool. I ignored their low-voiced conversation, because as I sorted through our purchases, I was also peering out the window, checking for signs that we were followed. By the time Ranolt had laced Torian into his new winter boots, I hadn't spotted any suspicious movement in the street.

That didn't mean there hadn't been any—my one-eyed vision had its limits—but at least no crowd armed with torches and pitchforks was storming the shop.

"Zal." Torian's tone was both fond and exasperated. "You've put everything in your pack."

"So?"

"So I'm perfectly capable of carrying my share."

"This makes the most sense," I grumbled. "Keeping the food together."

"Yes, but my new clothes are not food. You haven't given me anything."

Because you've already given me so much.

Torian revealed new wonders every night around the campfire, split the journey's chores, shared warmth with me in our common bedroll so that I wasn't cold and alone when I awoke every morning.

What did I have to offer?

Without my Stone, all I had was my physical strength, and even that was compromised by my blind side. Carrying more was the least I could do.

Ranolt hustled over with the other knee-high boots draped over his arm, the ankle boots in one hand and two pairs of slippers in the other. One set of slippers was noticeably larger than the other.

"Here you are. As promised."

I held up a palm. "Thank you for the work you've done on Torian's behalf, but I don't need slippers."

Torian stepped in smoothly and took them from Ranolt's hand. "Yes, you do. You deserve to be comfortable too, Zal, and we won't always be on the road."

They hesitated a bit, biting their lip, and I could almost hear what they didn't say: *Not anymore.*

I'd never be on the road again, at least not as a circuit mage.

With a quirk of one dark eyebrow, Torian stowed all the footwear in his own pack, and then shouldered it under his cloak. I laced the flap on mine and did the same. I nodded to Ranolt.

"Our thanks."

He tucked his hands in his apron pockets. "My joy to serve." He winked. "Particularly when I'm so well paid. Safe journey to you both."

I opened the door, and before I could stop them, Torian had stepped out onto the wooden walkway in front of the shop. They turned to me as though to say something, and then gasped, staggering sideways.

Damned blind side.

Because someone had come barreling up on my left and collided with Torian, sending them stumbling back to teeter on the edge of the walkway. Before I could move, the assailant had grabbed Torian's wrist, yanked them forward, and leaned in to growl something right in their face.

I roared, lunging out the door, but too late. The person slapped something into Torian's hand and bolted, jumping straight off the walkway and into the muddy street to disappear behind a team of draygurs pulling a travois loaded with stacks of split logs. I was about to launch myself in pursuit, but Torian's surprisingly firm grip on my arm stopped me.

"Zal. Please. There's no need."

I looked down at them, blood still surging in my veins. "But he attacked you."

"I'm unharmed. I'd much rather leave town than cause any further disturbance." Torian smiled crookedly. "I've had more than my share of disturbances in my life, and I'd prefer to avoid as many as possible in future."

"If you're sure?" I grasped their shoulders and scanned their face, looking for signs of injury. "Your wrist? Your hand? He hit you."

Torian's gaze shifted to a point beyond my shoulder. "I'm fine. But I would like to go now."

I glanced behind me. Ranolt was standing in the doorway, observing the scene avidly, as were all the townsfolk who'd been close enough to either witness the attack or be drawn by my own shout. Torian had the right of it—the fewer people we made privy to our business, the better.

"You're right." I nodded to Ranolt again. "A good day to you."

With a hand on Torian's back beneath the bulge of their pack, I set a brisk pace out of the village and up the hill toward the spinney of winter-bare paperbark trees that had probably given the town its name.

Once the path narrowed enough that we had to walk single file, I let Torian go ahead of me, the better to guard their back should anyone follow us.

That was how I noticed that their right hand was fisted.

Reaching out, I touched their arm. "Torian. You *were* hurt. What's the matter with your hand?"

Their steps faltered and their hood dipped as though their chin had fallen to their chest. They turned slowly to face me. "I had hoped to wait until we made camp to talk about this."

I lifted a brow. "But?"

"But I know you don't let anything go when you're worried." They raised their fist and uncurled their fingers. In their palm was a crumpled bit of white.

I touched it with a finger. "That's… That's paper."

Torian's eyebrows drew together. "Yes. Why do you sound as though it's a novelty? The populace can manufacture paper. I know. I saw references to it in the observers' reports back in the Lab."

"Aye. But so few need it, especially in the outer cantons, that it's rarer than a warm day in winter. Mostly they make do with slates and chalk."

"But you have books." Their frown deepened. "Don't you?"

I snorted. "You've an unreasonable notion of a circuit mage's wealth if you think I could afford any of my own."

"But the… the planet has books," Torian said a little desperately.

"Aye. Some of the Sun-born who don't have mage potential or who decide not to follow the path train as scribes. They work mostly in the capital, though, where the library is."

"*The* library?" Torian's voice dipped low. "You make it sound as though there's only one."

I nodded. "Aye."

"There's only *one* library on the whole fucking *planet*? And all the books are *hand-lettered*?"

Torian's anger was more than a bit alarming. I'd only seen them truly angry one other time, and that had been after they'd been assaulted by Farren and the other miscreant apprentices from Corvel-on-Byrne.

"Why are you so bothered, love? The library is open to all."

Torian's fist closed around the paper again. "But you have to *go* to it. How likely is it that people in… in Market Spinney, in

Corvel-on-Byrne, or any remote village will make the trip to the capital just to consult a book? Is everyone at least *literate*?"

"What?"

They huffed, but then took a slow, deep breath. When they spoke again, their tone had evened out. "Are you taught to read and write?"

"Oh, aye. Earth-born children go to the temple schools until they're ten and ready for apprenticeships. If they've got leadership ability, they'll spend three years at the academy run by the College of Seigneurs over in the delta. The Sun-born go to schools operated by the College of Mages, since we all have to be trained and tested to see if we've mage potential. Those are all in the southern cantons, though." I shrugged. "The Sun-born aren't fond of the cold."

"I saw some Sun-born in Corvel-on-Byrne when we left town, though. Are you saying their children would go to the Earth temple schools?"

"Of course not. They need Sun-born teachers. But the mage schools are all boarding schools, anyway. We all leave home at six and live there until we decide whether to take the vows or not."

Torian looked away, their face going stormy once more. "Do the Earth temple schools all have the same curriculum? The same textbooks?"

I laughed at the outlandish notion of any scribe allowing a precious book to be taken to someplace as remote as Corvel-on-Byrne. "They've no need. The priests run the schools and they're priests because they've passed the test."

Torian's narrow-eyed gaze snapped back to me. "What test?"

"The Remembrance. They take it when they're done with their regular schooling. If they can recite their lessons perfectly, word for word, they're taken in by the priesthood."

"Remembrance. You mean it's a memory test? The priests all have perfect recall?"

My brows drew together, uncertain why Torian still seemed unsettled. "They're *priests*."

Torian heaved a sigh, their shoulders slumping. "That isn't as clear an explanation as you might imagine, Zal. It may be obvious to you, but..." Torian sighed. "That's another thing the Infomancers were unaware of. It's not in the reports." Torian's eyes clouded. "Not any reports I'm able to access, at any rate." They sighed again. "So you're saying that Earth-born children learn lessons by rote in the temple schools."

"Aye."

"And if they've perfect recall, they'll go on to become priests and, in turn, teach others by rote."

"Aye. It's not so different from the way masters teach their apprentices, except the children are younger." I held up my palms. "And the children aren't *forced* into the priesthood. They still have a choice if they'd prefer to remain in their village and take a different apprenticeship."

"Has no one ever objected to this system? Expressed the desire for change?"

"Why would they? It suits us."

Their jaw tightened, throat working, and they stared down at the ground for a long moment before lifting their chin to meet my gaze.

"Then tell me this, Zal. If everyone is so satisfied with the status quo, why would someone in an Earth-born village go out of their way to give me this?"

They held up their hand, unfurled their fingers, and smoothed out the paper. On it were four strings of twenty-six letters—the alphabet, twice in upper case and twice in lower case. But the ink was dark and even, the letters between each copy were absolutely identical, no differences between them at all, and not a smudge, not a blot, not a wobble of the pen.

I touched it in wonder. "Our scribes are skilled, but I've never seen anything this perfect."

"This wasn't lettered by a scribe, Zal. It was made by a printing press."

I blinked, brow furrowing. "A printing press? What's that?"

"I'll explain later." They sighed heavily again, running a finger across the lines of letters. "But the real question is this: Why is it a secret?"

I rested my hands on Torian's shoulders. "Nay, love. The real question is why did someone in this out-of-the-way village tell that secret to *you*?"

Chapter Four

Torian

Although Zal wanted to put some distance between us and Market Spinney, he called a halt well before our usual camping time.

I glanced around the little clearing. Granted, it was a perfect spot—a stream burbling nearby for water, trees encircling it three-quarters of the way with a good amount of deadfall for firewood, and a tumble of boulders to close the circle, blocking the wind but not the sun.

Zal jerked a thumb at the sky. "Sky's clear. Hasn't been for at least a week, but I smell snow coming. You'll need to charge yourself now while you've got the chance."

I didn't argue. For one thing, he was right. If the weather was about to turn for the worse, I wanted my reserves topped up as much as possible. But for another, Zal had been quiet and withdrawn ever since I'd shown him evidence of the printing press. I hadn't been inclined to break the silence myself, fury and confusion still warring in my middle until I'd had to run a quick system flush.

That paper, those four simple lines of print, had disturbed me more than I wanted to admit.

I wasn't certain what it meant. Was there a conservative contingent among the planetary inhabitants who preferred things to remain as they were? Who objected to change for its own sake? Why else would anyone want to suppress the printing press, arguably the most important invention of societal advancement from old Earth, granting as it did wider access to ideas and stories previously controlled by church gatekeepers or hoarded by the wealthy?

Well, I supposed that was one answer. The church and the wealthy liked things the way they were. Except... From what I'd seen so far, the Earth-born temples had more in common with charities and old-style guilds than the monolithic church infrastructure of old Earth Europe. Likewise, I hadn't seen any evidence of truly unequal wealth here, either. Granted, my exposure had only been to small villages, so income disparity might be more prevalent once we headed into more populous areas, but for some reason, that didn't feel like the right answer.

The other answer chilled me down to my control circuits.

The Infomancers.

They'd decided, for some reason, that it suited them to keep their subjects at a more primitive level, and so had done something to quell innovations like the printing press.

But to do that, they'd have had to reach out of the Lab and interfere directly with the populace, something that was strictly against their project design and observation protocols.

What else had they manipulated? What fundamental ethical and scientific standards had they compromised? What were they willing to sacrifice?

Edric certainly hadn't had any scruples about exposing himself and his advanced tech to Zal, threatening to kill him. In fact, the entire team was ready to destroy this whole world, a world with hundreds of thousands of inhabitants.

From what Zal had told me, regardless of the inhabitants' firm belief in *choice*, roles and options were still limited here, not only by where a person happened to be born, but by their strain. By coding specific traits and abilities into the genome for the Sun-born and the Earth-born—and presumably the Moon-born as well, although with only myself as an example, I couldn't draw significant conclusions—the Infomancers had effectively created a society that was predicated entirely on race, which was incomprehensible considering the diversity of the galaxy from which they came.

Maybe that was the entire point of this experiment. If so, how absolutely *monstrous.*

However, if so, that might also explain their need to destroy the evidence.

I wanted—no, I *needed* to find out the truth, not just for the sake of my own curiosity, but for Zal's safety, for the safety of the planet. The Infomancers had gone so far as to plan mass genocide to hide their involvement, to hide their reasons, their eventual goals. There had never been any mention of such scorched-earth protocols in the Lab charter or articles of incorporation or in any of the reports I'd scanned.

I shuddered. Was that data also hidden behind a firewall in my system stores, shunted away from me along with my ability to refuse a request to *submit* when it was couched in the right terms?

If I wanted to dig any deeper, though, to run at least a surface diagnostic to see if my rough self-surgery had removed more from my circuitry than just my tracking device, I needed a full charge, and this might be the only opportunity.

So as Zal arranged fist-sized rocks in a circle and built up our fire, I slipped off my pack and climbed onto one of the boulders midway up the pile. Stone rose up behind me, blocking the wind, and the whole jumble still retained heat from the sun, which still fell on my perch as it dipped toward the horizon.

I removed my cloak and folded it under me to pad out my seat a bit. I gave it an affectionate pat. The new clothes had been far warmer and more comfortable, the new boots so well-fitted that my feet weren't tired and sore at all.

"Zal," I called as I stripped off the woolen jerkin, "what sort of magic do the Earth-born have?" The Lab reports had always referred to them, the A-3 strain, as the *control,* but I'd never seen any definition of their attributes.

Frankly, I hadn't looked. I'd *assumed* that a control group would be a baseline, as close to old-Earth standard as possible. But then, they were A-3. So what happened to A-1 and A-2? I'd never bothered to look before, since the data had never been pertinent to any of my Lab tasks. And now, I was afraid to try.

Zal glanced up at me from where he was crouched next to the fire ring, arranging the wood he'd gathered in a rough pyramid, ready for him to strike a spark with his flint and steel, since he couldn't ignite the kindling with his solar magery any longer.

"The Earth-born? None."

"None at all?"

"Nay. They never seem to feel the lack. They're all about their crops and their crafts." He chuckled. "They enjoy a good time, too. I suppose you might call the ale they brew a bit of magic, but they insist it's just skill."

I pulled the shirt over my head and inhaled sharply when the sun hit the lattice on my back. "Are you sure? Because these boots fit perfectly. Whatever Ranolt did to them while we were at the market was as much like magic as to make no difference."

He smiled up at me. "Mayhap it's like those Infomancers of yours. His skill is enough advanced that it seems like magic to anyone who doesn't know how to do the same. He was an older man, so he's had many years to practice his trade."

That made me pause. This planet was on the technological level of about fifteenth century Europe. Infant and child mortality kept the average life expectancy low, although if a person survived childhood, they had a reasonable chance of reaching fifty, or at least the mid-forties, absent death in battle. But medical care had been so primitive that anyone who'd become ill or gotten injured was just as likely to die from the treatment as recover.

Granted, the mages were able to dispense a higher level of care here, but still…

"Zal? How old are you?"

He paused in the act of unlacing the cook pot from his pack. "Me? I've counted thirty-two summers. You?"

I blinked. Zal was actually younger than me by almost two planetary years. I suppose that made sense. He was born after the Lunaria virus had wiped out the rest of my race, and, as its last remnant, I'd clearly been born before or during the outbreak.

Yet I appeared at least a decade or more younger. Part of that was due, no doubt, to the harsher conditions on the planet's surface, conditions that Zal weathered for most of the year, while the Lab's environment was precisely controlled, and the nutritional needs of its inhabitants carefully monitored and adjusted.

Another factor was the Infomancers' own genetic inclination to longevity, some of which they might have passed to me during one of my many modifications. The average life expectancy for their sort of human was at least a century and a half with no appreciable deterioration in physical or mental capacity, and some managed into their third century. Edric, for instance, had been well past his first century when he…

When I…

Suddenly, my breath stalled as though the microprocessors driving my cybertronic lungs had gone offline. My vision began to iris in as though a system shutdown was imminent.

I dropped my head to my knees and gasped, mouth working like one of the landed fish Zal often caught for our supper.

"Torian? Shite!"

Then Zal was there, solid and warm at my side, his big hand splayed on my hip. Even after so short a time together, he knew not to block the sun from my solar grid, and that brought the tears prickling in my eyes, further clouding my vision.

Fuck, I hated crying.

"What is it, love?" Zal's voice, which I knew could be loud and forceful enough to scatter a pack of campsite invaders, whether human or animal, was low, soothing, a balm to my nerves.

"Nothing." My voice was thick. I sent a terse command to reduce the swelling in my throat and tried again. "Nothing." That was better. I sounded eighty-nine percent optimal at a minimum.

Zal hummed low in his throat, and though it was as tuneless as the Earth priests' chants, it resonated in my circuits, more effective than one of my healing protocols.

"I'll let that pass for now, because I don't want to distress you further. But later? I think we'll have a wee chat." He hummed again. "Let me get the fire started. Then I can see what the stream might yield in the way of fish."

"No." My proximity sensors were attuned to him now, so without lifting my head, I reached out and gripped his arm. "Not yet. It's early. I'd rather wait."

"If you're sure?"

I nodded, my forehead rubbing against the nubby wool of my new trousers. "I just need a moment."

"Very well." His weight shifted as though he were about to stand.

Panic swamped me again and my head jerked up. "Where are you going?"

He stroked my hair. "Only to get a few things from my pack. I'll be gone naught but a moment." He kissed the top of my head. "I'll bring your waterskin. You sound as though you could do with a drink."

I wrapped my arms around my knees and watched him, wondering yet again how his presence could warm me more than even the sun being absorbed into my solar lattice. But it was so.

In that moment, as though a background query had suddenly returned its results, I realized that it wasn't the fact I'd ended Edric's life that had caused my malfunction.

It was the thought of Zal's life ending. And mine going on. Without him.

If the Infomancers had indeed spliced the genes for their own longer lifespan into my DNA, I didn't want them. Not if it meant decades, centuries, without Zal.

I laughed weakly at my own lack of foresight. What had I imagined when I escaped the Lab? Clearly nothing to the purpose. Perhaps the Infomancers had engineered imagination out of me, along with targeted curiosity and the ability to refuse sex.

A beautiful friendship, I'd told Zal. But it was more. It was a true partnership. A perfect partnership. If I were lucky, a *long* partnership.

And at its end, if I were left alone? Well, I'd instigated a system shutdown before. I could do it again.

I had calmed enough that I was able to smile at Zal when he returned, even to accept the waterskin and take a few sips. He settled beside me on my left with a groan and several bundles from his pack that I'd learned contained his mage supplies.

"I'm not certain why I'm so knackered lately."

I glanced at him in surprise. "But that's obvious."

He turned his face fully toward me, the eyebrow above his eyepatch quirked. "To you mayhap. Care to share that secret with me?"

I leaned into him, letting his warmth soak into me from the side, even though the sun was doing a perfectly good job of heating me. "I'm sorry. I don't mean to be as supercilious as the Infomancers." I bit my lip, trying to find the right words, words that would make sense in the context of his world.

Then I realized that was ridiculous. He already knew *me*, he'd seen Edric and the shuttle, he'd been told of the Infomancers' tampering with his planet and his people. If he wasn't precisely conversant with the technological concepts, he accepted them on faith because he trusted me.

"The way that your"—*what word makes sense?*—"nature was designed by the Originators, the bit of you that makes it possible for you to manipulate solar energy through chrysocite..." At the quirk of his lips, I mock frowned. "Fine, to work magic with your Sun Stone. I think it's probable that you've become so used to having that energy at your fingertips, available to you at all times, that you subconsciously draw on it to maintain your own welfare." When his brow puckered, I scanned my data stores for the correct analogy. "The healing stones. The one you gave me. The ones you traded to Netta for my first clothes. You imbued those with power that could still work without you being present to specifically activate it. It's like that. Your Sun Stone was like a perpetual healing stone, granting you stamina, energy, and probably accelerated healing."

His jaw sagged and he blinked once, twice, three times. "Shite, Torian. If that's true... You think it worked like the prosperity stones too? That it made me... luckier?"

I shrugged. "It's possible, even probable." I nudged him with an elbow. "Maybe that's why you're always able to catch enough fish for supper as fast as you cast your hook in." At Zal's bleak look, I dropped my smirk and laid my hand over his. "What is it?"

"It's just... This is the worst time to be without my Stone, then. Because when we face the Trine, I'll need all the luck I can get."

Chapter Five

Zal

Torian's words had chilled me to my marrow. I'd always depended on my Stone for my spells. What mage didn't? But had I been leaning on it for more than that? Had it become a crutch, one that I couldn't manage without?

Now that I was aware of it, surely I'd be able to adjust. Compensate. Adapt. I snorted softly. *Better do it right sharpish, then, before I face the Trine.*

I considered our journey so far. It hadn't been *so* bad. Granted, I was more tired of an evening, but we'd been forcing our pace a bit so we could reprovision in Market Spinney before winter loomed so close that our trip to the capital would need snowshoes as well as boots.

I'd still *reached* for my magic often during the day before I'd remembered. But that was instinct. Habit. Just as I'd fashioned a walking stick—on Torian's advice—to aid my gait, I would have to find new, nonmagical ways to handle tasks that had been second nature to me for fifteen years.

It wasn't as though I had much choice.

Still, the Earth-born could live without magic. Shite, I'd done so as a child before I'd left home to go to school, and even there until I began training in earnest. I just needed to *remember*. Practice. Become accustomed.

And stop bloody moping about it.

I carefully picked up the leather roll containing the Sun Stone shards. Now that I knew how valuable they were in trade, I wanted to secure them better. I didn't want to chance losing any if they spilled like they had in Ranolt's shop.

When I unrolled the leather across my lap, the double handful of shards winked in the sun like the golden tracks under Torian's pale skin. I lifted one long splinter and laid it across my palm with a sigh.

"Do you reckon I've enough here to last us until I master a new skill or two?"

"Hmmm." Torian's hum was as sweet as a bird's trill. They touched the shard with a tentative finger. "Have you tried to manipulate any solar power…" They smirked at me, and I didn't take them to task because I was so relieved they'd recovered from their earlier upset. "Excuse me, *work any magic* since it shattered?"

"Nay. There was no point."

"Try it now."

I frowned. I'd never known Torian to be needlessly cruel, yet pretending I hadn't lost a part of my soul wasn't kind. "Torian —"

"Please, Zal. Humor me." They took the shard from me and scooted a little way across the boulder to hold it up in the sun, where it sparkled and glowed and made my throat close as a pit of loss opened in my belly.

"All right," I croaked. "What do you want me to do?"

They nodded at the pile of twigs and small branches next to the fire ring. "Pick up a twig and… start the fire."

"Start the fire," I said woodenly. "Just like that?"

In the past, I could have done that without a second thought. Sun and stars, I'd hefted a boulder the size of the House of Mages out of the Byrne the day I'd met Torian. Lifting a twig and setting it alight would have been nothing, needing only a scrap of my attention.

But now? I curled my fingers into fists and pressed them against my thighs. I took in a shuddering breath. Held it against another wave of loss. *I can't. I don't want to. How can they ask it of me?*

Yet Torian asked me for so very little, the least I could do was *humor* them as they'd pleaded with me now.

So I stared at a twig that was precariously balanced atop my pile of kindling and reached for that place in my core that had always answered me before.

Aaand... nothing. The twig moved not a whit. My shoulders slumped and I exhaled, letting my chin drop until my braids curtained my face. "I'm sorry."

"Don't be." Torian lifted my right hand. "Open your fist, please, Zal." When I did as they asked, they laid the shard across my palm and carefully folded my fingers around it. "Now try again."

My eye widened as I stared at them, understanding what they were saying. Perhaps I didn't have an *intact* Stone, but I had its *parts*. I'd always used a shard in my divination, so it wasn't as though using one was new. Part of me wanted to rejoice, but another part wanted to kick myself for being so dense.

I gazed at the twig and didn't even have to think twice. It rose, catching fire midair, and sailed into the ring. The wood ignited, its pop and crackle drowned out by my whoop.

"I did it!" I said, grinning so widely that my eyepatch dug into the top of my cheek.

They smiled back warmly. "You did."

"I want to do it again."

"Zal—"

"Watch." But when I tried to move a second twig, nothing happened and my grin faded. "Shite." My fingers tightened around the splinter until I could feel it slice into my palm. "Do you suppose it failed because I don't have all the shards anymore? Because I traded some away?"

"Please don't be discouraged." Torian laid their palm against my cheek. "That tiny piece can't hold much energy and I didn't charge it for long. You probably just depleted it." When I uncurled my fingers and Torian spotted the bright gash of blood, they made an unhappy croon. "Let's try another experiment, okay?" They selected a slightly larger chip and held it up to catch the sun.

I set the noticeably dimmed shard aside and tipped a little water from Torian's waterskin onto my palm to sluice away the blood. "What do you want to do?"

"I'd like you to do whatever"—another smirk, although I was positive this one was simply to bolster my spirits—"magic you ordinarily do with your healing stones, what you did to the water when you treated my feet that first day, but do it to yourself. Localized on that cut. See if you can close it up."

I peered down at my palm. Sun Stone was sharp—Ranolt had been right about that—but the cut wasn't long or deep. I hadn't gripped it hard enough to drive it far into my flesh. A surface wound only.

Torian hummed again, holding the chip up and squinting at it. "Still just a low-level charge, approximately ten percent, at a guess. But if this works, we can spread the lot out and keep going until you're good as new."

I took the chip in my other hand and... sure enough, the cut knitted nearly all the way closed. I met Torian's gaze, and I could almost swear that the hope shining from my eye bathed their face in a golden glow.

But that was probably only the power grid under their skin absorbing the light of the sun.

I gathered the edges of the leather together and stood carefully, not willing to risk losing a single piece of my shattered Stone, of my past, and possibly of my future. I arranged it atop the flat boulder at Torian's back, making sure all the pieces were exposed in a single layer, then sat down next to Torian again and wrapped an arm around their hips below their bare back.

"Thank you, love. Thank you for thinking of it and thank you for not letting me drift into despair."

"It's one of the things I'm trained to do." They leaned against me, gesturing with both pale, elegant hands. "Frame a question. Test the hypothesis. Evaluate the results. Reframe the question. Test again." They tilted their head to gaze up at me. "This was an easy one. I just wish there was a way to... to..." They cupped their palms and brought them together as though they were shaping a ball of dough. "I don't know, daisy chain them, or link them in parallel."

I chuckled. "I'm sure that made sense to you, but I'm still in the dark."

They smiled crookedly. "Sorry. Always call me on it when I don't provide sufficient context." They bit their lower lip, brows drawing together. "I can't think of a way to join them all, to merge their energy into a larger pool. I'm concerned you'll be limited to the small energy in each segment individually."

I kissed their temple. "Don't fret about that. This is more than I had before. I'm content."

They pulled away and glared up at me. "Well, I'm not. I don't want you exhausted when we get to the capital. The shards are sharp, right? Maybe we can thread them onto your cloak so they can recharge as we go. That way, you'll feel stronger when we face the Trine."

"That would be a boon, and no mistake."

"What is the Trine, anyway? There's nothing in the..." Torian's expression shuttered, in that way it had now and again since Edric's death, but they only paused for a moment before shaking their head. "I don't know anything about them. I don't know anything about the capital at all really, other than it's smelly and noisy—thanks for that, by the way—including why it doesn't have a name. Corvel-on-Byrne has a name, so does Market Spinney. But the capital has got to be a lot bigger, and it doesn't have one?"

I shrugged. "I guess nobody saw the need. There's only one capital but there are hundreds of villages and towns."

"I suppose that's fair." They tilted their head, considering, and chuckled. "I expect *the capital* is as good as a more whimsical name, given it's unique. Otherwise mail could go seriously astray."

I looked down at them. "Mail?"

"Mail. You know, correspondence." They grimaced. "I forgot. No universal access to paper. I suppose that could be a problem. How do people communicate with those who live far away?"

"If the folk live far from each other, chances are they're not acquainted and would have nothing to say to one another, anyway. Other than Sun-born circuit mages, we tend to stay close to our homes."

"Is that from necessity or choice?"

"It's always a choice. But nearly everyone chooses to remain where they're known, where things are familiar, where they know how to manage. Since they're usually trained up in an apprenticeship from the time they're ten, they've already got a place to belong."

"But surely some must move away. If there are too many apprentices for a particular craft, for instance, or if another village lacks someone with an essential skill?"

"It happens, but not often."

I stared into the trees, frowning, trying to remember something I'd heard in passing, although I couldn't recall where. Something my parents said of an evening by the fire, when my sister and I had already retired to the loft and they thought us asleep? Gossip in the dorms after I'd gone to the House of Mages for schooling? Something muttered in an inn on my rounds?

Somebody *somewhere* had hinted that things used to work differently. But that scrap of memory had no... What would Torian call it? Context? So even if I could call it to mind, it would remain meaningless.

"So how would that kind of arrangement get made? How *do* you communicate?"

"Well, we circuit mages—" My belly tumbled and I had to swallow twice before I could continue. "That is, circuit mages pass on the latest news and decrees from the House of Mages when we make our rounds."

"But you only visit a village once a year, correct?"

"Aye."

"The news must get awfully stale."

I chuckled weakly. "It does and all. But the Congress of Mages and Seigneurs doesn't move too speedily—they're too busy arguing with each other for that—so once a year is usually soon enough. Then every three years, there's a conclave in the capital. All the mages and the reeves from all the villages who want to make the journey converge on the capital." I pushed my braids back and knotted them at my nape. "It's bloody pandemonium, with all the inns at capacity, and merchants hawking their wares on every street corner."

"Do you like that?" Torian sounded a little wistful. "The excitement? The novelty? The festivity?"

"Me? Nay, it gave me a headache when I had two eyes. This next one will be the first since I was half-blinded, and I'm not looking forward to trying to make sense of the chaos when I won't be able to see what's happening on my left. I nearly got bowled over by a stilt-walker last time, and I had both eyes then." I squinted up at the sky, remembering. "Although that might have been due to all the ale I'd drunk with my supper."

"So you don't miss... other people?" This time, their voice was laced with hope.

I turned to face them fully. "Are you worried that I'll forget you? That I'll let you fend for yourself?"

"No," they said hurriedly. "But you might want to spend time with friends. Do things for which it would be... inconvenient to have a hanger-on that causes as much comment as I do."

I captured their hands between both of mine, gazing into their eyes. "Circuit mages tend to be solitary by nature. We have to be, because we spend so much time alone. Those who crave more company stay in the capital and work in the hospitals, the library, the scribe houses. This life"—I gave our hands a little shake—"*our* life suits me fine." I dropped a kiss on Torian's knuckles and let go of their hands. "Although I'm not certain what that life will look like after I report in and let the Trine know they're down a circuit mage and will have to assign someone else to my rounds."

"There's the Trine again." Torian smiled, seemingly comforted by my words, so I must have been successful at hiding my true worry about that report.

Once I'd been removed from the active mage rolls, and once I'd introduced Torian to the Trine, the chances were very good that we'd be separated. Perhaps forever. Because Torian was unique. Their wealth of knowledge, their experiences, their intelligence... Well, I wasn't fool enough to imagine that the Trine would ever let a disgraced former mage like me deprive them of such a rich and singular resource.

But I refused to burden Torian with my fears. So instead I stood, brushing off the seat of my breeks.

"Let me make us some supper and I'll tell you all about them."

Chapter Six

Torian

After we ate, Zal strung the hammock from his pack between two sturdy trees. He'd begun doing that a couple of nights after we'd started sharing our bedrolls, the first time it had rained overnight. He suspended oilcloth above it, pegged down on either side to form a tent to keep the rain off from above as the hammock raised us off the wet ground below.

The first time I'd tried to climb in with him, I'd dumped us both unceremoniously to the ground, but he'd just laughed and we'd tried again until I'd managed to join him.

Hammocks, particularly when one is nestled against a warm, solid presence like Zal, are surprisingly comfortable. I always slept as well or better than I had in the Lab.

Tonight, though, I wasn't quite ready to sleep. "The Trine, Zal. You promised you'd tell me all about them."

"I would have," Zal said, pulling the blankets up over our shoulders and settling me against his chest, "except you distracted me when you started singing that song about climbing over rocks when you were actually climbing over rocks."

I chuckled. That had led to "Poor Wand'ring One" and then to "When the Foeman Bares His Steel." When Zal asked, I'd gone back and started from the beginning, sung the entire libretto from *The Pirates of Penzance*—with two encores of "With Catlike Tread"—and we'd never gotten back to the Trine.

My questions had remained, of course, but I'd sidelined them with end-of-day alerts because the look of wonder in Zal's eye, the rapt attention on his face... Well, when I finished a song and he said, "Another, please?" always careful to phrase his request so I could refuse if I wanted? How could I possibly disappoint him?

"Yes, I sang, but you're the one who..." I paused, frowning into the dark as rain started to patter against the oilcloth overhead. "Zal, why *did* you keep getting up and peering into the woods?"

His big chest rose and fell, his breath ruffling my hair. "It was naught, love. Only my nerves. Before, I could set wards and be sure we would be protected. Now that I can't... Well, I imagine bogeys behind every tree and boulder."

"Will the fire keep animals away?"

His chuckle rumbled in his chest, vibrating my bones. "Hear that?"

"Hear what?"

"The rain has changed to ice."

I listened to the *pick* of the current precipitation, scanning the library of environmental sound clips I'd amassed on our journey so far. There were a lot of samples. Growing up in the Lab as I had, I'd never imagined the *variety* of noises out here. Not even the *silence* was the same, and rainfall had its own subdirectory. But my scan didn't return a match.

"Does snow sound different, too?"

"Snow is silent. At least until enough piles up on the branches above you to *whump* down on your head. But tonight, animals with any sense will stay snug in their burrows."

"That didn't stop you from hanging our packs from the tree again," I said dryly.

"Aye. That's what *people* with any sense will do, since it's best not to depend on the sense of animals."

"All right. Stop stalling. The Trine."

Zal's arms tightened around me, not with amorous or intrusive intent, but because he shifted in the hammock and had to adjust my position to keep us stable.

"Truly, I'm not trying to be difficult, but you always want to know the *why* of things. The Trine has just always *been*, and I haven't got a good explanation for them."

I tilted my head back until I could see the strong angle of his smooth jawline. "I only ask reasons because that's how I've been trained to approach a problem. Not that you're a problem," I said hurriedly. "I've only had the Lab's methodology to teach me how to learn. That doesn't mean I'm judging you or your society. Only that I want to understand."

"It's all right, love. I know you're not asking to find fault. But I want to do right by you as well as do justice to my world." He kissed the top of my head. "The Trine are the three mages who administer our order. They're in charge of the College of Mages and are responsible for all Sun-born with magical ability, regardless of whether we choose to take the mage vows."

"Are they hereditary positions?" I tried to keep the censure out of my tone. Power that was defined purely by bloodline was a recipe for authoritarianism at best and totalitarianism at worst.

Zal laughed, setting the hammock swinging. "Shite, no. We hold elections every three years, at that conclave I was telling you about, to fill the positions—Speaker, Scale, and Scribe."

"Okay," I said slowly. "So what—"

"You say those letters often. Why is that?"

"What letters?"

"O and K."

"Ah." I chuckled, nestling closer as the *tick* on the oilcloth increased in tempo and force. "It means the same as your *all right*. It's a verbal artifact in the historical records I was cataloging for the Infomancers that appealed to me."

"What about that other word? The one you say when you're upset. What does *fuck* mean?"

I shook my head. Given that the Originators had seeded a common language into this world, as well as the three primary genetic strains, I was constantly surprised by the omissions.

Whoever the first linguist was, they must have been rather prudish.

"It means, well, sexual intercourse, although it's also one of the strongest of expletives, and it's in that context I've been using it. I won't do so anymore if it bothers you."

"Nay, don't stop on my account." He laughed again, almost sub-vocally, but I could feel the vibrations in his chest. "I like knowing when you've reached your limit."

"If you don't want me to reach my limit now," I said with mock severity, "back to the Trine."

Another warm chuckle rumbled through him. "*Okay.*" One of his hands stroked my arm, although I suspected he didn't realize he was doing it. "The Speaker, well, speaks for all mages. They preside as head of the College, represent us in the Congress of Mages and Seigneurs, hand out circuit assignments, that sort of thing. Our current Speaker is Obeila. She's about a decade older than me, so pretty young to hold the post, especially since this is her third term, and she looks likely to be elected again since nobody else seems interested in stepping up."

"Why is that?"

"Because the job is a pain in the arse, keeping all us stubborn sods in line. *I'd* never want to do it. But Obeila is terrifyingly organized, and manages it all while maintaining an unruffled serenity. I suspect we'd elect her even if she chose not to run."

I scanned my databanks for equivalencies. The Speaker sounded like the CEO of an old-style company, or the Prime Minister of a country, or an on-site project director. "Got it. Please continue."

"The Scale… Well, the Scale is another story. They're in charge of enforcing the rules, keeping order at meetings, and adjudicating conflicts between mages, so they're more remote and intimidating. Have to be, if they don't want to be accused of bias. Gerd, our present Scale, had to take over the post in the middle of the term because the fellow who'd held the job for the last two sessions sickened and died unexpectedly. Since he'd been the Scale years ago, back before I was assigned my circuit, he stepped in." Zal shivered, although it felt exaggerated and intentional, like a dramatic comment, rather than an involuntary reaction. "Now there's an intimidating man. But perfect for the job, since I don't think he's spoken more than six words to anyone outside his duties for the last decade."

"That sounds... lonely."

"Aye, well, that suits some folk. Obeila offered to appoint someone else, gave him plenty of opportunity to refuse after his name was put forward in the Congress, but he agreed to return until the next election."

"Do you think that's a good thing?"

I felt Zal shrug. "Gerd's a hard man, but I've never known him not to be fair. Although he's nearly a generation older than I am, he's at least as fit. Some would say more so, since he still has all his body parts."

I frowned into the dark. I hated it when Zal thought of himself as defective, as *less*. "I find it hard to believe that anyone could best you."

"Wait until you meet him. You'll see." He settled his shoulders, making the hammock swing. "Brylun's our Scribe. They're like you. Two-natured. Although I suppose you've more than two, haven't you?"

"I don't mind two-natured, although nonbinary is what I use if I've needed a label."

In a way, that was ironic, given that so much of me was precisely binary—nothing but ones and zeroes, defining my nature. My earlier failed queries still haunted me. Had those ones and zeroes betrayed me? Or had they been hijacked by others who wanted to describe my every function in binary terms?

On. Off. Yes. No. Free. Captive. Or maybe... Alive. Dead.

Zal patted my arm, diverting my darkening thoughts.

"Nonbinary then. They're an historian, our official record keeper, and preserve the proceedings from all our meetings, although they've got a staff to do the legwork while they coordinate and collate. They're the head librarian and were even before they were elected Scribe. They took office for the first time right before Obeila's first term, so they've served together for almost ten years. I expect Brylun will want to keep you all to themself once they realize how much you know."

Without my conscious will, my hand crept to Zal's sleeve, and I clutched at the fabric, the rough homespun wool so different from the characterless synthetics in the Lab. "Zal?"

"Yes, love?"

"What if... What if the Trine won't listen to you? What if they judge that I'm a rogue mage? Will they condemn me the way they did Loriah?"

His arms tightened around me. "Loriah was a threat. She was about to slaughter an entire Earth-born village, a village not too far from here. A dozen or so leagues beyond Market Spinney. This was her circuit."

He was silent then, perhaps remembering his friend, the one who'd betrayed him, the one who'd injured him. However, I also noted that he didn't say that the Trine *wouldn't* condemn me.

In a way, I found that more reassuring than if he had immediately denied the possibility. From my work in the Lab, both prepping and cleaning up after the Informancers' experiments, I had learned that evaluating all possible outcomes, from optimal to catastrophic, was far better than optimistically expecting success.

It allowed one to prepare.

"We mustn't forget that they might consider me a threat as well. After all, I did k-k-k..." I frowned. Was there a problem with my vocal subroutines now? "I did k-k-k..." I tightened my middle and *pushed* the words out. "*Kill* a man."

"You did. However, you made a choice in that instant that Edric's threat was greater. That's where Gerd will be the deciding voice. He can weigh whether your choice was justified, whether allowing Edric to live would have caused more harm than his death." He sighed. "When they sent me to fetch Loriah, I was told that her death, while not ideal and certainly not what any of us could wish, was better than the deaths of hundreds of innocents."

"The needs of the many," I murmured.

"What?"

"It's from another ancient film. One set in space, actually. 'The needs of the many outweigh the needs of the few.'"

He snorted, ruffling my hair. "That sounds like something Gerd would say."

I didn't tell Zal the rest of the quote: *Or the one.* What if the Trine decided the one—in other words, me and what I represented in terms of information about the very nature of their existence—constituted the greatest threat of all? One well-placed knife thrust and they could go on as they always had.

That had been my intent as well, hadn't it, when I'd chosen the planet over Edric?

Be honest. The planet's safety, the safety of the many, was incidental. You chose Zal over Edric. You chose the one.

"When they hear about the Star-born—"

"But how much *should* they hear?" I said, a little desperately. "Will they even believe any of it? They'd have to take my word for everything. You said yourself that nobody in memory has ever seen a Star-born."

"Other than me?" he asked dryly.

"Well, what if they don't believe *you*?"

His breath caught. I could hear it, could feel the constriction in his chest under my cheek.

"You never thought of that, did you?" I said softly. "That they might think you were lying?"

"No." His chest rose and fell with a sharp breath. "But I should have. You threw that at me yourself, back when we first left Corvel-on-Byrne. That I wasn't inclined to listen to what others, like Loriah, had to say. That duty has to be tempered with mercy."

"That the ones who give the orders might be the ones who are lying?" I said gently.

He started at that. "No. There was evidence. From many. I saw it. I wouldn't have—"

"Zal. I'm not saying you were at fault with Loriah, or that you're at fault for taking me to the capital now. All I'm saying is that we need to consider our approach carefully, from all angles."

"And our escape as well, should things not go to plan?"

I was relieved that his voice once more held a hint of amusement rather than panic. I nestled against him. "We simply need to keep our options open."

As well as all three of our eyes.

Chapter Seven

Zal

In the two weeks it had taken us to travel the rest of the way to the capital, I hadn't been able to shake Torian's warnings.

Yes, I'd known that our audience with the Trine would be awkward and painful, since I would have to confess to the loss of my Stone. But it had never entered my head before that my testimony about Torian might be disbelieved.

So as we'd made our way south, I'd concocted dozens of plans and discarded just as many when I'd discussed them with Torian over our nightly campfire.

At least the weather had improved as we left the harsher north behind us, with only a few days of snow the week after we left Market Spinney, and that not too heavy. Torian had managed to work slivers of my shattered Stone into the fabric of my cloak in a pattern very like the one under their own skin.

"It's simply an efficient layout," they'd said dismissively when I couldn't keep from praising them every time we stopped for the night. "I only wish I could connect them somehow, so you could access a well of power rather than a sequence of minor trickles."

"It's more than I had, love. Don't reproach yourself." In the firelight, I'd admired the sparkle of gold across the cloak's shoulders, where it caught the sun as we walked. "It's doing the job to keep fatigue at bay, and it's beautiful on top of that."

In fact, my energy had improved steadily as we'd gotten nearer to the capital, so much so that I had to consciously slow my pace. Because *Torian* seemed to be flagging now, waking every morning with dark circles under their eyes that hadn't been there since Corvel-on-Byrne.

I'd insisted that we stop every midday when the sun was at its height so that they could recharge, and that seemed to help. But the next morning, they'd be dragging again.

I was aware they weren't sleeping well. We'd nearly fallen out of the hammock twice when they'd woken with a wheeze and a gasp, arms flailing.

I had little doubt that despite the plans we were making, Torian was still worried about what would happen when we faced the Trine.

As we stood on the hill, looking down at the capital under the perpetual haze of smoke that only cleared when the wind was out of the west, I made a silent vow that somehow I'd make the Trine understand. Should Gerd's rigid principles interpret Torian's behavior as rogue, I'd appeal to Obeila, who had a far broader view and had always been more open-minded. Or to Brylun. How could a librarian resist what Torian had to offer?

The stories they could tell alone were a wonder.

Every night after we'd hashed out what Torian called *scenarios*, they'd recited one of those old *films* for me. They'd been humble, of course, claiming what they offered was only a shadow of the true performances, the true *filmic experience*.

But I didn't see how that was possible. While Torian didn't prance around the campsite, their face always reflected the emotions in the story, just as their voice changed for each character. I'd heard them mimic Edric's voice, of course, but this was different. They'd *known* Edric, probably heard him speak many times during their life, but this? Torian almost *became* these other people.

And sometimes—the best times—they would sing. Torian called those films *musicals*. Those were my favorites. They'd even taught me a few songs, although I always sounded as flat as the Earth temple priests with their chants.

I glanced down at Torian now. They were gazing, wide-eyed, at the capital spread out below us, at the guards whose shoulders and leather helms were visible behind the curtain wall parapets, at the red-tiled roofs of the buildings in the merchant quarter that gave way to weathered shingles the further the distance from the main square, and at the bulk of the House of Mages and the House of Seigneurs, taller by half again than any other building, looming in the center of it all like a bloated spider in a web.

Odd. I'd never thought of the capital exactly that way before. It had always just been the capital, the place I'd been educated, the place I had to endure at least once a year to make my circuit report. Now, seeing it as though through Torian's eyes, it seemed... forbidding, somehow. Why did the merchants rate nicer homes than the folk who worked for them? What had they bartered to earn their privilege?

Surely, if our most sacred principle was the right of every citizen to choose, could someone from the workers' quarter choose to move to the merchant quarter, provided they had something to barter for their new lodgings?

Mayhap it wasn't only Torian's concerns that were coloring my view. Wasn't I about to try the same thing, choosing to leave the life, the occupation, the calling that had been mine my entire adult life? I couldn't deny that it had been my choice to bring Torian back, and I didn't regret the loss of my Stone if the alternative was not having Torian by my side.

But would the Trine see it that way? Would I be allowed to choose to step away now and retreat to my cottage by the sea with Torian? If they asked me to take a position here in the capital the way other Sun-born who'd decided against mage vows had done, would I be allowed to refuse?

Ah, well. Standing up here on the hill, I'd never find out, and I still had one last duty to perform.

Make that two: In addition to informing the Trine that I was no longer a mage, I had to introduce Torian to them. I refused to consider that I'd be putting Torian at their mercy, that I might never see them again.

I straightened my shoulders. *No.* I wouldn't let that happen. If it looked as though the Trine were unreceptive, we could fall back on one of our *scenarios*.

"Zal?"

"Yes, love?"

"Are there always so many soldiers here?"

One of the films Torian had recited for me was the same one they'd quoted after Edric's death and the shuttle explosion, so I knew about war and soldiers, at least in theory, although it made little sense to me. It was a waste of lives and property, and it wasn't as if any reasonable citizen, if given the choice, would slaughter strangers for something as ridiculous as their leaders' conflicting statecraft.

"Those aren't soldiers. They're naught but guards."

I squinted at the parapets, spotting tabards in the scarlet livery of the College of Mages as well as others in the College of Seigneurs' peat brown. That wasn't out of the ordinary. Guards from both Colleges regularly shared patrol duties. Although Torian was right—there did seem to be more than the usual complement, both atop the wall and at the gates.

Then I remembered.

"Shite. Judgment Day."

The trip back to Corvel-on-Byrne after Star Mountain exploded and the side trip to Market Spinney had put me behind schedule more than I'd realized. The time passed so pleasantly on the trail with Torian that I'd lost track.

"Judgment Day?" Torian shivered, despite the warmth of the sun that made our cloaks almost too heavy for comfort. "That has an unfortunate meaning in the Lab annals."

I laid an arm across their shoulders. "Another film?"

"Among other things," they said darkly.

"Here, Judgment Day comes around four times a year, on the solstices and the equinoxes. It's the day that sentences are pronounced and carried out for any citizen who's been tried and convicted in the previous quarter. Guard patrols are always heavier around Judgment Day, since emotions can run high."

My own hadn't been especially low on the day of Loriah's judgment and execution. I'd been shocked at the brutality of it all, as had the rest of the watching crowd. They'd gone dead silent at the end. When the headsman raised his axe at the last, a child had cried out and been hurried away by their parents. I'd have hurried away too, if the Congress hadn't insisted I stand on the dais next to the Trine, my eyepatch proof, they'd said, of her guilt.

"Is today Judgement Day?" Torian asked.

"Nay. The solstice isn't until tomorrow, but this complicates things, not that they weren't complicated already." I sighed. "Ordinarily, I stay in the circuit mage quarters at the House of Mages, but we knew that wasn't going to work this time, not with you along. But all the inns near Judgment Square will be booked now. We'll end up quite out of the way, probably in the workers' quarter."

"Do we need two rooms? We've been sharing a hammock on the trail. Surely inn beds aren't quite so..." A smile eased the nervous set of their lips. "...adventuresome. And does it have to be close?" Torian asked. "I'm used to walking by now."

I tapped one finger on my walking stick. "A single room wouldn't strain our resources quite so much. As long as you don't mind? And to be honest, rooms in the workers' quarter will be less expensive, anyway. Although it means we'll have farther to run if our audience with the Trine goes poorly."

"I haven't minded so far. And I suspect if the audience goes poorly enough that we have to run, distance will be the least of our concerns."

I chuckled. "I suppose that's the Sun's honest truth. Well, then. Let's get on with it, shall we?" I eyed Torian, who'd pushed back their hood and flung their cloak back over their shoulders. I wasn't certain whether it was because they were over-warm or whether they were taking advantage of the bright noon sunlight to recharge before we headed into the city.

I wanted them to take advantage of what sun we could, but exposing both their skin and their short hair wasn't the best strategy for remaining unnoticed.

I pointed to the trail ahead of us with the tip of my walking stick. "This path leads to the main road, where we're bound to encounter more traffic, especially with Judgment Day so close. It might be best if you were to pull up your hood and don your gloves."

Torian gazed down at their hands and sighed. "I suppose you're right. Although it's a shame to waste the solar exposure." They glanced over at me, their gaze focused in that intense, swirling way that meant they were... what did they call it? Recalibrating their vision. "I think it might also be best if you were to turn your cloak inside out."

"What? Why?"

They ran a gentle finger along the pattern of Sun Stone shards on the oiled leather where it lay across my shoulders. "Until you know what the Trine has to say about the destruction of your Stone, do you really want to advertise its loss this way?"

I smiled crookedly. "Given that I don't have my staff anymore, its loss won't be a secret to anyone we meet. But I take your point."

With Torian holding my walking stick to free my hands, I unclasped the agate pin that fastened my cloak and swung it around, settling it over my shoulders with the lining facing outward. I could feel the *fizz* of the shards through my shirt and jerkin more strongly now that they weren't further muffled by the cloak's leather and lambswool.

"I'll look a right fool wearing it turned about this way," I grumbled.

"Better a fool than an outlaw," Torian said as they returned my stick. "Better a fool than a robbery victim." They flipped their hood up. "If the avaricious way the Market Spinney townsfolk salivated over those bits of chrysocite is any indication, that could be a very real danger."

Torian's prim tone made me laugh. "Mayhap if we were in the hinterlands. But here in the capital, we're at the center of Sun magics. Nobody would dare."

"If you say so." Torian sounded dubious, but followed me readily enough, pulling on their leather gloves as we marched down the trail.

I didn't want to mention it to Torian, but as soon as those Sun Stone chips were hidden from the light, I felt them depleting. I was drawing on them to preserve the brace of coneys and the string of goldenfin that I'd caught last night, redirecting the magic away from my own comfort. For now, keeping my catch fresh was more important, since it was the way we'd be paying for our food and lodging. And since we'd be staying farther from Judgment Square, the inns wouldn't be as expensive. I ought to be able to bargain for baths as well as our room and supper.

When our trail joined the main road, stepping onto the paving stones from the dirt path was almost a shock. I had intentionally taken us through the wilderness as we'd traveled. It would have been faster and more direct to take the main roads once we'd gotten closer to the capital, but I wanted to give Torian as much respite as possible, given how uneasy they'd been in Market Spinney.

I hardly admitted to myself that I'd been avoiding scrutiny as well. A mage without a staff, without his Stone? That was an explanation I wasn't eager to make often. Confessing to the Trine would be trying enough.

The road was clotted with folk heading for the main city gates, some in chattering groups, some trudging along behind barrows piled high with goods, some stalking along, staring somberly ahead as though barely registering their surroundings.

Torian studied the groups from inside the shadow of their hood. "These people clearly have different expectations of their upcoming experience in the city," they murmured.

"Aye." I took their elbow and guided them to the side of the road, out of the way of a cart loaded with peat. "Judgment Day always brings in folk from the nearby cantons, those with goods to sell or those hoping to buy. I hear that some folk will purposely wait until after the last sentence is carried out before they visit the market stalls, in hopes of driving the best deals from vendors not wanting to haul unsold goods back home."

"Isn't that a risk? What if everything is sold out? And wouldn't they have the same trouble? Transportation back to their village?"

I shrugged. "They're willing to take the risk for the chance of a bargain. It's mostly the folk who live in the capital who use that scheme." I chuckled. "I'm told that there's a whole lane in the workers' quarter that stocks their shops in exactly that way, providing their neighbors with second-hand goods bartered from city dwellers."

Torian made a thoughtful sound and gestured covertly to a Sun-born striding past as though on a mission. "What about him? No staff, no chrysocite, so he's clearly not a mage."

My smile faded. "Nay. I expect he's here to witness a judgment."

"He doesn't look happy."

"No." My belly took a dive, remembering Loriah, being forced to stand there and expected to display satisfaction at the justice dispensed with my assistance and at least partly on my behalf. "He wouldn't."

Chapter Eight

Torian

I had braced myself for more stares when we joined the steady stream of people heading for the city gates, but oddly, we were largely ignored. I supposed part of that was the way my clothing now masked my obvious physical differences, but I was conversant enough with the Infomancers' socio-political data to see it in another light.

These people *expected* to encounter strangers. This wasn't their home. Furthermore, based on my observations from the hillside, the city was orders of magnitude larger than Corvel-on-Byrne or even Market Spinney. I doubted its inhabitants knew everyone else who lived there any more than the citizens of the home world metropolises were acquainted with other residents in a meaningful way.

As we neared the gate, Zal led me away from the edge of the road and more toward the center, where we were flanked by a boisterous group of young adults on one side and an older couple leading a smallish quadruped that resembled the donkeys from the home world data files, its panniers loaded with rough-skinned tubers, a hybrid of potato and yam that the Originators had propagated across the continent before introducing human inhabitants.

I wondered at Zal's tactics at first, but then I realized what he was doing.

Camouflaging himself.

Not from the other visitors, but from the guards. A pair stood on either side of the wide main gate, one with a red surcoat secured with a wide amber sash, and the other in leather-belted brown. According to what Zal had told me about the way the capital's magical and non-magical populations shared jurisdiction, it meant that both mages and seigneurs were represented at the gates.

One of the guards in the red mage livery was the J-4 strain like Zal, but the others were all A-3, like the inhabitants of Corvel-on-Byrne or Market Spinney. I knew from the Infomancers' files that the J-4 population was smaller than the A-3 control strain, and of course there were no remaining C-28 specimens other than me. Perhaps it wasn't possible for the mages to completely staff their guard complement with J-4 citizens, since the majority of them were destined for mage work.

Also—and apparently unknown to the Infomancers—as many of the J-4 were celibate, the breeding pool would be even more limited. I wondered briefly if that was why the Lab directors had resorted to something as scientifically unsound and borderline unethical as the quick genetic manipulation of the C strains. After all, the A strain only had three iterations, the J only four. The C had twenty-seven before its extinction with C-28.

That made me wonder about the missing letters: B and D through I. Had they all been unviable genetic manipulations? Or had the Originators simply chosen the letter designations for other reasons?

I shelved that query for later. We were nearly at the gates and I couldn't afford to be distracted, especially by another null result.

Beside me, Zal had moved closer, hunching his shoulders, as though attempting to make himself smaller and less obtrusive. I grimaced inside the shadow of my hood. The sheepskin lining of Zal's cloak seemed to glow amid the duller homespun or cured leather clothing of the other travelers, even in the shadow of the tall city walls. It caught the attention of the guards, I had no doubt, because all of them squinted at Zal.

None of them unhooked their thumbs from their belts, though, or made the least move to approach. In fact, for guards, they didn't seem to do much guarding. Their belts held nothing more lethal than the equivalent of a police baton. No bladed weapons at all. The only projectile-type weapons this world boasted were heavy, rather unwieldy spears and the bow and arrow. However, those were only used for hunting, and infrequently at that.

Zal had explained it over the fire one evening, the flames glinting in his dark eye, explaining that the populace considered such practices immoral, since prey animals didn't have any natural way to protect themselves against an arrow fired from a distance.

"If I lay a trap for a coney, or bait my hook for a goldenfin, they have a choice whether or not to step into the trap or take the bait off the hook. Shooting a pointed stick at them from inside a bush doesn't even give them the choice to run away."

Even hunters who used spears always shouted before their throw to give the prey a chance to bolt. From their perspective, if a hunter couldn't bring down an animal on the run, he didn't deserve it.

I didn't think the Infomancers had any notion of how deeply the *consent* liturgy permeated this culture. I sincerely doubted it was anything they set in motion themselves, considering their entire installation here was the antithesis of consent, tinkering as they did with the very engine of evolution.

If my efforts had been successful, that wouldn't happen any longer. My system conflict monitor pinged an alert at that thought, and I winced. Had my choices—to kill Edric, to destroy the shuttle, to warn the Infomancers off—been tantamount to the same type of tampering?

Another worry for later. Particularly since I couldn't do anything about it now.

We'd drawn even with the gates, and although the J-4 guard continued to observe Zal with a perplexed frown, the others had lost all apparent interest and turned back to scan the wide avenue again.

Once we'd passed the gates, the sounds hit me like a blow. People calling, metal clanging, animals bleating, neighing, honking, squawking.

A line of brown-robed Earth-born priests paraded past, droning one of their interminable chants, the last priest in line banging a wooden drum in a funereal rhythm, apparently to keep them in step and on chant amid the surrounding cacophony.

And the *stench*. Zal had warned me that the capital would be worse than Market Spinney or even the noisome Corvel-on-Byrne gaol. But the sheer variety of smells overwhelmed me, sending my evaluation and classification subroutines close to crashing.

Smoke was everywhere, making my eyes burn. I managed to identify not only wood but peat fires as well, commingled with the stench of burnt organic materials, both meat and vegetation.

Fur and feathers and human sweat added their pungent notes, although oddly, no animal dung, or at least not much. I realized why when the donkey-equivalent lifted its tail not far from us. Almost before the droppings hit the paving stones, an A-3 person wearing a flat leather cap and sturdy boots, their workaday breeks and jerkin covered with a heavy canvas apron, scurried over and scooped the manure into a battered metal bucket.

I supposed continual refuse removal would be necessary for even marginal comfort in a city this large, and I was grateful, but I still adjusted my olfactory sensitivity, throttling it down to its lowest setting. I was tempted to disable it altogether, but if I did that, I could miss something critical.

More critical than donkey-equivalent shit, anyway.

We moved forward along with the wave of people entering behind us. Once we got farther from the gates, the main avenue branched off in a sunburst of smaller roads, and the crowd thinned as people went their separate ways.

When Zal led me down the road at two o'clock, we weren't precisely alone, but the people striding along with us were in less festive attire than those who'd headed in the nine o'clock direction. I assumed that meant we were aiming for an inn in the less affluent section of the city.

I braced myself for accommodations similar to the gaol in Corvel-on-Byrne, but instead, Zal stopped in front of a neat brown-shingled three-story building with green-painted window boxes sporting what I recognized as herbs rather than flowers. The wooden sign swinging above its matching green door held a faded but surprisingly accurate painting of a Terran rooster and a thick-necked longhorn steer with a stylized ampersand between them.

I choked back a laugh. "Is this... Are we truly staying at an inn called the Cock & Bull?"

"Aye." Zal peered down at me. "Why? Do you not like the look of it?"

I sucked in a wheezing breath and waved a hand. "No, no. It's fine." If Zal didn't react, probably that colloquialism hadn't made it into the planet's lexicon. I was beginning to think that linguist had not only been a prude but totally lacking in humor.

"Okay, then." He grinned at me, and as he opened the door, I wondered how long it would take for *okay* to permeate the language.

Zal led the way inside into a low-beamed room with a high wooden counter across the wall opposite the door. Behind the counter, a sturdy Earth-born man in a bibbed green apron, loops of grizzled braids flopping out of his messy topknot, was dispensing ale from a cask into a wooden flagon decorated with the carving of some kind of winged creature.

"'The flagon with the dragon,'" I murmured, and added *The Court Jester* to my list of films to introduce to Zal.

The aisle from the door to the counter was flanked with long plank tables, their benches possibly a quarter full, although the smaller tables under the windows were all occupied.

I nudged my olfactory sensors up, the better to assess the environment. The aroma of roasting meat and the hoppy scent of the ale was overlaid by the citrusy scent rising from the bucket of water that a young woman in breeks, her braids bound up in a length of linen, was using to scrub the floor in the corner.

Another young woman, this one with both an apron and knee-length kirtle over her breeks, braids coiled in an intricate knot on the back of her head, was weaving through the tables, balancing a tray holding at least half a dozen steaming bowls on the flat of one hand.

The bartender smiled at us and wiped his hands on a bit of toweling. "Good morning, my fine citizens. Welcome to the Cock & Bull. I'm Ibb, your host. How may I serve you today?"

Before he had a chance to set the toweling aside, an even sturdier looking Earth-born woman pushed through a swinging door behind the bar, scowling like a thundercloud. She snatched the toweling out of Ibb's hand and placed a fresh one on the counter.

She nodded to us, her scowl morphing into a tight smile, and then disappeared behind the door.

Ibb just chuckled and picked up the clean towel. "My wife, Jocosa. She keeps me honest, she does. Now, how may I serve you?"

"We'd like a room, please, if you've one available."

Ibb's jolly demeanor faded. "You're not staying in the mage's quarter? Most of the Sun-born lodge there, even though a fair few grace our establishment now and now." He patted the cask. "For the excellence of the ale as well as Jocosa's cooking. But lodging? Never."

Zal tensed next to me. "So you're not able to—"

"No, no! Don't mistake me. We've a fine room free that I'm pleased to offer your honor. It's only that I was surprised, seeing as Sun-born housing is provided by the House of Mages around Judgment Day." Ibb's voice rose on the last words, so it didn't take my sentiment analysis sensors to deduce that he was asking how we intended to pay.

"We've our reasons." Zal pulled his wicker fishing creel from under his cloak, as well as the string of coneys. "Will this do for payment? We'd like a meal and baths today, and perhaps breakfast tomorrow."

Ibb's eyes widened and he all but snatched the offerings from Zal's hands. "That's a gracious plenty. We can arrange the baths and a nice luncheon for you right away." He winked, brandishing the coneys. "And you'll enjoy the magic Jocosa can work on these beauties with supper tonight, just you wait and see."

As though her name conjured her, Jocosa barreled through the door again. "What are you— Oh!" With an expression that combined reverence with avariciousness, she took the coneys.

Ibb tipped the lid on the creel. "Goldenfin too, and fresh as fresh. They'd like a room, baths, and a meal or two."

The way Jocosa studied us with shrewd eyes, I had no doubt who truly managed the inn. "The payment's ample, but we've had trouble before. I won't let a room to anyone I can't look in the face."

Zal straightened, jaw tightening, and reached for the game. "Then we'll go elsewhere."

I laid a hand on his arm. "No. It's all right. We have to start somewhere."

I lowered my hood, keeping my gaze fixed on the polished wood of the counter until I'd settled the folds on my shoulders. Then I looked up and met their gazes with what I hoped was confidence.

They both gasped, eyes and mouths rounding in almost identical unison. I was prepared for questions about my Moon-born nature, but instead, Jocosa whispered, "What did you do?"

I frowned, blinking. "I... Do?" Had my actions, Edric's murder, somehow marked me so that anyone could see my guilt?

"They did naught but fall ill in the north, at the foot of Star Mountain," Zal growled.

For some reason, that made both of them relax. "Ah, I see," Ibb said. "Those folk out in the hinterlands don't understand the two-natured. Probably treated you like you'd poisoned the well, eh?"

"Something like that," I said faintly.

"You needn't worry about that here. Our youngest is two-natured. My sister's child too." Jocosa turned toward the door and bellowed, "Darej."

A person, probably in their late teens, stuck their head out the door. "Yes, Mam?"

"Take these folk up to the back room." She winked, just like Ibb had. "Quieter back there, away from the street, with a nice view over the kitchen garden."

Darej looked at me, wonder in their eyes. "You're like me, aren't you?"

Although I wasn't really like anyone anywhere, I nodded. Darej hurried out of the door and around the counter to gesture toward a claret-colored curtain in the far corner.

"Stairs this way, if you'd be pleased to follow me."

Zal rested a hand on my shoulder. "You go ahead, love. Have your bath and eat a bit. I've our audience to arrange, but I'll be back as soon as may be." He nodded to Ibb, Jocosa, and Darej. "I thank you for your hospitality. Please take good care of Torian. They're very dear to my heart."

My own heart felt as though it were lodged firmly in my throat as I watched Zal stride for the door.

"Zal!"

He turned. "Yes, love?"

"Leave your cloak. You can take mine if you're cold."

Zal met my gaze, understanding what I was saying. "I'll be warm enough without." He shrugged out of his cloak and handed it to me. "Don't worry. Everything will be fine."

And he vanished into the street, leaving me alone among strangers for the first time since Edric's death.

Chapter Nine

Zal

Torian's caution, their warning to me about parading through the streets with Sun Stone shards winking on my shoulders, was understandable, but I was bound for the House of Mages. They'd know soon enough what had befallen me.

Nevertheless, if it weren't for the fact that I'd call more attention to myself, I'd have run all the way to the House of Mages because I didn't want to leave Torian on their own any longer than I had to. Ibb and Jocosa seemed honest and trustworthy as far as I could determine without the power to do a divining spell, but with Torian, I wanted to take no chances.

As I strode through the streets, I had to dodge dawdling groups of visitors as well as troops of guards from both Houses who were quick-stepping over pavers worn smooth by many feet over many years, forcing all to step aside with shouts of *Make way!*

After the third squad in mage livery trotted past, I slowed for a moment, staring after them. I'd never noticed so many patrols in the capital before. Was this normal for Judgment Days? Ordinarily, I was in and out of the city as quickly as I could make my circuit reports and escape. The only time I'd stayed longer was after Loriah's attack, and then it was only because the healers wouldn't release me until they were certain they'd done as much for me as they could.

Walking through the streets then, I'd been disoriented enough because my depth perception had nearly vanished. I hadn't had time to notice who exactly was on the streets with me, guards or otherwise.

Judgment Square, when I reached it, was ringed around by flimsy booths canopied with brightly colored cloth. My stomach churned because I knew full well these weren't *permanent* market stalls—no structures were allowed to stand overnight atop the intricate stone inlay of the square. Sod it, the law decreed that the Square's vast mural depicting sun, moon, and stars should greet the dawn unhindered. Not even foot traffic was allowed until the rising sun had touched every corner.

So these vendors had erected their stands *after* that, expressly for this occasion. Yes, Judgment Day meant that more citizens descended on the capital, but... but *fuck*, this wasn't a *festival*. Today, people would be punished or cleared, as the tribunal decided. Some might be executed, which should never be cause for *celebration*.

Scowling, I skirted the stalls and approached the postern door between the House of Mages and the Library, where the Scribe's administrative office was located. I wouldn't see Brylun themself, of course, only one of their many assistants who handled routine duties, one of which was accepting requests for audiences with the Trine.

When I stepped inside, the place was packed. Three clerks stood behind the wide marble counter. If I recalled correctly, each clerk handled different duties—the one on the right was for permits for businesses, both temporary and permanent. The center one handled registrations of other sorts, such as partnership licenses and land leases. The one on the left—the one where most people waited, of course—managed the Trine's public calendar.

I took my place at the back of that line, standing out because I was both the only Sun-born in the queue and at least a head taller than the rest. I drummed my fingers against my leg as the clerk handed a wooden token to an Earth-born wearing a grimy snood in a vaguely familiar crocheted pattern. The cap was saggy and misshapen, looking more like he'd stuffed it with leaves and rocks than hair. I wondered idly whether he'd done something to warrant a shearing and was trying to disguise his crime.

That sort of trick wasn't illegal, precisely, and I kicked myself for not thinking of it for Torian. Even Jocosa was more shocked by Torian's shoulder-length, unbraided hair than she was by their pale skin. Maybe after meeting with the Trine I could—

"Next," the clerk called, as the fellow hurried out, shoulders hunched and face turned away, and another person entered to take their place behind me.

By the time it was my turn, I'd lost even the illusion of patience. I stepped up to the counter and slapped both hands on it with a *thwap* that made the clerk wince.

The man was actually someone I recognized—a Sun-born several years younger than me who'd chosen to renounce the Sun Mage path in favor of children of his own and another sort of service, although his mage abilities had never been above the average.

I nodded to him. "Natin. I hope your family is well."

He stared up at me, his hands clutching the edge of the counter, a very odd expression flickering over his face. His glance cut beyond my shoulder and I turned to follow his gaze, but the only thing in that direction was the doorway, and it was clear.

I faced him again. "Natin? Is aught amiss?"

"What? No. I..." He swallowed. "Nothing."

I gentled my tone, since he seemed so on edge. "Surely you remember me. It's Zal."

"Y-yes. Of course." Natin patted the neat coil of braids at his nape. "Why have you— That is, what is your pleasure?"

"I'd like an audience with the Trine. It's urgent."

Natin attempted to regain his usual aplomb, but it settled over him like an ill-fitting jerkin. "You realize that urgency is in the eye of the beholder. The Trine is quite occupied with Judgment Day duties. They have little time for mundane requests."

I leaned forward, resting a forearm on the burnished wood. "Have I ever made a frivolous request?"

He tugged at his shirt as though it were too tight. "To my knowledge, you've never made a request at all."

"Then don't you think I might know the difference between something that's urgent and something that can await the Trine's convenience? Trust me when I say that I have information that they will want to hear, and the sooner the better."

Natin pressed his lips together as though trapping words behind them. "Very well." He consulted a slate on the counter next to his elbow. "You may have your audience in… two hours' time. Present yourself at the House vestibule and the Trine can spare you twenty minutes."

I suspected that they'd clear their schedule for longer than that once they heard what Torian had to say about the Infomancers, and what *I* had to say about Torian. "Thank you. We'll be here."

He raised his eyebrows. "'We'?"

"Yes. I'm bringing someone with me." I flicked my fingers at the slate, where he'd chalked my name. "You'd best add that, so we're not delayed by all these guards."

After he did so—rather begrudgingly, I thought—I nodded sharply. By the time I'd shouldered my way out of the crowded office, I was sweating, my skin prickling with the need for space and air.

Of course, once outside, it wasn't much better. The air was heavy with the dueling smells of wood smoke, roasting meats, and far too many bodies, along with the pung of animal droppings that steamed on the pavers until someone from the night soil guild could clear it away.

Two hours' time. That didn't give us much grace. I hurried through the streets, breaking into a trot when the way was clear enough. I hoped Torian had been able to eat and bathe by now, since we'd be hard pressed to make our appointment otherwise. I had no wish to appear before the Trine in all my trail dirt, and my belly was so hollow it was cleaving to my spine.

Of course, it was also twisted like a wood snake from worry over how the Trine would take our news.

When I turned the last corner and spotted the Cock & Bull's green door, I could finally draw a full breath, my scowl relaxing at last.

But my relief vanished the instant I stepped inside.

The common room was completely empty. No customers. No Ibb or Jocosa. No maids or Darej. The tables were all littered with half empty tankards and abandoned bowls and loaves.

My stomach dove for my boots. *Torian.*

Why had I left them? I should have found another way to arrange our audience. Gripping my walking stick in a palm damp with sweat, I raced for the curtained doorway and pounded up the narrow stairs, my footsteps booming hollowly on the treads. I launched myself off the landing and through another curtain, only to stagger to a halt.

Because everyone missing from downstairs was *here*, packed into the hallway and crowded as close to the door at the far end of the corridor as they could manage. I caught the sound of a muffled sob and shifted my grip, ready to flatten anyone who'd dare make Torian cry.

But then I heard it: Torian's voice, not crying but soaring in song, faint words drifting out from behind the closed door. *Sail,* I heard, and *bridge* and *troubled water.*

The sobs weren't Torian's. No, it was the folk jammed together, straining to hear, who had tears streaming down their faces.

I could understand why. Torian's voice was a wonder at any time, but this? My own eye prickled, throat catching. Although I couldn't hear the words, the unfamiliar melody nigh on broke my heart.

I lowered my staff. "Pardon me," I said as I edged my way through. Ibb, Jocosa, and the two maids who must be their children were standing right outside the door. Darej was actually leaning against the door, eyes closed, with their mother's hands on their shoulders.

Jocosa looked up at me and swallowed twice. "Stay as long as you like. There'll be no charge for your meals or lodging. Whatever you want for your supper tonight, I'll make it special." She sniffed mightily, then dashed her hand under her eyes and straightened her shoulders. "Your bath's waiting inside, but we can hot up the water in a trice. Darej?"

I held up a palm. "There's no need for that. I'm used to the trail. Anything warmer than the river is an unlooked-for boon."

She narrowed her eyes. "If you're sure?"

"Absolutely."

"Then I'll make you a dulaberry tart." She turned and glared at everyone who was still standing about in the corridor, straining to hear Torian's voice. "What are you lot loitering about for?" She flipped her apron at them. "Don't blame me if your soup's gone cold. And Maer, Lafi? Off with you. There's dishes to wash and tables to clear." She poked Ibb in the chest. "Unless I miss my guess, there'll be a gracious lot of ales to pull, so you'd best get behind the bar."

She chivvied all of them off through the curtain to the stairs, but before she followed, she turned back to me, and an almost shy smile lit her face. "Thank you. And thank your partner. I haven't heard such like since I was a tiny child, and never thought to again."

I blinked at that. There'd never been anybody like Torian, of that I was certain. Jocosa and Ibb seemed older than me by a good few years, although not as old as Ranolt in Market Spinney. Had *this* been the Moon-born's magic? Is *that* what the world had lost when they all died? Temple chants were all right in their way, but *song* was completely different, touched something else inside us.

The Infomancers hadn't just committed genocide with the Lunaria virus. They'd killed part of my world's soul.

When I slipped inside the room, Torian broke off their song. Half-naked, they were sitting cross-legged on the bed with their back to the window, the cross-hatched light from the mullioned window spilling over their smooth, pale skin. A meal was laid out on a table in the corner and a copper slipper bath stood opposite the bed. If its water wasn't steaming, at least it wasn't thundering over rocks or limned with frost. I sighed contentedly.

Torian's smile was both welcoming and relieved. "You're back."

"Indeed." I leaned my walking stick in the corner. "We've an audience in somewhat less than two hours."

Torian scrambled off the bed. "Then you'll want to eat and bathe. I'll get out of the way. I'm sure I can—"

"Stay. We've no secrets between us any longer. There's naught but skin under my clothing, and you've seen it often enough on our journey." I paused with my hands on the collar of my jerkin. "Unless you want to leave."

They shook their head. "No. But the lack of privacy on the trail was unavoidable. I thought perhaps you might prefer a bit more while you have the opportunity."

"Nay. By now, privacy means being alone with you, so I'm okay." I stripped off jerkin and shirt and started to unlace my breeks.

"You've been gone longer than I thought you'd be."

I paused at the hesitation in their tone. "Were you worried?"

They smiled crookedly. "I believe worry is my new baseline. But in this case, it's only that the bathwater is tepid now."

"Tepid is better than frigid."

Torian gave me a stern glare, the equal of any from my old mage teachers. "You deserve a hot bath, Zal. I'll handle it." They stood, took the two steps to the tub, and plunged both arms into the water to the elbow.

I watched, my jaw sagging, as they swirled their hands through the water, a look of fierce concentration on their face, and the golden lattice under their skin glowing.

"W-what are you doing?" I croaked.

They shot me a mischievous grin that made them look absurdly young. "Heating the water. Didn't I tell you? I figured this out right before..." Their face shuttered and they stood, shaking droplets off their fingers before they picked up a length of toweling, looking down as they dried their hands. "It's nice and warm now."

I strode over to them and wrapped my arms around them. Although both our chests were bare, the contact wasn't lascivious, not on my part, and not on Torian's part either. It was comfort, pure and simple. Because I knew what they hadn't said.

Before I killed Edric.

Chapter Ten

Torian

In the end, I asked Darej to bring us a couple of extra buckets of water and the soft, scented soap necessary in a society where cutting one's hair was tantamount to being a criminal, and keeping that hair in hundreds of tiny braids was de rigueur. I'd needed the distraction of washing Zal's hair while he scrubbed himself ruthlessly, because his report of the encounter with the clerk made me decidedly nervous.

"Why do you think he had such an odd reaction? Was it guilt? Shock? Hostility?" I asked as I massaged Zal's scalp.

"I expect it was nothing more than— Shite, that feels good."

"Mmmm." I decided not to mention that I was releasing a trickle of energy through my fingertips to compensate for reduced chrysocite chip exposure. He'd left his cloak behind at my suggestion, and I didn't want him to suffer for it.

"When you run into someone in a place you don't expect, sometimes it takes a moment to recognize them, even if they're somebody you've known for years. And Natin and I haven't seen one another since before I left on my first circuit."

"If you say so."

But I couldn't shake that feeling of *wrongness* as we both dressed in clean clothing and ate our meal far too quickly than its excellence deserved. The stew was thick and hearty, the bread fresh, and the dulaberry tart that Darej delivered with a shy smile was better than anything I'd ever tasted. But then, food in the Lab was formulated for maximum nutritional value with minimum effort as nobody in the Lab considered cooking an efficient use of their time, and our food on the trail had been limited by what I could gather and Zal could hunt.

Jocosa had promised us what she'd called a more *worthy* meal for our supper, but every time I thought about supper, I couldn't avoid thinking about what had to happen before we arrived at that point.

This audience with the Trine, their assessment, their *verdict* was the fulcrum on which my life balanced. Zal accepted that my abilities were the result of science, not magic, although the concept of *science* still gave him pause. I had seen the look on his face when I'd heated the bath water, evidently still struggling to fit *technology* into his world view, a worldview that didn't even have a printing press.

Zal had weeks of getting to know me, and if he could still doubt, I stood no chance with strangers. I vowed silently not to reveal any but ordinary abilities to the Trine.

My conflict alert pinged again. *Definition: ordinary; refine parameters.*

Ah. That was a problem, wasn't it? I still wasn't entirely sure what constituted *ordinary*, particularly for a Moon-born. Would the Trine have *that* information at their disposal? If so, I would be at even more of a disadvantage.

Look what had happened when I'd tried to soothe myself with a song. Just as Zal had done, the Cock & Bull's staff and customers had reacted as though they'd never heard anyone sing before. They'd been... entranced.

If all they'd ever heard was tuneless Earth temple chanting, an ancient folk-pop ballad might well seem like magic to them.

And I didn't want to *think* about what could happen if my fucking involuntary *seduction* modules were activated by an unfortunately worded question.

"Ready?" Zal asked, startling me out of my spiraling thoughts.

"Yes." I tucked my pack with its incriminating tech in the clothespress at the foot of the bed.

When I straightened, Zal was swinging his pack onto his shoulder, although his cloak still hung from its peg. Alarm sparked along my circuits.

"Zal. I think you should leave your pack here, too."

"Nay, love. I can't. The Trine will need to see my shattered Stone. It's evidence."

"I suppose."

I pulled on my leather gloves, donned my cloak, and pulled the hood up. The moment we stepped outside the inn, the sun beating down from above and the heat rising from the paving stones made sweat prickle along my hairline and dampen my armpits.

As I kept pace with Zal, I took a moment to wish irritably that in all their tinkering, the Infomancers had bothered to give me a better temperature regulation module.

When we reached the House of Mages, I stumbled to a stop, my chin lifting up and up until I had to clap a hand on my hood to keep it from falling onto my shoulders.

The building was *enormous*. Made of bricks the color of the earth, it was easily taller than the walls surrounding the city. Broad stone steps led up to massive wooden double doors with heavy wrought-iron hinges, guards in the mage's red and gold stationed on either side. Its soaring walls were pierced with so many windows that I questioned its structural integrity.

But then, solar power manipulators would need to arrange as much light as possible to work their magic and could probably keep their headquarters stable with it too.

Instead of heading up the steps, though, Zal led me down around the side to a low structure that joined the House of Mages to the next building along.

"Where are we going?" I asked, hurrying to keep up.

"We're to enter here at the vestibule. It links the House of Mages to the Library where the Scribe has offices."

I studied the connected building with interest. So this was *the* Library, the only one on the planet. It was built of the same brick as the House of Mages but wasn't as tall—maybe three stories to the House's six—but it seemed to stretch on forever. Both of them were a far cry from the buildings in Corvel-on-Byrne or Market Spinney, or even the Cock & Bull.

It made me wonder who'd constructed these edifices, what they'd been paid, and how they'd been treated during the process. On the other hand, perhaps both had been erected by magic. I couldn't discount it out of hand.

"Where do the other Trine members keep offices?"

"The Speaker's chambers are on the top two floors of the House."

"That seems like... a lot."

Zal smiled down at me, although I could detect the strain around his eye. "It includes meeting spaces that are impressive enough to awe the Seigneurs when they come to negotiate. The Speaker's assistants all have offices there too. The Speaker alone can't handle administration for the lot of us."

"I suppose not."

"The Scale... Well, those offices aren't as grand. They have one in Capitol Hall, where the College meets, and where the tribunal holds court. But here in the House, their offices are down below, where the cells are."

I shivered despite my over-warm cloak. "Cells. You mean like the gaol in Corvel-on-Byrne?"

"A bit more well-built than that, but if you're incarcerating a Sun Mage, you can't very well give them access to sunlight." He laid a hand on my shoulder, his light, firm grip comforting. "The central gaol is a bit less gloomy. That's where any prisoners who aren't mages are held."

"I see." I swallowed thickly. If the Trine ruled against me, I'd technically be a mage. Would they lock me in one of those lightless underground cubicles? I wouldn't last a week before emergency shutdown, and total system failure would follow in short order if I couldn't recharge.

"All we need do is follow the plan and all will be well. Come." Zal's voice was gentle, his smile soft and knowing, as if he could detect my worry. He tucked his hand under my elbow. "The Trine appreciates punctuality. We don't want to be late."

He led me into the vestibule. The room was cheerful enough, considering the door was flanked by diamond-paned windows easily my height. The floors were polished wood and a long table stood opposite the entrance, with smaller interior doors to either side.

Two A-3 guards in mage livery flanked the table, but the person sitting behind the desk was J-4 like Zal. Skin, hair, and eye color were as far as the similarities went, however. Whereas Zal, even when he was at his imposing Sun Mage best, was clearly kind and approachable, this person could have been carved of stone.

"Name and business?" they asked.

"Zal. Audience with the Trine," Zal said.

The J-4 consulted a slate. "The guards will escort you."

The two guards stepped away from the table. One of them opened the door on the House side and stepped through while the other stood back, not looking at us but clearly waiting for us to enter. When we did, he followed, closing the door with a hollow boom. I wasn't certain whether it was the finality of that sound or the guard's presence at my back that made the hair on my nape stand up.

Zal seemed mostly unconcerned, though striding along behind the lead guard as though this was business as usual, and perhaps it was. I mentally cursed the Infomancers for their tunnel-vision focus on genetics to the neglect of cultural observation. If they'd spent less time on germline editing and more on societal monitoring, I'd have more data at my disposal now.

On the other hand, maybe they had, and it was stored behind one of those maddening blocks. I really needed to run a complete diagnostic, but since that required Lab facilities, it would always be impossible.

The guard halted outside a door in a narrow corridor near the rear of the building. "In here."

This got a reaction from Zal. "Our audience is with the Trine. Surely the Speaker's offices—"

"Our orders are to bring you here." The guard shrugged, clearly uninterested. "Busy time."

Zal frowned, but nodded. "Very well."

The second guard held out a hand. "We'll need that pack."

Zal clutched at its straps. "No. This holds evidence important to our audience."

"The pack or you're on the street," the second guard said, tone implacable.

"I said—"

"It's all right, Uhtrig," a plummy voice called from beyond the second guard's shoulder. "The pack can stay, but you both may go."

Both guards pivoted smartly and marched away like automatons, revealing a tall J-4 with a round face, dimpled hands folded across her middle. Her gray-shot black braids were coiled over her ears, reminiscent of one of the more ridiculous hairdos from one of the films I'd recited to Zal during our journey.

While the citizens of Corvel-on-Byrne, Market Spinney, and even those I'd seen in the capital, wore clothing that favored practicality, clearly this woman had no plans to go anywhere more rough and daunting than the nearest staircase. Her brocade robe glinted with gilt thread and trailed on the floor behind her. The bells of her sleeves reached nearly to her feet, where curly-toed slippers peeped from under her hem.

Zal inclined his head, a polite obeisance, but not so deep I'd call it a bow. "Speaker."

"Zal. I was surprised to hear of your request. I apologize that we must conduct our meeting in such quarters, but"—she shrugged—"Judgment Day. What else need I say?"

"I appreciate you making the time for us."

"Hmmm." She tilted her head. "Us. Yes, that is the crux of the matter, isn't it?"

Zal chuckled weakly. "Perhaps not. But we've a tale to tell the Trine, if you're ready for us."

"Please." She gestured to the door, clearly not planning to open it herself. With both guards dismissed, it fell to Zal to do the honors before stepping aside to allow her to enter first.

Zal gripped my shoulder and gave me a tight smile. "Not long now. Everything will be... okay."

I smiled a little shakily at his evident attempt to ease my nerves. "Thank you."

Our plan was to minimize details about the Infomancers' planetary interference as much as possible, and not mention Edric at all. In theory, that was fine for me—I never wanted to mention Edric again. In practice, I wasn't certain if I'd be able to hold up my end of the bargain. If one of the Trine should ask me a question that I wasn't free to answer—or not to answer with words I chose myself—I might condemn us both.

The room we entered was narrow, and though not especially long, the closeness of the walls made it seem endless. A table sat across the far end, and two J-4s were seated there on either side of a third empty chair. The wall to our left was stone, blank and dark. The one on the right was pierced with three tall, narrow windows, but since they faced north, they let in little light. Most of the illumination in the room came from three fist-sized lumps of chrysocite arranged before each place at the table.

Obeila swept forward and took the center chair, arranging the folds of her robe to her satisfaction before beckoning to us. "Please. Approach. We are eager to hear your tale."

The way she couched that—*your tale*—raised my hackles. It was as though she had already decided that what we were about to tell them was fiction. But Zal strode forward confidently, so I hurried to keep pace.

He stopped about two meters from the table, and as there were no other chairs, we had no choice but to stand. He inclined his head to the austere J-4 to Obeila's right. "Scale."

So that was Gerd. Zal had called him remote and intimidating, hard but fair. Hard I could certainly see—his jaw might have been carved by a Cubist sculptor, and his eyes were like chips of obsidian. His skin was darker than Zal's or Obeila's, and his braids were drawn tightly back from his face, pulling the skin at his temples taut.

Gerd returned Zal's greeting with a barely perceptible dip of his square chin.

Zal turned to the third person with another nod. "Scribe."

If Gerd was all uncompromising angles, and Obeila was soft, deceptively yielding curves, Brylun was one giant question mark.

Their eyebrows were quirked over wide eyes, their lips slightly parted, their narrow frame leaning forward just slightly. *Avid.* That's what Brylun was. Their braids flopped messily over their shoulders, some spilling across the slate at their elbow and onto the table in front of Obeila.

Obeila brushed Brylun's braids aside and replaced them with her folded hands. "Now. Let us begin."

Zal turned to me. "Torian?"

As we'd agreed, I reached up and lowered my hood.

While Obeila blinked, and Gerd did nothing, Brylun sucked in a breath and murmured, "So. It's true."

Chapter Eleven

Zal

Brylun had said something when Torian revealed themself. I'd seen their lips move and felt Torian tense beside me, but didn't catch the words. Since asking one of the Trine to repeat themselves simply wasn't done, though, I continued as Torian and I had agreed.

"Near the end of my circuit, as you may have heard, there was a cataclysm at Star Mountain. A large part of the mountain was destroyed, and one large piece fell very close to Corvel-on-Byrne, the northernmost village in my charge. When I arrived at the village to assist the citizens with any damage, I found that a piece of the mountain wasn't all that had arrived."

I turned and put a hand on Torian's back. When Brylun's eyebrows rose further, I realized I should have avoided an action that might be construed as infringing on Torian's choice to be touched. But too late now.

"May I present to you Torian, Moon-born, the only one of their race to survive the Lunaria virus."

Brylun leaned forward, spilling more of their braids onto the table. "But how? How could you survive when all perished?"

This was Torian's part of the story, so I turned to them. Torian glanced up at me, swallowed once, and raised their chin, gazing briefly at each of the Trine in turn.

"I was rescued as an infant. By a group of Star-born who lived in a... an enclave on Star Mountain."

Obeila and Brylun exchanged a glance. Gerd's stony glare remained fixed on Torian.

Obeila smiled kindly at Torian. "We are naturally thrilled to find that at least one Moon-born survived that terrible plague. But could you tell us how?"

Torian shook their head. "The procedures were extensive. Invasive. And continued on throughout most of my life, since so many internal systems were affected by the virus."

Again, Obeila and Brylun exchanged looks, but this time it was more as though Obeila were asking Brylun for clarification. I could relate. While I'd had our entire journey to accustom myself to Torian's manner of speech and was able to deduce their meaning from context, this was the Trine's first exposure.

"What Torian means is that the Star-born have different healing methods than we do."

Obeila gave me an admonitory look. "Torian can speak for themselves, Zal. You needn't interpret."

Heat washed through me, leaving hollowness in its wake. I bowed my head. "Of course, Speaker. Please forgive me."

She smiled and returned her attention to Torian. "So the Star-born were able to sustain you with their magics for… how many years?"

"I am thirty-four planetary years old, but you misunderstand me. The Star-born do not wield magic. Not as you do. They use technology." At their blank looks, Torian said. "Science." Still nothing. Torian sighed. "Craft. Think of them as very advanced blacksmiths."

"Ah!" Obeila sat back with a satisfied nod. "That explains much. Although that doesn't explain why Zal took it upon himself to bring you here to us."

Torian held up both gloved palms. "I had nowhere else to go. When the La— When the cataclysm hit Star Mountain, the Star-born's enclave was destroyed."

Well, *that* got their attention. Obeila sat up straight and Brylun leaned so far forward that their chair tipped up on its front legs.

"Destroyed?" Obeila said. "The whole installation?"

Torian nodded. "I escaped, but was woefully underprepared for the weather conditions. I passed out near Corvel-on-Byrne."

"Did no one else survive?" Brylun asked.

"I couldn't say. Certainly nobody else entered Corvel-on-Byrne, at least not that they told me." Torian laced their fingers together, but not before I noted them trembling. "However, as I was incarcerated before I ever awoke, I suppose it's possible."

"Incarcerated." Gerd's deep voice held no inflection. "Why? What had you done?"

Torian spread their hands again, but quickly reclasped them. "Passed out on the riverbank? Truly, at that point, I'd had no opportunity to do anything else. Shock, exposure, and subsequent unconsciousness, you understand. I didn't see any of the citizens until I awoke already inside the cell. There... may have been misunderstandings."

"Misunderstandings." Gerd didn't couch it as a question. "Explain."

"My job in the... enclave was the equivalent of the work provided in a Comfort House. However, the techniques used there were unfamiliar to the Corvel-on-Byrne citizens, and they misconstrued them as coercive sex magic."

"And were they not?" Obeila asked.

"No. I was merely trying to exchange the only asset I possessed in exchange for my freedom." Torian shuddered. "I did not enjoy gaol."

"Who would?" Brylun murmured.

"The reeves informed me that they were harboring a rogue mage," I said. "At first, I didn't understand Torian's nature either, however, it was clear that I needed to escort them here to the capital to explain the situation and state their case."

"I see." Obeila sat back, steepling her fingers. "I believe this is the point where the tale turns more toward you, Zal, and the reason why you appear before us today without your Sun Stone." She turned to Brylun. "Perhaps you could escort Torian to your study. What follows doesn't pertain to their situation."

She smiled at Torian. "Some of what we are about to discuss are secrets privy to Sun Mages alone. You understand, don't you, my dear?"

"Of course," Torian said, but I could detect the uncertainty in their tone.

I gripped their shoulder gently. "It's all right. Go along with Brylun, love." Torian's eyes widened slightly, and I realized what I'd said. Shite. Another misstep, but I wouldn't retract it if I could, if only to reassure Torian. "I'll be fine."

I stood, hands clasped behind my back, as Brylun rose, tossed their braids behind their shoulders—slapping the back of Obeila's chair in the process—and led Torian away.

I had to grit my teeth to keep my protest inside and forced myself not to turn around and track their progress. At the click of the door latch, I could swear it was as though the sun had been eclipsed or swallowed by a storm.

Calm down. Don't overreact. While Torian speaking with Brylun was part of our plan to convince the Trine of Torian's innocence, of their harmlessness, of their worth, I'd expected to be present during the conversation.

But since I could scarcely countermand Obeila's orders, I'd best do my own part, and do it well. Then we'd be free. Free to choose a quiet life together in my cottage overlooking the inland sea.

When Obeila's smile dropped, rendering her as implacable as Gerd, though, I swallowed hard. This plan might not be as simple as we'd hoped.

"Well?" she said. "We are quite interested to hear your explanation, Zal, of how you come before us without your staff." I opened my mouth to respond, but she held up a palm. "And let me be clear. We will countenance only the full and complete truth. We will tolerate no excuses, no prevaricating, and above all, no lies."

I bowed my head. "Of course not, Speaker. That has ever been my intent." My nape prickled, and I had the urge to bolt from the room and find Torian immediately. I wasn't sure I could do this without them at my side.

When we'd first embarked on our partnership directly after Edric's death, they'd told me I needed somebody to watch my blind side. And in this moment, I definitely felt that need.

I unslung my pack and pulled out the bundle containing the Sun Stone chips that remained after Torian had threaded nearly half of them into my cloak. "If I may approach?"

When Obeila gestured impatiently, I paced forward and set the bundle on the table between her and Gerd. When I untied the thong and unrolled the leather to expose the shards, Obeila recoiled and Gerd's jaw tightened.

"While we were on the trail, Torian experienced a"—what had they called it?—"near-death experience. In reviving them, I drew on too much power, too quickly. My staff split and my Stone shattered." I gestured to its remains. "As you see."

Gerd extended a finger and touched one sliver, although he drew back sharply, as though he'd been burned. "It is still bonded to you, even though it's fragmented."

"So it would seem." Despite my assurances to Obeila that I would be completely forthcoming, I didn't want to confess that I could still use the pieces individually.

"Let me be sure I understand this." Obeila's tone chilled me like a plunge in the Byrne in midwinter. "You, an experienced mage with hundreds of circuit judgments to your credit, made the decision that a single person—and a Moon-born at that—held more value than your Sun Stone?"

"I... Surely our duty is to all citizens, to their safety, to their right to choose their path?"

She waved an impatient hand, the gold rings that circled each of her fingers glinting. "Yes, yes. But it's *your* choice that we are discussing now. Are you certain that the destruction of your Stone and forsaking your calling truly *was* your choice?"

I frowned. "I don't understand. Of course it was."

"Perhaps you are not aware, as most of our citizens are not, what the Moon-born were capable of, and why we are far better off without them."

This time, my jaw dropped. Was she actually countenancing genocide? *Approving* it? "The Earth temples teach that all life is sacred, which is why we all have the right to make our own choices. Surely the Moon-born were no different."

"Ah, but that's where you're wrong. The Moon-born were able to ensorcel entire *crowds* of people..." She drew herself up, braids quivering. "With their voices *alone*."

It felt as though a fist had closed around my throat. *Torian's songs.* "How do you know this? I've never heard of it."

"Because it was better for our citizens to forget. There are many journals in the Library's restricted stacks, available only to Scribes, that recount it. Brylun discovered them when they took office."

The pressure around my throat increased. Torian was alone with Brylun now, alone in a building bristling with guards, alone without me to protect them. "What are you saying?" I croaked.

"I'm saying that you could be under this same kind of enchantment now. Why else sacrifice the heart of your power to save a near stranger? Why else break the sacred vows you took when you bonded with your Stone?"

"I didn't break my vows," I said hotly.

"No? Yet you called the Moon-born *love*."

"That doesn't mean aught but that we are friends. Partners on the trail. But not lovers."

"Yet Torian admitted that comfort work is all they know. How else convince you to take them along with you, bring you to the very people"—she spread her palms—"the very place they would need to bring their schemes to fruition?"

"What schemes? The only scheme they had was to escape the enclave, where they had no choice but to agree to comfort house work. They have no desire to continue that, no more than I have any desire to indulge in it myself."

"No? Yet we have testimony from two witnesses that claim you conducted an unwarranted shearing because you were under the Moon-born's influence, and that afterward, you shared bedrolls with the Moon-born nightly all the way to the capital."

Anger built in my chest. The fellow in Natin's line ahead of me, the one with the ill-fitting hat that hid his braids—or lack of them. I *thought* there was something familiar about that snood. I'd seen the same crochet pattern in the village the day I met Torian, and again the night our campsite had been invaded.

"If you mean those louts from Corvel-on-Byrne, their shearing was completely warranted. They weren't able to distinguish silence from denial, a lesson they should have learned before their trials. They were about to force Torian to take all of them, right there in the open." I snorted in disgust. "I daresay they followed us all the way here, spying along the way."

The disgust was for myself as much as for the accusation. I'd *known* something was off. I'd felt eyes on us every night, but had never spotted anyone, despite checking our surroundings so often that Torian remarked on it.

Shite, could they have witnessed Edric's death? Torian's resurrection? The shuttle explosion?

"They claim they were invited," Obeila said, her tone hard. "That the Moon-born coerced them."

"Coerced them into a gang rape? I don't think so."

Her eyes narrowed, probably at my disrespectful tone. "I note you don't deny sharing a bedroll."

"For warmth! It's bloody cold on the trail this time of year, which you may not know, seeing as you've never walked a northern circuit."

She stiffened at that, then seemed to relax with a visible effort. "Zal. You must understand. In all the history of our order, no Sun Stone has ever shattered without a mage breaking their vows. It is easy to lie, easy to leave out pertinent information, so it would be easy for a mage to hide such transgressions. The Stones, however, do not lie. Yours shattered, ergo, you broke your vows."

"But I didn't!" My voice broke with my desperation. "I did not!"

She shook her head, and her sorrow could almost be real. "In a way, I don't blame you. The Moon-born enchanted you the way they enchanted the citizens in Corvel-on-Byrne. Therefore, *you* were deprived of choice. However, it doesn't change the law. You broke your vows, therefore tomorrow on Judgment Day, you will be executed. However, since there could be extenuating circumstances, we will show mercy and at least make it swift."

Chapter Twelve

Torian

The route to Brylun's study was ridiculously circuitous—unnecessarily so, given what I recalled of the layout of the building when we'd entered. I knew precisely where we were—on the second story above the vestibule, between the House of Mages and the Library. I wondered briefly if they were trying to disorient me, confuse me so that it would be more difficult for me to escape.

But that was also ridiculous. The place was full of people, many of them guards. I wouldn't be able to leave unnoticed even if I wanted to.

And I didn't want to. Not without Zal. It felt *wrong* to be here without him, as though an entire sector of my grid had gone dark. I'd been on edge anyway, ever since we left the inn. My hazard alerts had been buzzing continually during that travesty of an audience, making my fingers twitch as we faced the Trine.

Three people who were wearing masks.

Not physical masks, but emotional masks, *intentional* masks. Clearly Zal didn't see it, but he hadn't been trained to read micro-expressions in body language as I had, nor did he have the visual acuity that I did when I recalibrated my vision for closeups.

The Trine were hiding their true objectives from us, and that had put me so on edge that I'd only half listened to the conversation, which had probably been a mistake. Because there was something—

"Here we are," Brylun said brightly as they pushed open another of those heavy iron-banded doors. "My little sanctuary."

They gestured with their staff. The guard who'd followed us from the audience chamber probably interpreted it as an invitation for me to enter, but I'd been around Zal's power long enough to recognize it for what it was: a solar energy-backed compulsion for me to move into the room.

I buried a snort. *So much for the concept of universal consent.*

While I could feel the compulsion's strength, it was configured for organics, not cybertronics, so I could have resisted it if I'd wanted. But this was another thing that didn't quite add up to Zal's opinion of the Trine. So I walked inside.

The room wasn't large and was only slightly off being a perfect square. Opposite the door was a pair of tall windows flanked with heavy velvet drapes in a deep maroon. A fussily ornate wooden desk stood in the center of the room, perpendicular to the window, and a throne-like chair upholstered in the same maroon velvet stood behind it. Bookshelves covered all available wall space other than a three-foot gap between the windows, which held a full-length oil portrait of a much younger Brylun.

The artist had been far too kind.

At the door, Brylun told the guard, "I'm sure you have duties to perform for Judgment Day. You needn't stay."

"If you are certain, Scribe?"

"Of course. Now toddle along, there's a good fellow."

As the guard's heavy footsteps retreated down the hall, Brylun shut the door, and I heard the *snick* of a lock.

Brylun sauntered behind the desk. "Do please have a seat." They gestured to the only other piece of furniture—a wooden chair with no arms or seat padding—with their staff.

I took note that its legs were shorter than those of the chair behind the desk, so it would put me lower than Brylun.

Nevertheless, I kept up the ruse of being controlled and sat while Brylun shed his rusty black, too-long robe, revealing close-fitting breeks, a rather crumpled linen shirt, and an embroidered waistcoat of truly astonishing brilliance and ugliness. They hung the robe on a coat rack and tied their braids at their nape with a jeweled ribbon.

They planted their staff in a purpose-built stand so that their Stone was directly behind their chair and sat. The Brylun who faced me now was orders of magnitude different from the scatterbrained person in the audience chamber, or even in the hallway.

"Now then." They laced their fingers on the desk's gleaming surface and fixed me with a steely gaze. "Let's do away with the pretense, shall we?"

I blinked. "I... I beg your pardon?"

Irritation flickered across Brylun's face. "Don't waste my time. I have far too much to do before tomorrow." They pointed a finger with a rather yellowed nail at me. "And you needn't try any of your voice enchantment tricks on me. I cast a protection spell on the room before we entered."

"I wouldn't—"

"I said, don't waste my time. Tell me the results of the test."

"Test?"

Brylun made an irritated noise. "The test. The *test*. I must say, I'm a bit annoyed with Mage Mohindes. The explosion was supposed to take place within sight of the capital. But we've had credible witnesses report the event, so I suppose I can let it go this time."

Mage Mohindes. Could Brylun mean Dr. al-Mohindes? *Edric*?

"It was unavoidable," I said, hoping for more information.

And then it hit me, the thing that had been niggling at my mind since the audience: Obeila had asked whether the whole *installation* had been destroyed.

Why would she have called it an installation unless she knew more about the Lab than Zal or the other planetary inhabitants?

We'd been careful to refer to it as an *enclave,* and I know we hadn't slipped up or my conflict alerts would have pinged.

"Well, I suppose he did manage to send you, so we must be ready to proceed."

"I'm sorry?"

Brylun blew out a breath. "Really, I'd think that someone with Mage Mohindes's resources would be able to arrange for a more intelligent messenger." Then they winced and followed up with an almost embarrassed chuckle. "Ah. I'd forgotten. The opening spell. Foolish of me."

Brylun pulled a small brass key out from under their shirt and bent forward to turn it in the desk's center drawer. Then they sat back, put a finger to the same spot—I detected another flare of solar energy—and the drawer sprang open. With an expression of concentration, they reached their entire arm into the drawer and pulled out...

A spiral-bound notebook with a red cardboard cover, the kind Lab assistants used to scribble notes before they transferred them to electronic storage.

For a moment, shock held me frozen, as if I truly were the automaton that Brylun seemed to think I was. That sort of notebook wasn't valuable, but the only way for Brylun to have one is if they'd actually been in contact with someone from the Lab.

"Mage" Mohindes, for instance.

Brylun rifled through the pages before tapping one with a finger. "Here it is." They peered closely at the page, lips pursed, and then looked up at me and said, "Retrieve directory zed alpha two seven five nine, authorization Mohindes three eight one, disengage."

I gasped, because suddenly the contents of a directory bloomed in my mind, one I'd never seen, one that had been hidden from me until this moment.

Horror pooled in my stomach as I scanned its files. *Gunpowder production. Firearms schematics. Explosive formulae.*

Edric was about to upset the entire power structure of the planet by arming the Trine—and presumably their adherents—with projectile weapons and ordnance.

Brylun beamed. "Good. You've remembered the message. Now, if you would—" A brisk knock interrupted them, and their smile immediately vanished. "Blast. What now?" they muttered.

They tossed the notebook onto the desk, rose, and strode to the door. When they were turned away to open it, I angled my head a fraction so I could watch the doorway in my peripheral vision while still appearing impassive.

Obeila stood in the corridor. "Do you have it?"

"I've just unlocked the message but haven't transcribed it yet."

"Why not?" she said testily. "You've had more than enough time."

Brylun *hmmmph*ed. "I'd like to see you do better."

"Well, I have. Zal is in his cell, and we're about to head to the Square to report his capture and announce the Judgment Day agenda. After that, we'll be busy until after the execution tomorrow."

"All right, all right," Brylun replied. "Keep your hair on." They grabbed their robe off the coatrack and shrugged into it before grabbing their staff. "I suppose we couldn't do anything with the instructions until afterward, anyway."

They peered at a shelf behind the desk, made a pleased sound, and grabbed a flask holding a murky brown liquid. They slopped a dollop, perhaps three or four ounces, into a rather dusty crystal goblet and held it out to me. "Drink this."

The compulsion flared, and once again, I chose to pretend it was working. I took the glass and downed its contents, grimacing at the bitter taste. Immediately, my ingestion analysis subroutines took over, identifying the chemicals and their properties, flagging it as harmful, and encapsulating it in an impermeable membrane. The packet was redirected to the compartment where my spleen used to be for neutralization and later elimination.

Since the analysis had returned a full report of the expected effects, I slumped in my chair and feigned unconsciousness.

"There." Brylun rescued the goblet from my lax hand. "It won't be going anywhere for at least forty-eight hours. By then, we should be able to study the files at our leisure."

"You're sure you can control it?" Obeila's tone was edged with skepticism.

"Please. It responded to the compulsion spell without a smidge of resistance. We'll have no trouble, not once Zal is out of the way. Let's go."

"What if it tries to escape?"

"I *told* you. It won't be moving again until day after tomorrow at the earliest, but if it makes you feel better, we can leave a guard posted outside the door."

My eyes pricked behind my closed lids.

It.

None of the people I'd met in the villages, on the trail, or here in the capital had ever referred to me as *it*. They had often misgendered me, yes, but I had never been an *it*. Only Edric referred to me as *it*. If I had had any doubt before, I had none now.

Edric had been in contact with the Trine.

Obeila sighed. "Very well. Come on."

More footsteps, then the door closed and the lock *snick*ed again. I waited for another excruciating few minutes to make sure, and then opened my eyes and surged out of the chair.

Zal imprisoned. Zal to be *executed*. No!

I couldn't allow that to happen, any more than I could allow the Trine to get their hands on advanced weaponry. But with a guard outside the door and more patrolling the corridors, it wasn't as though I could traipse through the House of Mages again, even if I had somewhere to go.

Then I remembered. I *did* have somewhere to go.

Ibb and Jocosa had accepted me, promised that our room was secure for at least tonight. Provided I could get to the Cock & Bull, I could count on at least that much help.

Getting there was the issue, though, wasn't it?

I hurried to the window and looked out. It didn't face the street where we'd entered. Instead, it faced the other direction. There didn't seem to be as much foot traffic in the rear, probably because everyone was already crowding the Square for the fucking *execution announcement*.

It was a sheer, two-story drop to the street. I doubted my bone structure, despite being fortified, could make that drop undamaged. In any case, the windows didn't open, and the leaded diamond-shaped panes were too small for me to squeeze through, even if I broke the glass.

I whirled and scanned the room. *My sanctuary*, Brylun had called it. As they were the head librarian as well as the Scribe, wouldn't it stand to reason they'd need sanctuary from both roles? But by the same token, their retreat shouldn't be located an inconvenient distance from either of their domains.

I prowled along the bookcases on the side of the room I knew was closest to the library, and I found it—an unobtrusive lever on the center case. When I pushed it, though, nothing happened.

"Fuck!"

Before I pounded my head against the frame or launched a book through the window simply out of frustration, I remembered: solar energy manipulation.

I carefully pressed the lever again while sending a trickle of energy through my fingertip, easy enough to do since my stores were almost completely charged from basking in the sun at the inn.

With a *click* and a rumble, the case moved back and to the side, revealing an open archway across a small, bare, wooden-floored room, which was deserted. I was about to step past the case, but stopped and darted back to Brylun's desk to snatch the notebook and stuff it into the pocket of my breeks.

Not only didn't I want the Trine to have access to it, but if Edric had provided any more passwords to hidden directories and secret files, I wanted *all* of them under my own control. Subject to *my* choice.

After all, they were stored in *my* data banks.

I spotted an identical lever on the other side of the bookcase and sent it rumbling back into place. I turned and took a deep breath.

Now… what? I still had to get through the library and back to the inn without being noticed, and how likely was that?

Nevertheless, I pulled my hood as far forward as it would go, tugged at my gloves, and peeked out the archway. The hallway on the other side was deserted, and I hesitated for a moment, uncertain. Because surely I couldn't be that lucky.

But it seemed that I was.

I made it down the stairs without encountering anyone at all. The library's ground floor didn't seem to boast any patrons at all, and its few staff members were plastered against the front windows, peering out into the Square.

Please let there be a back door. Please let there be a back—Ah!

I found it in the corner between two massive cases, helpfully labeled *Exit*, and slipped out into an empty alley.

I called up my memory of the capital layout, or as much as I'd already mapped through either walking it or observing it from above. I followed a path that avoided the Square, although the sound of amplified voices and muffled cheers followed me all the way to the inn.

When I burst through the door, the common room was empty of customers, although Ibb was polishing tankards behind the bar while Jocosa and their children scrubbed down tables. They all looked up when I stumbled to a stop.

"Please," I wheezed. "I need your help."

Jocosa tucked her rag in her apron pocket and met my gaze calmly. "Tell us what we can do."

Chapter Thirteen

Zal

It didn't matter how many times I'd sworn that Torian hadn't bespelled me, that they weren't a mage, that I hadn't broken my vows, Obeila and Gerd wouldn't listen. Finally, they'd called in a pair of hulking guards.

"Take him to the judgment holding cell."

"What? No! I didn't do anything. You can't—"

But the guards, both of whom were half a head taller than me, yanked my arms behind my back and looped bespelled cuffs around my wrists.

"Please. Please don't hurt Torian," I nearly sobbed. "They've done nothing wrong."

Gerd regarded me stonily, but Obeila's lips twisted in a parody of her usual smile. "Really? Nothing at all?"

Obeila flicked her fingers at me and I felt it hit my chest—a truth compulsion. Our Stones prevented mages from using offensive magics against one another, which was why my battle with Loriah had been hand to hand—or in the end, knife to eye. But I didn't have a Stone anymore. I wasn't a mage any longer. So I had no hope of resisting.

Although I knew the gesture was futile, I clamped my lips together, determined to make them *work* for every incriminating scrap of information. But somehow, the truth about Edric's death didn't crawl up my throat to condemn Torian and me both. My knees nearly buckled with relief and I closed my eye briefly to send thanks to the Sun.

Obeila frowned, clearly annoyed. "It appears that the enchantment works even when the Moon-born isn't present."

"I'm not enchanted," I growled. "They didn't enchant me. They're not like that."

"For the Sun's sake," she said, her tone dripping disgust, "take him away."

Obeila stood and bustled out of the room. Gerd merely nodded curtly to the guards and turned to regard the Stone shards spread out on the table in front of him.

The guards frog-marched me out of the chamber and down the corridor that led to the underground levels. Two flights of stone steps yawned at our feet—wide so prisoners could be flanked by guards; shallow to allow for the shortened stride of someone in leg shackles.

Iron sconces holding bespelled fist-sized chunks of quartz marched down the walls. While the white light they cast was bright, it was also cold. Impersonal. Distant, like the stars.

As the guards hauled me down the steps, we cast no shadows. There was nowhere to hide.

At the bottom of the stairs we turned right, passed Gerd's office and the guards' ready room, and continued on until the corridor ended in a wall made of stone blocks as big as my torso. To our left, a narrow door led to more stairs, these narrower and poorly lit with flickering torches.

My throat closed and for a moment, I couldn't breathe. Although the bottom of those stairs was swallowed in darkness, I knew what lay at their foot: the cells expressly for Sun Mages, dark, dank, windowless, and enough to cause any of us to go mad even without the threat of death hanging over our heads.

They'd taken Loriah down there after I'd hauled her in. Between the pain of my wound and the infection that had set in by then, I was in no shape to visit her even if it had been allowed. Only the guards and the Trine were allowed near those cells.

Well, guards, the Trine, and the prisoners, but they had no choice.

"You got it from here?" one of the guards asked his partner. "I'm due at the Square."

"Go on," the other replied, gripping my biceps tightly enough to crush muscle to bone. "Not like he can do anything in those cuffs."

The first guard strode off, boot heels clacking against the stone floor, as the remaining guard yanked me onto the top step.

Halfway down the flight, the line of torches ended. The guard fisted his hand in my braids and shoved me, face first, against the rough wall.

"Don't move."

Since the darkness below was almost palpable, seeming to creep toward my feet, I was frozen in place even without his weight pressing against my back.

He tugged at a chain around his throat and pulled a lump of quartz the size of my thumbnail from under his shirt. When he touched it to his lips, it flared to cold, white light, and he shifted his grip to my arm again.

"I know how you Sun mages are about the dark. You try anything with me and the light goes out, understand?"

I nodded, the flesh on my back creeping as he jostled me around to face forward, his bespelled quartz only bright enough to light the next few steps below.

"Good. Walk."

The stairs weren't quite wide enough for us to walk comfortably side by side, but I suppose he wasn't interested in my comfort. He crowded me against the wall all the way down that endless flight, the stones getting rougher as we descended, bruising my flesh, tearing my sleeve, scraping my skin.

The stairs ended in a narrow corridor, unlit except for the guard's light which barely pierced the gloom. The shadows beyond its wan circle looked thick enough to repel an axe. The wall on the left was solid, more huge stone blocks and crumbling mortar. The right, however...

The right froze my blood.

A metal door, its dark surface seeming to swallow the light, loomed at my elbow, another one half-visible a few steps further on. Both were pierced by two hatches, each secured with sliding bolts, one at eye level and one on the floor. They were inset at least half a meter into the wall, and close enough to one another that it was clear the cells behind them were narrow, the width of my arm-span or less.

The guard shoved my back, sending me stumbling toward the shadows. "Move."

I shuffled forward, not moving too far ahead of him because my depth perception was poor even in good light. Down here? I was nearly blind.

We passed the first two cells, so they apparently weren't for me. Were they already occupied by other mages awaiting Judgment Day? If so, they had given up so far as to stop protesting their innocence, because the corridor was silent except for the sound of our breathing.

We passed a third cell. And another. And a fifth. When we reached the sixth, the guard stopped and in the faint glow, I could see the corridor ended two steps beyond, in another wall of hand-hewn stone.

I'd heard the rumors, of course. Everyone had. The last cell in the block was for those condemned to death.

The guard shoved an iron key into the lock. From his muffled curses as he wrestled with it and the scrape as it turned, this cell hadn't been used lately.

The door swung open into utter darkness. The guard's quartz illuminating nothing inside, cut off cleanly at the threshold. I knew what that meant.

Magic null.

Somehow, the College of Mages had rendered this cell— perhaps all of them in this block—impervious to spells. This was further brought home to me when the guard shoved me hard between my shoulder blades and I stumbled over the metal strap bolted into the stone floor. Because as soon as both my feet were inside, the cuffs dropped off my wrists.

I whirled, if only to have one last glimpse of light before the door closed.

"Please. You can't leave me here in the dark. I didn't do anything wrong."

"They all say that." He grinned, not pleasantly, and dug in his belt pouch. "Here." He tossed something onto the floor and it rolled to fetch up against my boot toes. "A candle." His grin grew. "You're a mage. Light it."

The door clashed shut on his laughter, leaving me in total darkness, panic gnawing at my vitals. I had no idea what else was with me here in the cell. Was I alone? Were there rats? Other vermin? Where was the slop bucket? I shivered in the damp chill. Would they have left me a blanket? Would it smell of anything but mildew and despair?

For a moment, I closed my eye and called up the memory of the gold threads running beneath Torian's skin, of the scent of ozone and petrichor that clung to their hair.

Torian.

Were they all right? Surely Brylun would protect them, not only because of the wealth of knowledge Torian contained, knowledge irresistible to any mage—especially a librarian and historian—but because the two of them were alike in nature.

I should be there, by Torian's side, protecting them. I didn't believe Obeila's claims that Moon-born magic worked through words. Even if it *was* true, Torian wouldn't. They believed just as strongly in choice as any of my people. Even if Torian *could* enchant me with their voice, they wouldn't. They—

Wait a moment.

Enchant had more than one meaning.

Enchant didn't always denote coercive spells.

Enchant could mean the feelings that overcame you when you beheld something beautiful, smelled something enticing, heard something impossibly heartbreakingly beautiful.

Something like Torian's voice lifted in song.

Whatever records Brylun had unearthed, they could have completely misinterpreted them. I'd suspected as much, but this was further proof.

The Moon-born had been *musicians*. Performers. Artists who shared songs and stories and imagination with others, the way Torian had sung and regaled me with the tales from those ancient *films*.

Urgency scaled my ribs to lodge under my heart. I had to tell them. I had to let them *know*. They could be making the worst mistake since the Lunaria virus swept away all Torian's people.

I crouched and groped on the floor until I found the candle, the only thing I knew for certain was in the darkness with me, so I wouldn't trip over it. Then I held my other arm in front of me and crept forward until my hand met the cold iron of the door.

I pounded on the metal. "Obeila! Gerd! I need to talk to you. Come here! Please! You've got it all wrong."

My fist against the door made scarcely a noise, as though my hand was wrapped in cotton wool. Was the cell bespelled to muffle sound as well?

"Sun forbid the guards be *inconvenienced* by the prisoners' suffering," I growled. "Fuck!"

Torian's expletive expressed my feelings exactly, the shape of it in my mouth, the hard edges of it, even if I had no true context of its meaning.

Suddenly, the candle flared to life in my hand. I was so startled I nearly dropped it. How…? I had no magic, and even if I did, the cell would have snuffed it out.

But who cared how it had happened? I had light now, and since the thing was barely a stub, I didn't have much time with it.

Hand trembling, I raised it above my head. A rough gray blanket lay crumpled in the far corner, directly on the floor, without even a straw pallet to cushion the uneven stones. The corner to my left nearest the door held the slop bucket, which my nose would have led me to eventually, anyway.

Standing in the center of the cell, I could probably touch each wall if I spread my arms. I turned slowly, squinting in the dim light.

Blanket. Slop bucket. Door.

Blanket. Slop bucket. Door.

Nothing else. The room was otherwise completely bare.

The slot at the bottom of the door indicated they might pass in food or water, assuming they felt I deserved it, or if they remembered. Clearly they removed all remnants of it afterward, though, because not a dented cup or broken plate remained.

I continued to rotate. Blanket. Slop bucket. Door. Bl—

Wait. What was that? Low on the wall next to the door…

Writing.

My candle near guttering, I dropped to my knees and held it close. The lettering was uneven, as though whoever wrote it had been struggling with their writing implement. What sort of implement *could* be effective against stone this rough? Slates were smooth for a reason. And the ink was oddly rusty.

I choked on a moan.

Not ink. *Blood.*

Whoever wrote this used the only resource available to them: their own body. Using their own blood—and I had to hope it had been spilled by their own hand and not the result of torture-inflicted wounds—they'd used their finger to scrawl the words.

the sun will scorch the earth the stars will devour the sun beware the stars beware the tr

That was all.

Despite the unevenness of the letters, driven by obvious desperation, I recognized the writing. The dip in the lower curve of the S. The Es that could look like Cs when the cross-stroke was slashed too carelessly.

Loriah.

She had been here, in this cell. Furthermore, I had put her here. Maybe I hadn't turned the key, but I'd delivered her to this fate all the same.

I remembered Torian's accusation that night when Farren and his gang had accosted them, when they'd berated me for not getting Loriah's side of the story, of not investigating her reasons:

"Because from where I stand, Zal, you're the one who failed to ask."

Yes, I'd followed my orders. I'd done what I'd been sent to do. But I hadn't truly *listened* to Loriah. Frankly, I thought her ranting, her talk of conspiracies and persecution and coercion, was the sign of her disordered mind, further evidence she'd gone rogue, although I'd scarcely needed any considering she'd already killed Wythael, the first mage who'd pursued her.

The Trine had warned me to subdue her quickly, else I'd suffer the same fate.

beware the tr

Had Loriah been about to write *trine* before she was interrupted? I shivered, not wanting to think about what that interruption might have been.

Last week—shite, *this morning*, I'd have taken that warning as the further ravings of a rogue. But now? Sitting in this cell, condemned for something I didn't do, *knowing* that the Trine was misinformed about Torian's nature, about the nature of the Moon-born in general, I wondered what else Loriah had known.

And what I might have learned if I had only stopped to listen before I'd launched my attack.

I let the candle drop from my lax fingers where it spluttered once before the flame died, leaving me in darkness as black as the stain on my soul. I covered my face with my hands and drew my knees to my chest, rocking back and forth.

"Sun, moon, and stars," I croaked between sobs, "what have I done?"

Chapter Fourteen

Torian

I huddled on a low wooden stool in the middle of our room at the Cock & Bull, wearing nothing but my smallclothes. The sun streaming in through the window was sending energy coursing through my grid, but I shivered nonetheless.

This would work. This *had* to work. I refused to accept any other outcome.

When someone scratched softly at the door, I said, "Come."

Darej slipped inside. The smell emanating from the deep wooden bowl in their hands was so astringent it burned the inside of my nose. They smiled a little diffidently.

"I'm sorry for imposing on your privacy, but this really goes on much better if somebody else handles the application of it. Besides, palms are usually paler than the rest of a person's skin, and if you get it on your hands, they'll be far too dark."

I motioned them to approach. "It's okay."

They blinked. "Oh. K?"

My chuckle held an edge of hysteria. "It means the same thing as all right."

Darej beamed. "Oh *kay* then." They set the bowl on the table next to my stool and I eyed the deep brown liquid inside it with some trepidation. "We'll do a test first, to see how many layers we'll need. The inside of your upper arm is best. It's not usually a place people look."

Obediently, I raised my arm. Darej dipped their fingers in the viscous solution and spread a thin layer on a palm-sized section of my triceps, where it was immediately absorbed, turning my pale skin a dark ivory.

"Won't it stain your hands too?"

They glanced up at me as they scooped another dollop and smoothed it over the first. "Of course. But soaking my hands in salted water with two parts vinegar to one part Mam's laundry soap for ten minutes will get rid of it." They smiled at me with a decided twinkle. "We've had a lot of practice with clawfruit rind stain. Clawfruit juice is the main ingredient in Mam's winter solstice punch, and collecting enough for the year's batch takes *ages* every autumn because the stupid things are mostly rind. If we didn't have a way to clean it off, Maer, Lafi, and I would go about looking as though we'd dipped our hands in tar." They studied their handiwork, head tilted. "Yes, two layers should do. There are enough Earth-born with skin that light that you won't attract attention. You don't want to go as dark as a Sun-born. That *would* catch a few eyes."

"You're the expert." I wondered briefly why Darej and their family knew about this process as I peered at my arm and poked it with a fingertip. The dye was already dry, the skin now a light golden brown, similar to the artificial tans some of the Lab assistants maintained. "How long will it last?"

"It will fade gradually over a fortnight, but the change won't be noticeable for at least three days." They bit their lip. "This will go much faster if Maer and Lafi could help. Do you mind?"

I shook my head. "The faster the better." After my time in the Lab as a combination sexual surrogate and test subject, my body shyness was negligible.

"I'll just call them, then."

Maer and Lafi must have been waiting outside the door, because they immediately burst in, swathed in canvas aprons, each holding another bowl of dye. As they hunkered down on either side of me, Maer looked up at Darej and shook her head.

"By the Earth, Dar. Use the cotton wool, not your fingers. You'd think you *liked* soaking your hands in that nasty cleanser."

Darej's brown cheeks pinked. "I forgot." They pulled a handful of white fluff from their apron pocket. "I'll do your face and arms while they work on your legs and we'll move toward the middle. Okay?"

Lafi squinted up at Darej. "What are you on about, Dar? Are we reciting the alphabet now?"

Darej looked down their nose and sniffed. "*Okay* means the same as *all right*. *Everyone* knows that."

Lafi exchanged a look with Maer, one I'd seen between Lab assistants when they were wondering whether to challenge someone's statement or pretend they'd come to the same conclusion themselves.

But then Lafi shrugged and said, "Okay."

While they worked, I hummed low in my throat, a martial tune from an ancient musical about rebellion and redemption, which seemed appropriate under the circumstances.

"Oh, please. I'm done with your face." Darej held the soaked cotton wool in both hands, dribbling stain onto their apron and guaranteeing they'd be soaking their hands in caustic cleanser when we were done. "That sounds so wonderful. Are there... are there words?"

"Yes. Quite stirring ones, as it happens."

All three siblings looked at one another and then at me, eyes pleading.

"Could you—" Maer said, at the same time Lafi said, "Would you—" and Darej said, "Is it asking too much for—" and they all said, "you to sing it for us?"

"It would be no trouble at all." I smiled at each of them in turn. "You are doing so much for me, it's a small enough thing to offer in return."

I stood to give them all easier access, and as Darej sopped stain onto my arms and Maer and Lafi moved on from my legs to my torso, I launched into "Do You Hear the People Sing?" Before I reached the end of the first verse, Jocosa slipped in to pour a steaming bucket of water into the washbasin and then stayed to listen, her eyes bright with unshed tears.

It only took a couple of encores before they finished, dying my skin everywhere except under my smallclothes. We'd agreed that if it got to the point where anyone saw me there, I'd have other problems to deal with.

While Maer and Lafi washed their hands and Jocosa, still sniffing, left with her bucket, Darej held up a mirror, their fingers stained nearly black. "What do you think?"

I studied my face, tilting my chin up to inspect my throat. The color was smooth and even, not in the least blotchy, and my solar grid—which the siblings hadn't mentioned—stood out less. I'd seen people in Market Spinney with skin this color, although I'd never seen anybody with gray eyes. I'd have to hope nobody would get close enough to spot the anomaly.

"It's perfect. Thank you."

Maer nudged my shoulder to make me sit on the stool again. "Not quite perfect. We have to braid your hair."

I winced. "Even braiding it won't make its length any less apparent."

Jocosa bumped the door open with her hip and re-entered, a bundle of cloth in her arms. "Never you mind. We've got something for that, too."

While Maer plaited my hair so close to my scalp I thought the skin on my temples would split, Jocosa bustled across the room.

"My sister's a tailor," she said. "Makes the livery for the servants in the best houses, including the House of Mages. Shirt." She teased a spotless white linen shirt with ties at the neck out of her armful and tossed it onto the bed.

"Mam!" Lafi protested as she retrieved it and shook it out. "You can't crease it. Those House folk are always neatly pressed. The mages insist on it."

Jocosa simply *hmmmph*ed. "Waistcoat." She handed Lafi a black knee-length garment, subtle gold and red embroidery edging its open front and followed it with close-woven russet trousers. "Breeks.

I reached out and fingered the fine fabric. "I thought the House of Mages livery was red and yellow?"

"That's the guards. Servants are different," Jocosa said. "Stockings." They were also blindingly white. Her eyes narrowed as her gaze shifted to the boots tucked halfway under the bed. "Those won't do, though."

"I've two other pairs. In my pack." I pointed to the satchel on the hook next to my cloak.

"Stop fidgeting," Maer said, "or your plaits will be crooked."

"Does that matter?" I asked.

"Yes," Jocosa said, "because we've also got this."

She held up the last item in her arms, some kind of knitted, pouch-like article, something dark coiled within it, visible between its loose stitches and weighty enough to make it swing in her grip.

My eyes widened. "Is that…"

"It's not anybody else's hair, if that's what you're worried about. That would be sacrilegious."

Maer snorted. "Like you care about that, Mam."

Jocosa glared at her daughter. "*I* might not, but others do."

"Why is it sacrilegious?" I asked, wishing again that the Infomancers had paid more attention to social customs and community life and less to their next gene splice.

"When a citizen dies, before their body is given to the Earth, their braids are always shorn and given to the Sun. Then those ashes are part of the fire that sends them back to the Earth."

Burial rituals. Something so intrinsic. How had the Infomancers missed this? The obvious answer was that they hadn't bothered to look, but now that I thought of it, I'd never seen a graveyard. Even Zal had apologized about burying Edric at first, before I'd used a different method of disposing of his body.

"This is carded wool that we braided and coiled inside the snood," Jocosa said. "But to attach it to your head, your braids have to be seated close to your head, tight enough to bear the weight."

"Fair enough." That didn't keep me from wincing as Maer finished her work.

Jocosa pronounced my ankle boots acceptable, especially since they were clearly new. They all helped me dress, although the other three deferred to Lafi, who made sure every part of my outfit was as perfect and unremarkable as possible. The snood was an odd, unfamiliar weight at the back of my head, the pins that held it to my braids pulling whenever I turned my head.

"You can't wear your cloak," Lafi said flatly.

My fingers twitched, an abortive reflex tied to the protective subroutine I'd burned into my short-term protocols.

If surroundings=public then conceal=true.

To keep my danger proximity alarms from pinging continual false positives, I disabled the command, although *that* raised a security vulnerability warning which I also had to suppress.

Because it made sense—a liveried servant running an errand in the capital wouldn't be garbed for travel, especially since the weather was so mild here.

"Don't worry," Darej said. "I'll bring all your things to you outside the city walls. Zal's cloak, too." They met my gaze with their trusting brown eyes. "For when you succeed."

I held out my hands and they placed theirs, stained palms and all, in mine. "I don't want you to put yourself in danger."

They shook their head. "I won't be. I can even leave through the main gate. The guards are used to me out and about to forage for Mam's herbs and such like. They won't look at me twice." They waggled their fingers. "Especially with these. Nobody likes harvesting clawfruit, but they all want to drink the punch, so they're happy to let me pass."

I glanced at the window where the sun was dipping toward the roofs of nearby houses at the same time that gray clouds were boiling up to meet it. I didn't want Zal to endure a night in gaol—I knew too well what that was like. The need to get started, the urge for speed sparked under my skin like fireworks.

I looked at my hands, touched my face. "Will this fade in the rain?"

Jocosa scoffed as she poked at the edge of my snood. "What rain?"

I jerked my chin toward the window. "The rain in those clouds."

"It won't rain until after midnight," she said, seating a pin more securely.

"You've a weather sense, then?"

She frowned at me as though I were simple. "It never rains during the day."

I stilled, stopping myself before I could launch an archive retrieval query, because that was clearly at odds with the meteorological patterns of the planet that the Infomancers had maintained for centuries, not that many paid attention to it anymore. "What, never?"

"Think how hard it would be on the merchants in the Square if they had to keep their goods dry while still on display, or folk shopping with water dripping in their eyes." She gestured to Maer, who approached with a covered basket. "Rain isn't your concern. These are." She handed the basket to me. "Dulaberry tarts. The guard on duty can't resist them."

I accepted the basket, sniffing appreciatively at the aroma of browned pastry and sugar and tart berries. "How do you know?"

"He's my sister's husband's cousin's boy. Quite the snatch-pastry he was growing up."

"But how do you know he'll be on duty?"

She shrugged. "It's his shift. But not for much longer. Change happens two hours before sunset. Once he takes these into the ready room to eat, you'll be able to slip downstairs to the cell block."

"But Gerd's office is down there. What if I run into him? Or another guard or one of the clerks?"

She waved that away. "It'll be deserted. After the Judgment Day announcements, the Congress of Mages and Seigneurs will be hearing petitions all evening, and the clerks'll be busy recording it all."

"Petitions for leniency?" Maybe I should have considered a more procedural way to free Zal rather than this extremely risky plan, which, according to the data at my disposal, had less than a nineteen percent chance of success.

Jocosa's expression darkened. "Not always. Depends on the crime. There's some as wants sentences to be harsher. But that's why you need to go now."

"Yes. Right. Of course." I glanced between Jocosa, Lafi, and Maer, who'd be staying behind at the inn, and Darej, who'd be accompanying me part of the way, to show me the best route. "Thank you. All of you. I can't tell you how much this means to me."

Maer and Lafi both giggled and blushed. Jocosa snorted and looked away, but I could detect that telltale shine in her eyes. Darej just smiled, a little wistfully.

There was something I could do for them in return, something that wouldn't take long, but hopefully would remain long after Zal and I had gone.

"Would you like to learn a song?"

Maer's eyes widened. "You can teach us? To sing? All of us?"

I shrugged. "I can't guarantee you'll be able to carry a tune. Not everyone can." From what I'd seen, nobody on this planet had bothered to try. "But the words, yes, and what the melody should be."

They all nodded eagerly. So I did it.

I taught them a song.

As Darej and I made our way down the stairs, the notes of "Frère Jacques," in a shaky, off-key round, followed us across the empty tap room and out the door.

"This way," Darej said, and led me farther into the worker's quarter at a brisk walk that was almost a trot, through tangled streets and narrow alleys and unexpected courtyards that, even with my mapping system fully online, I struggled to capture.

"Are these streets always deserted like this?" I panted, hard pressed to keep up with Darej even though they were half a head shorter.

"Not always. Most folk will be at the Square, either waiting to present their petition or else shopping at the market stalls. Besides," they gestured to the dingy walls of the buildings that pressed in on either side of this narrow cobbled street, "visitors don't come this way. This is for us as live hereabouts."

"I see."

When we reached the next corner, they put out a hand, stopping me. "This is as far as I can go." They pressed a flat wooden disc into my hand. "Remember. Give this to the guard at the side gate behind the tanner's guild hall."

I peered at it. "What's it for?"

They smiled crookedly. "It allows you to leave by that gate without a barrow full of shit."

A laugh caught in my throat and I pocketed the token. "Then I thank you deeply." I gazed down at them. "Not only for that. For everything you and your family have done."

They met my gaze, their eyes shining. "You've given us something too, something that no one can take away, so the debt is ours."

They hummed the first bars of "Frère Jacques" and then held out their arms, clearly asking for permission.

I stepped into the embrace and they squeezed me tightly for an instant before releasing me and stepping back.

"I'll see you outside the walls, at the place where the main road meets the path off the mountain. Earth keep you safe."

And they were gone.

Chapter Fifteen

Zal

I lost track of time as I sat in the dark, shivering, my back against the unforgiving metal door, my arms around my legs, and my head on my knees.

Loriah. The Trine. Torian.

Meeting Torian had made me question many things about my world that I'd always taken as given. But this?

The Trine's impartiality, their commitment to justice, to the welfare and prosperity of all our people—that was at the very foundation of the Sun mage's creed, instilled nearly as deeply as our belief in choice, in hospitality, in the very Sun itself.

My breath shuddered as I fought down a sob.

If the Trine wasn't to be trusted what did that say about me, about the way I'd followed their orders without question, about what I'd done to a woman who'd been not only a colleague but a *friend* for most of my life?

If it weren't for Torian, I'd submit to judgment willingly, although not for the reasons Obeila was no doubt announcing even now from the steps of the College, where her voice would carry to every corner of the Square.

Mayhap the harsher punishment was living with the shame and guilt that I'd never suspected, never questioned, never even *imagined* the Trine might be as corruptible as anybody else. They'd made me *complicit*, damn them.

Missing one eye didn't give me an excuse not to *look*.

My breath hitched and tears leaked down my cheeks from my eye as well as from the empty socket, my heart drumming so hard that my whole body juddered.

How dare they? How *dare* they? It wasn't only grief that burned in my middle. It was rage, too. Rage at the Trine, rage at myself, rage at...

Then I realized it wasn't me, but the door that was vibrating. Clearly somebody was pounding on it, but the cell was silent except for my own labored breathing and the blood pounding in my ears. Evidently the noise suppression spells worked on both sides of the threshold.

The slot above my head slid open with a *screech*.

"Oy! Mage! Get away from the door if you want supper. Your arse is blocking the food slot."

Even though my belly was so empty it was cleaving to my spine, I didn't move. I didn't deserve to eat. Not now. Not when the very Earth had collapsed under me. Not when Torian was at the Trine's mercy.

Not when I couldn't get my hands around their throats.

"I said— *urgh*."

The guard's voice ended in a gasp and a gurgle, followed by a heavy weight hitting the ground outside.

A soft voice whispered, "Zal?"

My head shot up. *Torian*. A faint golden glow bloomed through the open slot above me, illuminating the miserable cell. When I scrambled to my feet, the glow bled through the lower slot too, gilding the scuff marks on my boot toes.

I flung myself against the door, dry lips nearly splitting with my relieved grin. But when I pressed my forehead to the cold iron and my eye to the peephole, my grin faltered.

The gray eyes that met mine were Torian's, the face was Torian's, as was the tracery of the golden threads gleaming under their skin.

That skin, though... The skin was nearly as dark as Netta's, the hair captured in a snood like Barkon's.

"Torian? Is it you then?"

"Who else would it be? Hold on. This key is a motherfucker."

I couldn't help it. Despite our situation, laughter burbled at the back of my throat. *Another Torian word.* It sounded like an extremely useful one, too, especially in these circumstances.

A moment later, the key grated in the lock and the door swung open to reveal Torian in clerk's livery. I surged through and wrapped them in a hug.

They returned the embrace. "Are you all right?"

"Now that you're here, I'm okay."

Their body trembled with their chuckle. "Good. Because we have to move fast."

They pulled away, stepping gingerly over the leg of the guard, who was sprawled on the floor amid a scatter of bread and beans.

I recalled Edric and the effect of his death on Torian as I peered down at the guard's body. "You didn't kill him, did you?"

"No." They laughed a little wildly. "I sort of panicked when he saw me and I tried this thing from an ancient entertainment out of reflex." They made a motion as though gripping a phantom neck. "I mean, I know where the nerve bundles are, and my hands are stronger with my skeletal mods, but I didn't think it would actually *work!*" They wrinkled their nose. "Although I suppose the jolt of electricity helped. Like a taser."

I didn't bother to ask what a taser might be. I gestured to their face and hair. "What happened to you?"

"Never mind that. We have to move fast, before he comes around."

With the glow emanating from Torian's skin, the corridor was easy to navigate. We ran forward and were halfway up the stairs when above us, a guard stepped into view.

He looked as startled as we did, but fumbled his night stick off his belt. "Halt!"

"Zal." Torian gripped my forearm. "I can't do anything without touching him. You need to throw him back, like you did with Farren and the others that night."

The guard began to descend toward us, both hands gripping his stick.

"I had my Stone then. I don't have it anymore, not even the shards. I can't."

Torian hissed through their teeth. "Don't you get it?" They let go of my arm and grabbed my hand in both of theirs. "You don't need your Stone. You've got me." They jerked their head at the advancing guard. "Now get him."

And I felt it then.

The surge of energy through my veins, pooling at my core, ready for me to shape to my will. Familiar, yet *different*.

More.

I'd been a Sun mage for more than half my life. I'd learned finesse and restraint and self-mastery through endless drills before I was ever posted to my circuit. But what Torian sent singing through our joined hands wasn't anything as tame and contained as what my Stone delivered at full charge. With my Stone, I could always feel its limits, sense the bottom, how far I could go.

But *this*? The bottom was so far away I couldn't touch it, because this power *had* no limit, like a dragon barely tamed to harness, a storm rolling in from the sea, an avalanche roaring down a mountain. Yet it was distinctly *Torian*, too. Sweet and awkward, knowing yet naïve.

And far, far too trusting.

I tried to free my hand. "No. I won't. You nearly died with Edric."

"It's *okay*. There are *failsafes*. Trust me. I'll throttle it down if it's too much." They glared at me. "I'm *choosing* to share it with you. Now just *do it*!"

So I did.

At first, I was afraid the power welling in me would be more than I could handle. That I'd lose control and incinerate the guard where he stood. But then I focused on Torian's touch, Torian's solid presence beside me.

Torian would never allow that to happen, not intentionally, not now, not after Edric.

So in the end, I simply extended a finger and *nudged* the guard, a stroke of power, no more than if I were brushing past him in the street. Even that small burst sent him flying back up the stairs to land on his back on the floor above.

Well, I wasn't a fool. I knocked him out, too. After all, we still had to get out of here, and now that I knew what the Trine thought of Torian—and what they might do to Torian if they knew what *true* magic lay coiled inside them—escape was even more vital.

"Will you be able to share that with me again when we encounter the next guards?"

"We won't," Torian said as they raced up the stairs behind me. "The place is deserted. The Trine is hearing petitions."

I stumbled as my bloody conscience weakened my knees.

Nobody had spoken for Loriah. Nobody had begged for mercy for her. Even if I'd known it was warranted, I couldn't have done it myself because I was half delirious, still under the healers' care. And since they'd already cut out her tongue, she couldn't plead her own case either.

Torian gripped my elbow. "You okay?"

I nodded and managed to croak, "Fine," before leading the way past the unconscious guard.

As Torian had claimed, when we reached the lighted corridors outside Gerd's office, there was nobody about. Even so, there were more obstacles ahead.

"I don't like to ask, seeing as how you've managed to get us this far, but how are we to leave the city? The guards at the gate —"

"We're not going that way. I've got a token that'll let us leave by the... the... Fuck, I don't know what it's called. The equivalent of sewage treatment. Where the barrows of shit get carted."

My brows rose. "The night dirt postern? They'll not let us out without a barrow."

"They will. I've got a token. All we need to do is—"

"Zal."

I froze at that implacable voice echoing down the stairs. I pushed Torian behind me and stared defiantly up at Gerd.

He stared back, his legs braced wide, his staff planted next to his booted feet, his Stone lighting the grim set of his mouth and casting his deep-set eyes into shadow.

"You've got it all wrong about the Moon-born," I said, chin raised defiantly. "They don't bespell people with their voices."

Gerd didn't move. "They tell you that, did they?"

"Wait. What?" Torian said, bewildered. "I can't bespell anybody."

I turned, Gerd be damned, because Torian was the important one. "I know, love. It's all a misunderstanding, I think. Brylun took a word at the wrong meaning in some old records."

"Brylun." Torian gripped my arm and lowered their voice. "I have to tell you. Brylun and Obeila, they've been in contact with the Infomancers. With *Edric*."

My belly dropped down to the cells below. "What? How do you—"

"Zal." Gerd's tone held unmistakable impatience. "What have you done?"

I glared up at him. "I *haven't* broken my vows, if that's what you're asking."

"I know that."

I blinked, my brows lifting of their own accord. "You do?"

"If you had, the bond with your stone would have broken, yet it is still intact."

"Then what the *fuck* are you doing chucking me in gaol?" I shouted.

"Zal," Torian said admiringly, "excellent work embracing new profanity."

Gerd shifted his staff to one side, out of immediate attack position. "It was necessary. I was coming to tell you so, but it appears I am behind the fair. Tell me. Did you kill my guards?"

"No. They're only unconscious."

He nodded curtly. "Good. If you had, I couldn't in good conscience have let you go."

"Y-you're letting us go?" Torian asked. "Both of us?"

"Aye." He held up his staff, and I tensed, but then he very deliberately propped it against the wall, a sign that he meant us no harm. "Although you were both fools if you imagined you could get through the streets without being stopped. The place is bristling with guard patrols."

"But isn't that your doing?" I asked.

He snorted. "It has more to do with the Houses of Mages and Seigneurs wanting to outdo each other. Every time a new mage patrol gets posted, the seigneurs match it." He shook his head. "I've no notion where they're finding the personnel."

"Conscription," Torian murmured.

Gerd's gaze sharpened. "Conscription violates choice. It's in direct opposition to our most sacred values."

Torian met Gerd's gaze levelly. "Then why did Brylun try a compulsion spell on me?"

"Shite," Gerd muttered, running a hand over his braids. "I knew it." He turned and leaned down, and when he stood back up, he had my pack in his hands. "Here." He tossed it down to me and I caught it reflexively. "Now we really do have to move, before the tribunal starts wondering where I've got to. This way."

He grabbed his staff and barreled down the stairs, passing us without a glance as he strode down the corridor. When he reached his office door, he turned and gestured for us to follow him.

Torian and I exchanged a look, then both of us shrugged and hurried down after him.

I halfway expected him to take us back to the cells, but instead, he tapped his Stone against the solid wall at the head of the stairs that led down to them. And the wall... opened, rumbling inward and to the side to reveal another set of stairs, darker, narrower, and twice as steep.

"What the..." I muttered.

"Tunnel under the curtain wall. Walk now. Questions later."

Gerd plunged down the stairs, his staff held high so his Stone could light the way. I gestured for Torian to precede me, and I noted that their grid wasn't glowing any longer. Fear cramped my empty belly. I hoped Torian had damped it down out of choice and discretion, and not because I'd depleted them when I'd downed the guard.

We followed Gerd for what seemed like hours, but was probably no more than thirty minutes before I noted the burn in my calf muscles that meant we'd been toiling up an incline so gradual that I'd missed it.

Gerd's staff suddenly illuminated another wall. As he'd done before, he opened it with a touch of his Stone. I took a moment to wonder if any mage could open the doors—assuming they knew they existed—or if they were keyed to Gerd alone.

Even with the wall gaping, the tunnel was only slightly less dim. But when Gerd extended his staff and pushed aside a screen of brambles, the late afternoon sun spilled in and burnished Torian's tight braids with gold.

Braids.

Who had braided their hair? Where had they gotten the snood? And their skin... I had thought that perhaps its color had been a trick of the chancy light in the gaol, but no. They could be taken for an Earth-born now by anyone on the street.

Gerd ducked through the brambles and held them aside so we could follow. We stepped into the light, blinking, onto the hillside overlooking the city in nearly the same spot Torian and I had stopped before we'd entered the gates that morning.

Gerd let the brambles fall and faced me. "I have been... uneasy since I resumed my place as Scale last year. I suspected that all was not right with the others in the Trine, that ill doings were afoot, yet I could find no proof. I know you have no reason to trust me, but I swear by my Stone, by the Earth, by Sun, Moon, and Stars, that I want nothing but the best for all our people."

His Stone flared brightly, making us all squint, a sign he spoke the truth.

"Very well," I said. "I believe you."

"They're trying to take over," Torian blurted. "Brylun and Obeila. They were conspiring with the Star-born to tip the balance of power in their favor."

"So." Gerd's hand flexed around his staff and he glanced down at the city. "It is as I feared. The danger is real, yet I'm not certain how to prevent them from—"

"You don't have to," Torian said. "Their contact is no longer... available. After the explosion, the Star-born all abandoned the planet. They've returned to the stars."

"So there's no danger from that quarter?" Gerd asked sharply.

I spotted the way Torian's jaw tightened, but they shook their head. "No."

Gerd stared down at his feet, swearing under his breath, and it almost sounded as though he said, "Fuck." Then he looked up, meeting our gazes again. "Then at least we'll be on an even footing. An ordinary coup I can handle, although I don't know who all I can trust."

"Don't discount the ordinary people in the city," Torian said, "or in the villages either. This world is theirs too. I suspect they'll help if you approach them properly."

His austere face softened in something that could almost be a smile. "A point well taken. Thank you." Then he looked back at me. "If you don't want guards dogging your trail, I'll have to tell the others I killed you as you were fleeing the city." Something that could almost be pity flickered across his face. "You know what that means."

My belly heaved and I would certainly have spewed on the sparse grass if my stomach hadn't been so empty. "You'll need proof."

Gerd nodded, reached into his belt pouch. When he withdrew his hand, sunlight winked in a Sun Stone nugget on the hilt of a twelve-inch dagger.

Chapter Sixteen

Torian

"Wait a minute." I stared from the enormous knife in Gerd's hand to Zal, all my danger alarms pinging at once. "What does he mean, proof?"

Zal let his pack fall next to his feet and placed his hands on my shoulders. "He needs to cut off my braids"—his hands spasmed on my shoulders and he swallowed—"and take them back to the city."

His braids? My fingers went numb. Without his braids, Zal would be practically a pariah, his shorn hair a physical manifestation of wrongdoing.

But at least he would be alive and out of the Trine's reach.

"That will convince them you're... you're dead? They don't need to see the body? How? Why?"

"I'm a condemned prisoner who ran from justice, love."

"You're not," I said hotly. "You're *not.*"

"As things stand now, that's exactly what I am, and as such, I'm not worthy of a sacred pyre."

"Sacred pyre? What does that even *mean*?"

"It means I can tell them I returned his body to the Earth without the Sun's blessing," Gerd said, his mouth set in a grim line. "No one will question it, but we'd best get on with it."

Although Zal had gone nearly gray, he nodded and then kissed my forehead and released my shoulders.

I pressed my knuckles against my lips as Zal unlaced his jerkin and pulled it over his head, followed by his shirt. My hands didn't muffle my whimper when I saw the scrapes and lacerations on his arms.

He knelt in front of Gerd and shot a glance at me. "It'll be okay, love."

Then he bowed his head and Gerd lifted one of Zal's long plaits and raised his knife.

The blade flashed in the sunlight and an instant later, one of Zal's braids lay on the ground by Gerd's feet. Then another. Then another. My legs gave way and I dropped gracelessly to the ground because Zal... Zal was trembling, his fists clenched at his sides, keening low in his throat.

Did Gerd have to cut so *close* to Zal's scalp? The knife was sharp enough that he didn't have to *saw* at the plaits, but Zal had probably never had his hair cut before. Pain wasn't always physical. Gerd was removing Zal's *life*, or at least the testament to his years. He could have left *something*.

When the last braid fell atop the pile of its fellows, limp and somehow forlorn between Zal's knees and Gerd's feet, Gerd stood back.

"It is done," he said.

Zal's fingers uncurled, and one hand crept toward the mound before falling to his side. He raised his head and took a shaky breath. "Thank you."

Gerd shook his head. "Do not thank me. Your road will be hard with your Stone in splinters and the mark of your disgrace for all to see."

"I thank you because you've returned choice to us. You've given us a chance. And above all, you've kept Torian out of their hands. That is a favor I can never repay."

Gerd helped Zal to his feet, steadying him when he wobbled. "All I ask is that you keep looking. Find the proof I need. Although, if I were you, I would have a care with whom I placed my trust. We don't know how far this conspiracy might reach, especially among mages, if it was indeed intended to raise us above the seigneurs."

"We'll be careful."

"Good." He turned away and began gathering Zal's braids, plaiting them together into a thick rope.

Zal watched him, shoulders slumped, listing to one side as though he couldn't quite adjust his balance. With every braid Gerd collected, Zal tilted more until I couldn't stand it.

I pushed myself to my feet and hurried forward.

"Let me help." I reached for the topmost braid.

"No," Zal and Gerd both barked at once.

"Zal may not touch them now, or the others will know he still lives. And no one but me may touch them or they'll suspect a ruse."

I glared at Gerd. "Do they keep count of everyone's braids? Inventory the hair on your heads?"

Gerd's eyebrows rose at the same time his lips turned down. "Of course not."

"Then I'm keeping this." With two fingers, careful not to touch any others, I lifted a braid from the pile.

"Why?" Gerd sounded truly mystified.

"Because..." I turned away as I twined the thick plait around my hand. "Because he doesn't deserve to lose everything. Not for me."

By the time I'd stowed the coil in my waistcoat pocket and turned back, Gerd had finished, the thick rope of Zal's hair hanging off his belt like some kind of hunting trophy.

He and Zal stared at one another, unmoving, until Gerd nodded sharply.

"Go with the Sun," he said.

"And you," Zal replied.

Gerd turned and disappeared through the brambles. A moment later, the tunnel door rumbled shut once more.

Zal sighed and then picked up his shirt. Before he could pull it over his head, I touched his injured arm with a fingertip.

"You're hurt."

His smile flickered once and then died. "'Tis naught. A few scrapes."

I extended a tentative hand toward his head. He didn't pull away, so I rested my palm there, the nubs of the shorn braids almost sharp against my skin.

"Will it be very bad?" I let my hand fall.

"A shearing is the sign of guilt. The shorter the shear, the more severe the crime." He smiled a little crookedly as he donned his shirt. "Looking like this, folk couldn't be blamed for thinking me a murderer." He winced. "Shite. I'm sorry."

"Don't be."

"Let's just say you won't be the one drawing the most attention on our travels any longer. Although…" He frowned as he pulled his jerkin over his head and laced it up. "I confess, Torian, I have no notion where we're to travel *to*. We can't very well go back to my cottage, nor can we go to any of the villages on my circuit, where folk know me. Word would certainly get back to the Trine that I'd been seen." He shivered. "And now I wish you hadn't talked me into leaving my cloak at the inn. Wherever we go, and it'll have to be somewhere in the hinterlands, we're deep in the bowels of winter now. With no money, and needing to say out of sight, we—"

"Psst. Torian?" The bushes rustled behind us and I whirled around to see Darej peering out between the few remaining brown leaves still clinging to the branches of a bush. "Is the Scale gone? Is it safe to come out?"

"Yes." I gestured for them to join us. "Although when you get back home, you should pass the word that Gerd is the one mage you can trust at the moment."

"I'll let Mam know. She'll make sure of it." Darej emerged from their hiding place and shyly handed Zal his cloak. "I spread it in the sun, like Torian said."

Zal bowed and solemnly accepted the cloak. "I thank you, young Darej."

Darej flushed and bobbed their head and then handed over my pack. "I put in another pot of the clawfruit stain, in case you need to go in disguise again." They glanced up at Zal's head, their eyes wide. "There's more wool, too, and another snood, but I didn't think we'd need more pins."

"Don't worry about that," Zal said. "I'm sure we'll manage."

They ducked back behind the bush and returned with Zal's creel, our bedrolls, and a basket with a long leather strap.

"How did you carry all this out without the guards noticing?" I said in wonder.

"Maer and Lafi helped. One of the guards is sweet on Maer." Darej snorted. "Not that it'll do him any good. Maer's got her eye on someone else. But she distracted him while Lafi and I made a trip or two." They wrinkled their nose. "We had to gather some clawfruit to keep up the ruse, but it won't go to waste."

"Very clever," Zal said, admiration in his tone.

Darej flushed again and pointed to the basket. "Mam sent along some bread and a few of those dulaberry tarts, since she said you wouldn't be able to manage those on the trail."

Heat built behind my eyes, as though I were about to cry. *Fuck.* I *hated* crying. I had no idea it could ambush you for reasons other than grief.

What was swirling in my chest and sending odd signals along my neural pathways wasn't grief. I had insufficient data for a full analysis, but there were several discrete components.

Gratitude. Determination. *Hope.*

Despite the plots and plans of people like Edric, Obeila, and Brylun, despite thugs like Farren and his gang, there were still good people, *kind* people, people who deserved to have their way of life preserved. One way or another, I intended to see that happened.

"Thank your mam for me. Thank your whole family and all your friends who helped us. We couldn't have done it without you."

Darej looked down at the city and then back at us, a bit wistfully. "Couldn't I come with you?"

I shook my head. "Although I'd be glad of your companionship, I doubt your mother would thank us for taking you away. Besides, we don't know what we'll be facing, so it's best if you go home."

"Will you come back?"

I didn't want to lie, so I just said, "Perhaps."

Then I smiled and began to sing. "Frère Jacques, Frère Jacques."

Darej brightened, joining in at the right spot, surprisingly on key, and by the time we'd run through the round three times, they were smiling.

Still humming, they headed down the path toward the main road, turning once to wave at us.

"By the Sun, love," Zal said, draping his arm over my shoulders, "you've changed another life."

I shrugged, but leaned into Zal's warmth. "I just taught them a song. It wasn't much."

Zal kissed the top of my head. "Unless I miss my guess, it might just be everything."

I glanced up at the sky. "We should probably get moving before it gets much darker. We don't want our campfire to be visible from the battlements."

Zal sighed and shook his head. "Moving where, Torian? I still have no idea where we can go."

"Don't you?" I looked up at him. "Tenner's End."

"Tenner's End? How do you know about Tenner's End? I'm not even sure it still exists."

"Do you know where it was purported to be?"

He waggled one hand. "More or less. But that doesn't explain why we should barge around in the wilderness looking for it."

I dug the scrap of paper out of the belt pouch that was part of my clerk livery, grateful I'd been able to keep it. I smoothed it out in my palm and gazed down at the printed alphabet.

"Because of this. The name of that village was the only thing the person who gave this to me said. Don't you think it would be a good idea to find out why?"

Zal's brows lowered in thought. "I suppose so." His expression cleared. "And it's not as though I have any better ideas. Let's get these packs sorted and we'll be off."

Zal began rearranging things in his usual manner, giving himself most of the burden. When he reached for Jocosa's basket, I pulled it away.

"Absolutely not. I'm carrying that one myself." I grinned at him. "I don't trust you around those dulaberry tarts."

As I hoped, he laughed. "Very well." He pointed to the northwest. "I believe we should head that way."

"All right. One moment. I need to change into my other boots." Zal sat next to me as I switched over my footwear. "This is likely to be a long march, love."

I glanced up from lacing my left boot. "I know."

"So we'll need a way to pass the time."

"You mean other than slogging through mud, sleet, and snow?" I laced the second boot and stood.

Zal chuckled as he shouldered his pack and lifted his walking stick. "Aye."

I looped the strap of Jocosa's basket across my chest, slid into my pack, and flung my cloak over my shoulders. "What do you suggest?"

"I think"—he nudged me with his elbow—"you should teach me a song."

I stared at him a moment and then burst out laughing.

So as we headed deeper into the forest, we startled more than one coney and at least two flights of birds as we filled the air with round after round of "Frère Jacques."

a message from
ej

Dear Reader,

Thank you so much for reading this omnibus collection of *Partnership* and *Principles*, the first of Zal and Torian's adventures in my Sun, Moon, and Stars story world. I'm so happy you've taken this journey with me! I'd be immensely grateful if you'd take a moment to leave a review at the retailer and any other site you use for reviews. Believe me, reviews make an *enormous* difference to the health and well-being of books (and not incidentally, to their associated authors!).

Pop on over to my website, https://ejrussell.com, for all the deets on my books—my paranormal rom-coms and mysteries, my contemporary romances, and my one lone historical. If you're an audio fan, you can find the audio scoop there too. (The QR code on the next page will get you there with your smartphone camera or other code reader.)

Would you like exclusive content and ARC giveaways, not to mention gratuitous dance videos? Then I'd love for you to join me in E.J. Russell's Reality Optional, my Facebook fan group (https://facebook.com/groups/reality.optional). My newsletter is the place to get the latest dish on new releases, sales, and more. I promise I only send one out when I've got…well…news. You can subscribe here: https://ejrussell.com/newsletter.

All my best,
—E

Also by
ej

Paranormal Romance
Mythmatched Universe
Fae Out of Water Trilogy
Cutie and the Beast
The Druid Next Door
Bad Boy's Bard

Supernatural Selection Trilogy
Single White Incubus
Vampire With Benefits
Demon on the Down-Low

Other Mythmatched Romances
Howling on Hold
Possession in Session
Witch Under Wraps
Cursed is the Worst
The Skinny on Djinni
Assassin by Accident (part of Carnival of Mysteries)

Quest Investigations Mysteries
Five Dead Herrings
The Hound of the Burgervilles
The Lady Under the Lake
Death on Denial

At Odds with the Gods (A Mythmatched / Purgatory Playhouse

crossover)

Mythmatchedlets (Mythmatched companion stories, free to
newsletter subscribers in ebook form, collected in one
paperback volume: *Second First Date, Rusty's Really Bad Day,
First Flight, Getting the Band Together, Purgatory Postscript, A Very
Quest Solstice*)

Magic Emporium Series (shared world)
Purgatory Playhouse

Enchanted Occasions Series
Best Beast
Nudging Fate
Devouring Flame

Ghost Townies Series
Ghostridden

Legend Tripping Series
Stumptown Spirits
Wolf's Clothing

Art Medium Series
The Artist's Touch
Tested in Fire
Art Medium: The Complete Collection (omnibus edition)

Royal Powers Series (shared world)
Duking It Out
Duke the Hall
King's Ex

Science Fiction
Sun, Moon, and Stars Series

Partnership
Principles

Interdimensional Time Bureau
Monster Till Midnight

Historical Romance
Silent Sin

Contemporary Romance
Camera Shy
Summer Kitchen
The Thomas Flair
Mystic Man
For a Good Time, Call… (A Bluewater Bay novel, with Anne
Tenino)

Christmas Kisses (holiday shorts)
The Probability of Mistletoe
An Everyday Hero
A Swants Soiree

Geeklandia Series
The Boyfriend Algorithm (M/F)
Clickbait

Writing as Nelle Heran
(traditional cozy mystery)

Crafty Sleuth Series (with C.K. Eastland)
Die Cut
Mixed Media
Found Objects (*coming soon*)

About the
Author

E.J. Russell (she/her), author of the award-winning Mythmatched paranormal romance series, writes LGBTQ+ romance and mystery in a rainbow of flavors. Count on high snark, low angst, and happy endings.

Reality? Eh, not so much.

She's married to Curmudgeonly Husband, a man who cares even less about sports than she does. Luckily, C.H. also loves to cook, or all three of their children (Lovely Daughter and Darling Sons A and B) would have survived on nothing but Cheerios, beef jerky, and Satsuma mandarins (the extent of E.J.'s culinary skill set).

E.J. also writes traditional cozy mystery as Nelle Heran. She lives in rural Oregon, enjoys visits from her wonderful adult children, and indulges in good books, red wine, and the occasional hyperbole.

News & Social Media:
Website: https://ejrussell.com
Newsletter: https://ejrussell.com/newsletter